Fool *for* Love

The Gansett Island Series by Marie Force

Book 1: Maid for Love
(Maddie & Mac)
Book 2: Fool for Love
(Joe & Janey)
Book 3: Ready for Love
(Luke & Sydney)
Book 4: Falling for Love
(Grant & Stephanie)
Book 5: Hoping for Love
(Evan & Grace)
Book 6: Season for Love
(Owen & Laura)
Book 7: Longing for Love
(Blaine & Tiffany)
Book 8: Waiting for Love
(Adam & Abby)
Book 9: Time for Love
(David & Daisy)
Book 10: Meant for Love
(Jenny & Alex)
Book 10.5: Chance for Love,
A Gansett Island Novella *(Jared & Lizzie)*
Book 11: Gansett After Dark
(Owen & Laura)
Book 12: Kisses After Dark
(Shane & Katie)
Book 13: Love After Dark
(Paul & Hope)
Book 14: Celebration After Dark
(Big Mac & Linda)
Book 15: Desire After Dark
(Slim & Erin)
Book 16: Light After Dark
(Mallory & Quinn)
Book 17: Episode 1: Victoria & Shannon
Book 18: Episode 2: Kevin & Chelsea
Book 19: Mine After Dark
(Riley & Nikki)

Fool *for* Love

MARIE FORCE

ZEBRA BOOKS
KENSINGTON PUBLISHING CORP.
http://www.kensingtonbooks.com

ZEBRA BOOKS are published by

Kensington Publishing Corp.
119 West 40th Street
New York, NY 10018

All Kensington titles, imprints, and distributed lines are
available at special quantity discounts for bulk purchases for
sales promotion, premiums, fund-raising, educational, or
institutional use.

Special book excerpts or customized printings can also be
created to fit specific needs. For details, write or phone the
office of the Kensington Sales Manager: Attn.: Sales Department. Kensington Publishing Corp., 119 West 40th Street,
New York, NY 10018. Phone: 1-800-221-2647.

First Zebra Books Mass-Market Paperback Printing: June 2018
ISBN-13: 978-1-4201-4688-2
ISBN-10: 1-4201-4688-2

10 9 8 7 6 5 4 3 2 1

Printed in the United States of America

Author's Note

My favorite place in the world is Block Island, located twelve miles off the southern coast of Rhode Island. A tiny slip of land with a Great Salt Pond in the middle, Block Island is the place time forgot. You won't find a stoplight on the island or a hospital. Internet connections are sketchy at best, and good luck finding a hotel room or a spot on the ferry for your car in the summer if you haven't planned months in advance. What you will find is peace and quiet and beaches and bluffs and quaint shops and a laid-back atmosphere that soothes the soul.

The island has played an important role in my life from the time I was a small child arriving on my parents' boat, through a college romance and now as a favorite family vacation spot each summer. I've never been anywhere that inspires me more. Block Island pops up often in my books, so I suppose it was only a matter of time before I made up my own version of the island and set a series there. Thus, Gansett Island and the McCarthy Family were born. "Gansett" is a tip of the hat to Rhode Island's Narragansett Bay, one of my favorite places to spend a summer day.

I love to hear from readers! Contact me at marie@ marieforce.com. Join my mailing list at marieforce.com to be notified of upcoming books.

Welcome back to Gansett Island! While this is intended to be a standalone story, you will enjoy it more if you read *Maid for Love* first. I so hope you enjoy Joe and Janey's story. Stay tuned at the end for a sneak peek at Luke and Sydney's story, *Ready for Love*.

xoxo,
Marie

Chapter One

The phone call Joe Cantrell had waited half his life to receive came in around nine on an otherwise average Tuesday evening. He'd put in a twelve-hour day on the ferries, done four round-trips to the island, and had just sat down to eat when his cell phone rang. Since he'd been in a foul mood all day, tortured by images of Janey in Boston with her fiancé, he'd almost ignored the call. Thank God he grabbed it on the last ring before voice mail picked up.

"Joe."

One word set his heart to racing. He'd know that voice anywhere. "Janey? Why are you calling me when you're visiting David?" He kept his tone light, but just saying the guy's name made Joe sick. He couldn't stand the way David went weeks, sometimes months, without so much as a visit to his fiancée. Sometimes Joe wished he didn't have front-row access to who came and went from the island. Some things he was better off not knowing.

He'd seen her earlier in the day, skipping onto the ferry on her way to surprise her doctor-in-training for their anniversary. Thirteen years together. Lucky thirteen, she'd joked. Joe had found nothing funny about it.

"I need . . ."

Was she *crying*? "Janey, honey. What do you need?"

"You."

Joe almost swallowed his tongue. How long had he fantasized about hearing those very words from her? Forever, or so it seemed. "What's wrong?"

"My car broke down on 95, just south of Foxboro."

Why was she south of Boston when she'd gone to visit David for a few days? "Where's David?"

"I'm calling *you*, Joe. Can you come?" More sniffling. "What was I thinking? It's too far—"

He was already leaving a cloud of dust behind his red pickup as he peeled out of the driveway. "Don't be ridiculous. I'll be there in less than an hour." Under normal circumstances, it would take much longer to reach her, but these were anything but normal circumstances. Something had happened. Something bad. If the bad thing was between her and David, then all of Joe's dreams had finally come true. But hers had been crushed. He had to remember that. No matter what this night might bring, he couldn't forget that she'd been with David for almost as long as Joe had harbored a secret, burning love for his best friend's little sister.

On the way, he tried to keep her talking and his heart from leaping out of his chest. "You want to tell me about it?"

"No."

"You aren't hurt or anything, are you?"

"Not physically."

Oh, man. *What the hell happened?* Joe was dying to

know, but he didn't ask again. He drove as fast as he dared and was stymied half an hour later by traffic in Providence.

"Are you still there?" she asked in a small voice. Janey McCarthy, *his* Janey, didn't have a small voice.

"I'm here, honey. I'm coming. Hang in there."

More sniffling.

Jesus H. Christ. Why the hell wasn't anything *moving*? Even knowing it wouldn't do an ounce of good, Joe laid on the horn. That earned him a raised middle finger from the guy in front of him. As his desperation to get to her inched into the red zone, he wished he could call Mac and get his take on things, but until he knew more about what had happened, he didn't think Janey would appreciate him cueing in her older brother that something was wrong.

As if she had read his mind, Janey said, "Don't tell Mac."

"Wouldn't dream of it." Traffic inched along, and Joe was certain his blood pressure had to be approaching stroke level.

Twenty minutes later, he flew across the border into Massachusetts. "Here I come."

"Good."

When he finally reached her location, Joe wanted to die when he saw her sitting in the front seat of her old blue Honda Civic, hunched over the wheel. Janey didn't hunch. She barreled through life with exuberance and optimism that brightened every room she entered.

He had to drive past her to the next exit, where he endured two of the longest red lights of his life before he was able to merge onto the southbound ramp.

By the time he came to a stop behind Janey's car, his hands were sweaty, his heart was racing and he realized he had absolutely no idea what to say to her. Women in crisis were hardly his forte. He took a deep breath and got out of the truck.

She didn't seem to know he was there until he opened the door and squatted down.

Turning to him, her ravaged face was like a knife to his heart.

Tears pooled in her pale blue eyes. "Joe."

"What happened, honey?"

"He was . . . He . . ."

Joe reached up to caress her soft blond hair. "Take a deep breath."

She gulped in air as a sob hiccupped through her. "He was with someone else. In *our* bed. In the bed I helped him buy. The bed he was going to bring with him when he moved home to the island to marry *me*."

"Okay, honey," Joe said through gritted teeth, not wanting to hear another word. If she kept talking, he wouldn't be able to contain the white-hot rage that possessed him, and he'd become an expert at hiding his every emotion from her. "You don't have to talk about it now."

"It's all I can see. She was on top of him, and he had his eyes closed. He didn't see me. I couldn't move. I just stood there watching—"

"Stop." Joe simply couldn't bear the raw pain he heard in her voice. He wanted her for himself. He wanted her more than he wanted his next breath. But not like this. Never like this. "Let's get you out of here." Joe slid his arms under her and scooped her out of the seat.

She clung to his neck, and in that one instant with

her soft and pliant in his arms, everything was right in his world.

"I can't leave my car here."

"I'll deal with it. Don't worry."

"I'm sorry. You probably had better things to do tonight."

"No, I didn't." Surrounded by the scent of jasmine, the scent of Janey, Joe wished he could hold her and never let her go. But he deposited her into the front seat of his truck and went back for the bag she'd packed to spend a few days with David. Joe wanted to hunt down that son of a bitch and teach him a lesson he'd never forget. But he figured Mac would take care of that when he heard about what David had done to his sister. Right now, Joe's top priority was Janey.

Before he joined her in his truck, Joe called for a tow truck. The operator asked for a contact number, and Joe rattled off his. He ended the call and rested his hand on the door handle, taking a moment to summon the courage he needed to get her through this—to get them both through it.

"I didn't even ask if you were busy," Janey said, swiping at the dampness on her cheeks.

"I wasn't. I'm glad you called me."

"I didn't know who else to call."

He reached over and rested his hand on top of hers. Even though it was summer and damn near eighty degrees, her hand was cold and trembling. "You can always call me. Anytime you need me. That's what friends are for." Her normally robust complexion was pale and wan, her eyes and nose red from crying, and looking at her in that condition, Joe discovered it was possible to feel someone else's pain almost as acutely as they were feeling it themselves.

She ran her free hand over her face. "I must look horrible. I didn't know it was possible to cry so much."

Tucking a strand of her thick ash-blond hair behind her ear, he resisted the urge to draw her into his arms. "You're as beautiful as always. He's a fool, Janey. Anyone who would disrespect you that way doesn't deserve you."

"Thirteen years," she said, shaking her head. "I've spent thirteen years of my life waiting for something that's never going to happen now." She gasped. "Oh, God, the wedding. I have to cancel everything." A shudder rippled through her petite frame, and he wondered for a second if she was going to be sick.

"You don't have to think about any of that today. Right now, let's just focus on getting you home."

A panicked look crossed her expressive face. "I can't go back to the island. Everyone will know. I can't—"

Joe couldn't resist any longer. He brought her into his arms and ran a hand over her silky hair. "You don't have to do anything until you're ready." Swallowing hard, he pushed the doubts and worries and despair from his mind. "You can stay with me for as long as you need to." The words were out before he could stop them. His mouth, it seemed, was operating on autopilot.

"I can't do that. It's too much of an imposition."

God, if only she knew . . . "Would you do it for me? If I needed a place to hide out for a while, would you let me stay with you?"

"Of course I would. You know that."

"Then why can't I do the same for you?" Even as he

said the words, Joe questioned the wisdom of opening his home to her. She'd stay a few days and recover enough to go on with her life, but her essence would linger in his home and heart forever. Well, he could always move, if it came to that.

A deep rattling sigh, the kind that followed a serious cry, echoed through her. "You really don't mind?"

"No, Janey," he said. "I really don't mind."

Janey focused on getting through each minute. Breathe in. Breathe out. Don't think. Don't remember. Don't go there. But despite her best efforts, the sight of her fiancé writhing in ecstasy beneath the enthusiastic hips of another woman was burned indelibly into her memory. He'd had his hands full of breasts that were much larger than hers. Had they been the draw? Or was it simple availability? Was it the first and only time? Or had there been others? Oh, God, she'd been such a fool!

She'd never suspected for one second that he'd cheat on her. He was always so busy with his internship and his life as a doctor. And she'd just accepted his many excuses because she wanted to be supportive and not add to his stress by nagging him for more of his time and attention.

All the lingering doubts from the last thirteen years came roaring back to remind her that there had been plenty of warning signs, and she'd ignored every one of them.

Like when he'd discouraged her from going to vet school. The loans will kill us, he'd said. Only one of them should go to medical school, he'd argued, because island practices won't generate enough income to pay off all those loans with enough left over to support them and the four kids they'd planned to have.

Like the fool she was, she'd gone along with him, settling for a job as a technician at the island vet's office when she'd had the undergraduate grades to get into a top veterinary school. Six years of cleaning up dog poop and grooming poodles, killing time until the day she'd be the wife of the island's only doctor and could stay home to raise their children: David Jr., Anna, Henry and Ella. They'd named them when they were just seventeen.

A sob erupted from her throat. All her dreams crushed to dust in one unbelievable moment.

Tuning into her misery, Joe unbuckled her seat belt and drew her over to rest her head on his shoulder.

For reasons they'd never discussed or acknowledged, he was probably the very last person she should've called. However, with her brother, parents and closest friends all on the island and her other three brothers out of state, there hadn't been much choice. Resting her head on his strong, dependable shoulder, Janey knew she could count on his discretion, even if she was putting him in the difficult position of serving as her knight in shining armor.

"I'm sure it doesn't seem possible right now, but you'll get through this, Janey. I know you will."

"I wish I was so sure."

"You deserve so much better than someone who leaves you alone for years and then cheats on you."

His gently spoken words reduced her once again to tears. Just when she thought there couldn't possibly be more, there were.

"I'm sorry," he said, sounding mad with himself. "I shouldn't have said that."

"S'okay," she said between sobs. "It's nothing I haven't already told myself."

He ran a comforting hand up and down her arm, and Janey sank into the warmth of his embrace.

"Hang in there. We're almost home."

Where was home now that David was no longer a part of her life? What would she do? Where would she live? Who would she lean on and make love with and laugh with? They'd had so many plans . . . Her head ached and her eyes burned, but still the tears continued to cascade down her cheeks.

The best part was that he didn't even know she'd seen him. He had no idea their life together was over. Would he even care when he found out? Did he still love her? If so, how could he sleep with someone else? How could he do that to her? To *them*?

Janey had never before wished so strongly for a switch she could flip to shut off her tired brain. Her eyes burned closed, and she didn't try to fight the darkness. In fact, she welcomed it.

Joe gnawed on his bottom lip until the taste of blood caught his attention. Tension coiled in his neck and back as he held her close to him. He suspected Janey had fallen asleep, which was just as well. She needed a respite from the pain, and he hoped she'd find it in dreamless sleep.

Twenty minutes later, he pulled into his driveway just as the moon was rising over Shelter Harbor. He sat there for a long time pondering the implications. Bringing her here was a huge mistake. A mistake, in fact, of epic proportions. Just being around her was sheer torture, and now she'd be under his roof for who knew how long. Heartbroken and shattered and unaware of all he felt for her.

He gritted his teeth and accepted the inevitable. He'd offered her a place to stay, and he couldn't undo the invitation. Besides, even if he could, he wouldn't. Perhaps he was some sort of masochist after all. Having Janey, even in her current condition, was better than not having Janey. A tiny spark of hope glimmered just beneath the surface of his current quandary, reminding him that he was the worst kind of fool—a man who'd spent a large chunk of his life in love with a woman he couldn't have.

But she was here now—in his truck, in his arms and in his house. Maybe this was all he'd ever have of her. As he lifted her gingerly from the truck and carried her inside, he told himself it was enough.

Chapter Two

Joe settled her into his bed, drew the covers up over her, and sat on the edge of the mattress. Her blond hair fanned out on his pillow, and her pink lips formed a perfect pucker. She was so beautiful, even with red splotches on her cheeks and a runny, wet nose. Her breathing continued to hitch with sobs, each one of them a spike to Joe's over-involved heart.

There was nothing he wouldn't do, nothing he wouldn't give to lessen her pain. He brushed the hair back from her forehead, and even though he knew it wasn't wise, he trailed a finger over her soft cheek.

She murmured in her sleep.

As if he'd touched something hot, Joe pulled back his hand and got up to leave the room while he still could. In the hallway, he leaned his forehead against the wall. The longer he stood there, the more ridiculous the situation became. Her scent would cling to his sheets and pillows. Anytime he glanced at that bed in the future, he'd see her there. He banged his head against the wall. Only when the pain started to register did he stop.

Rubbing the sore spot on his forehead, Joe went to the kitchen to clean up the remnants of the dinner he hadn't gotten to eat. Normally, he'd be starving by now, but he was so churned up that the thought of eating made him sick.

Even though he'd promised he wouldn't call her brother, Joe took his cell phone and a beer with him to the back deck. He cracked open the beer and scrolled through the numbers on his phone until he found Mac's.

"Hey, buddy," Mac said. Happiness all but radiated from his friend since he fell for Maddie Chester, and Joe couldn't be happier for both of them.

"How's it going?"

"Busy. Wedding craziness and the marina is cranking."

"The big day will be here before you know it."

"Maddie's mother is due home in a few days, and then we'll be down to the seven-day countdown."

"Have you ever met her?" Joe asked, stalling. "The mother? I've heard she's a piece of work."

"No, but I've gotten the high-maintenance impression from Maddie. Of course the whole prison thing paints a certain picture . . ."

Despite the tension that gripped him, Joe laughed. "Imagine writing enough bad checks to get thrown in the can."

"I can't. The whole thing is so embarrassing to Maddie."

"I'm sure. So, um, listen . . ."

"What's going on, Joe? You sound kinda funny."

Joe closed his eyes, sucked in a deep breath and took the plunge. "Janey's here."

"What do you mean? She's with David."

"No, she isn't. She's here. At my house."

"What the hell?"

"Something happened with him. She's not hurt, at least not physically, but she's pretty shook up."

"Wait a minute," Mac said, his tone tight with frustration. "Start at the beginning."

"I know this'll piss you off, but you'll have to hear it from her. She didn't even want me to call you, but I thought you should know where she is." In the back of Joe's mind was a bit of self-preservation, too. If Mac entrusted his sister's care to Joe, there was no way he would allow his own emotions into the equation. As crazy as it sounded—even to him—Joe saw this call as an emotional insurance policy of sorts.

"How did she end up with you?"

"Her car broke down, and she called me."

Mac was silent for a long time.

"What?" Joe finally asked. "Just say it, will you?"

"You really think you're the right person to nurse her through a crisis with David?" Joe had expected the question. After all, Mac was the only other person on earth who knew how Joe felt about her. Mac had kept the secret for almost as long as Joe had.

"I'm the one she called, Mac. What was I supposed to do?"

"Exactly what you did, I suppose. I'll be over in the morning to get her."

"No."

"Excuse me?"

"You heard me. She needs some time to get herself together before she has to face everyone on the island. It's what she needs right now."

"And you're suddenly an expert on what she needs?"

"Don't push me on this. One of us will call you in a few days. Until then, butt out."

"I swear to God—"

"Save it, Mac! If you can't trust me to take care of her, who *can* you trust?"

Apparently, his oldest and best friend had nothing to say to that.

"I don't want to see you hurt, either," Mac said quietly.

At that, some of the wind left Joe's sails. "I'm dealing with it."

"Be careful, man. You don't want to end up worse off after the dust settles."

"How could I be worse off?" Joe asked with a sarcastic chuckle. "Can you tell me that?"

"Yeah, I guess you're right. I wish you'd tell me what he did."

"Use your imagination. Go to worst-case scenario and take it from there."

"Son of a bitch," Mac muttered.

"Exactly."

"Since you're taking care of her, maybe I'll go take care of him."

Joe expected nothing less from Janey's doting older brother. "I know it's hard for you to sit there and do nothing, but you have to wait and take your cues from her on this one."

Mac released a rattling deep breath, and Joe had no doubt his friend was calling upon every ounce of self-control he possessed to keep from renting a plane and flying to Boston that very minute. It was a good thing for David Lawrence that Mac McCarthy was stuck on an island right then. For that matter, it was a good thing for David Lawrence that Joe Cantrell was more concerned with caring for Janey than he was with killing her wayward fiancé.

"I'm going to hurt him," Mac vowed.

"When the time is right, I'll help you."

After retrieving her bag from the truck, Joe checked on Janey and found her sleeping soundly, which was a relief. He couldn't deal with any more of her suffering just then, not when he was managing a good bit of his own. Leaving her bag next to the bed where she could find it if she woke up in the night, he took a pillow and a light blanket from the closet.

In the living room, he stripped down to boxers and stretched out on the sofa. Off in the distance, the moon silvered the harbor, but all Joe could see was Janey, hunched over the wheel of her car, devastated and alone. His hands rolled into fists. Oh, how he'd love five minutes alone with David Lawrence! However, while one part of him wanted to pound the cheating dog into the ground, another part wanted to send him an engraved thank-you note.

Maybe now . . . Maybe after she recovered from the blow and got back on her feet . . . Maybe there'd be a chance for them. He let the idea run around in his mind for a good five minutes, the fantasies coming to vivid life before reality came crashing back to remind him it was hopeless. Who did he think he was kidding? She saw him as an extra older brother, no different than the four others her parents had provided. Never would she see him as anything other than what he'd always been—a close friend of Mac's and, by extension, a friend of hers, too. Despondency crept over him like a heavy, wet blanket.

Damn it! Why'd she have to call *him* of all people? Why couldn't he have gone on with his evening, none the wiser to the drama unfolding in Boston? Of course he would have found out eventually, but he wouldn't have had to witness her devastation firsthand.

Most of the time, he dealt just fine with his unrequited love for her. Sure, there were times—like earlier today as she'd boarded the ferry on her way to surprise David—when it was agonizing to love a woman who loved someone else. But most of the time, it was something that was just *there,* as much a part of him as the birthmark on his thigh or the funky pinky toe on his left foot that curled inward.

He'd long ago accepted that she was a part of his DNA. She owned his heart, even if she didn't know it. That didn't mean his life was meaningless. Quite the opposite. He had great friends, owned a thriving, successful business that he loved and had no shortage of women willing to warm his bed on cold New England nights.

No, loving Janey McCarthy hadn't ruined his life. At least not yet. But now . . . Now that she'd been here, in the house he'd built with his own hands . . . Joe rested an arm over his eyes, wishing he could hide from the myriad emotions storming around inside him. Everything he'd ever wanted was asleep in his bed. And he was out here, one room away but light-years from what he most desired.

Against all odds, Joe dozed off and woke much later to the sound of wrenching sobs. He was up and off the sofa before he was fully awake. In the bedroom, he found her curled into the fetal position, crying her heart out.

If he'd taken the time to shake off the sleep stupor,

he might've contemplated the implications of crawling into bed with her while wearing only thin boxers. He might've stopped himself from easing her into his embrace and cushioning her head on his chest. He probably would've seen the error of his ways before she curled around him and held on for dear life. In his right mind, he would've examined the consequences in time to stop himself from acting so impulsively. But by the time he finally got a clue, it was far, *far* too late.

Janey McCarthy was in his bed and in his arms, and Joe Cantrell was ruined. Completely and utterly ruined.

Janey couldn't remember a time when she needed anything more than the sweet comfort of Joe's love wrapped tight around her. Somewhere deep down inside, in a place she rarely ventured, she had suspected he cared for her as more than his best friend's bratty little sister.

When she'd been blissfully happy as David's girlfriend and then fiancée, it hadn't occurred to her to delve too deeply into the heated looks she sometimes received from Joe or the odd vibe she'd experienced whenever they were together over the last few years.

In fact, more than once she'd been almost frightened by the intensity of what she felt coming from him, so she'd done what any loyal, faithful fiancée would do and acted like it didn't exist. Just yesterday, when she'd thought her life was set and her future secure, she wouldn't have dreamed of entertaining thoughts about her brother's sexy best friend.

But as he held her close to him, she was suddenly and acutely aware of not Joe, her friend, but Joe, the man. Had she ever noticed he was ripped with muscles? Or that he smelled so amazing? Right now, he wasn't her brother's friend or her longtime friend. No, right now he was here, he was warm, and she had no doubt, no doubt whatsoever, that he loved her.

"Joe."

"I'm here, honey." He tightened his hold on her, while under her ear, his heart pounded out a rapid beat. "I'm right here."

She drank in his clean fresh scent as well as the lingering spice of his beloved clove cigarettes and salty sea air. In her current state, it wasn't fair, she knew, to take advantage of him and all he felt for her. It wasn't fair to manipulate his care and concern, to turn it into something bigger than either of them could handle just then. She knew all that, but knowing didn't stop her hand from setting out to learn the curves and planes of his muscular chest.

He sucked in a sharp deep breath. "Janey." His hand on top of hers ended the exploration.

"I can't bear it," she whispered as new tears filled her eyes. "I can't."

"I know." He caressed her hair and massaged her shoulders. "It'll take time, but you'll get past it. I promise."

"I need to feel something else." Since he had a firm grip on her roving hand, she turned her face into his chest and nuzzled the soft blond hair.

As if an electrical current had hit him, he stiffened. "What're you doing?"

"Make me feel something other than devastated, Joe."

He tried to get up, but she stopped him.

His hazel eyes found hers in the moonlight that

seeped in through the open blinds. "You have no idea what you're asking of me. No idea."

"I'm asking someone who loves me and who I love to hold me and love me and make this awful, unbearable pain go away."

He shook his head. "I can't, Janey. I just can't."

"Joe." Her lips found his, her hand sank into his thick sandy hair, her fingers caressed his scalp, and he trembled. "I need you. Don't say no. Please don't say no."

His hands framed her face as he drew back from her. "You can't ask me for this, Janey. I'll get you anything else you need, but not this."

"No one else could give me this." She caressed his chest and belly, his rippling muscles responding to her touch even as he continued to resist. Emboldened, she rose up to shift on top of him. The press of his erection against her belly told her his body was with her even if the rest of him wasn't.

His hands traveled over her back and stopped at the waistband to her shorts. He studied her as if he was making some sort of decision.

"We can't, honey," he said softly. "It's not going to make anything better. It'll only make everything worse."

"No. It won't."

"You're using me to get back at him. Evening the score won't make you feel any less devastated."

She shook her head and slid her lips back and forth over his. "I'm not thinking about him right now. I'm thinking about you, and I already feel better." Straddling him, she sat up and reached for the hem of her shirt.

He stopped her. "You'll hate yourself in the morning. And worse yet, you'll hate me."

"I could never, ever hate you."

"You don't think so now . . ."

"I know so."

She tugged her fingers free of his grip and pulled the top over her head.

Joe's eyes flared with heat and desire at the sight of her lacy bra. His fingers dug into her hips.

"Take it off me." She rolled her hips, pressing her heat against his steely length.

"*Janey* . . ." He groaned and fumbled with the hooks.

Watching him react to her, Janey had a moment of hesitation. After all, she'd never done this with anyone but David. But he was gone now, dead to her in every way that mattered. Since she had no choice but to go on without him, she may as well get started on the rest of her life.

With her eyes fixed on Joe's handsome, familiar face, she slid down and took his boxers with her.

Chapter Three

With every fiber of his being, Joe knew this was wrong. Well, one part of his being wasn't listening to the rest, but he'd never been one to think with that part of his anatomy.

Until now.

Janey McCarthy was naked in his arms, and nothing in his wildest fantasies—and his Janey fantasies were quite something—had come even remotely close to the reality. Her hands and lips devoured him, rendering him helpless to deny her, even though he had no doubt he'd regret this. She claimed she wouldn't have regrets. He didn't believe that, either.

Despite the whir of thoughts and doubts and emotions, her lips on his belly required his undivided attention. Soft strands of silky hair tickled and tempted. Then she dragged her fingernails over his inner thigh, and his cock jerked. Before he'd recovered from that heart-stopping move, she took him into the heat of her mouth, and Joe felt like a virgin who was experiencing this particular act for the first time.

He buried his fingers in her hair and tried to hold

back, tried to summon some semblance of self-control. As if they had a mind of their own, his hips surged, and she took him deeper. And then he was coming harder than he ever had before. In the aftermath, he couldn't seem to catch his breath or find his equilibrium. With his fingers still buried in her hair, he guided her up to his chest.

Once there, her lips kept up the teasing and tormenting. When the tip of her tongue connected with his nipple, Joe grasped her hips and turned them so he was on top. He told his conscience to shut up and let him enjoy what was a dream come true, even if it wasn't happening the way he would've preferred. It *was* happening, and he could either let guilt ruin it or he could make sure she'd never forget the night she spent in his arms.

While Option A was without a doubt the wiser of the two choices, Joe chose Option B. As he cupped her sweet breast and sucked her nipple into his mouth, he set out to make sure that she'd remember him—she'd remember *this*—for the rest of her life. Years of loving her from a distance, of thinking about what he'd do if he had just one night with her, had left him well prepared to satisfy her every desire.

He left hot wet kisses on her belly and nibbled on both hip bones, which drew soft gasps from her. Settling between her slender thighs, Joe blew on the small thatch of blond hair that covered her. Her hips lifted and her thighs fell open. His finger traced a line over the damp seam until he was inside. He dipped his head and added his tongue at the same instant he slid a finger into her moist heat.

"Joe!" She pushed at him and tried to pull back.

"Shhh, honey."

"I've never . . ." Her voice hitched on what sounded like a sob. "Not like that . . ."

"You've never been loved like this, sweetheart?"

Eyes wide, she shook her head. "He didn't like it."

Joe closed his eyes and took a moment to absorb yet another burst of anger directed at David Lawrence. That selfish, arrogant *bastard*! However, good old David had once again made things easier for Joe. He had no doubt she'd remember *this*. Mindful of her hesitance, he started all over again with kisses to her calf, the inside of her knee and the silky softness of her inner thigh. By then, she was trembling uncontrollably.

"Relax, honey," he whispered. With his free hand on her belly, he urged her to stay still. "Just try to relax. I promise you'll like it."

He added a second finger to the one sliding in and out of her.

Janey moaned and lifted her hips to meet the thrusts of his fingers and tongue.

Her quivering thighs told him she was close, so he rolled the heart of her desire between his lips and sucked.

She came instantly, her muscles clenching tightly around his fingers.

Joe couldn't wait another second to be inside her. "Are you protected, sweetheart?"

Still gasping, she nodded. "I'm on the pill."

He raised her leg over his hip and entered her slowly, giving her time to accommodate him.

Her expression held such awe and wonder that if he didn't already love her with his whole heart, he would've fallen for her right then and there.

He flexed his hips, seating himself to the hilt.

Janey cried out and gripped his backside, holding him there as she came again.

Joe gritted his teeth, holding off as he rode the storm of her orgasm. *God, she was so hot and so responsive.* "More."

Her eyes flew open and met his. "I can't."

Bending his head, he captured her nipple between his teeth and pumped into her, determined to prove her wrong. He kissed his way to her mouth, his tongue mimicking the in and out action of his hips.

She wrapped her arms around his neck and met the thrusts of his tongue with soft caressing strokes of her own that made his head spin.

Joe had never experienced anything even close to this. He'd thought earlier that loving Janey hadn't ruined his life, but after this . . . God, after this, he'd never be the same. He gave her everything he had, and by the time he brought them both to an explosive, life-changing finish, he was sweating and breathing hard and more in love with her than he'd ever imagined possible.

"Janey. Janey." He couldn't stop kissing her, tasting her, loving her. *At last,* he thought, *at long last.* "Janey."

She combed her fingers through his hair, over and over, as if she couldn't bear to stop touching him, either. A guy could dream.

Trailing kisses from her neck to her jaw to her soft cheek, he encountered dampness that stopped him short. "Are you sad, Janey?"

"No," she whispered. "That was . . . It was amazing. I didn't know it could be like that."

His heart swelled with hope—fragile, but hope nonetheless. "It's never been like that for me, either."

She looked up at him, her face open and trusting. "Really?"

"Really," he said against her kiss-swollen lips. "In fact," he said, his hips already moving, "I think we need to do it again, just to make sure that wasn't a one-time moment of magic."

Janey laughed and ran her hands down his back in encouragement.

Thrilled to have made her laugh after hours of despair, Joe captured her mouth in a searing kiss and made love to her all over again.

Joe woke up facedown alone in bed with the sun streaming in the window. He shifted onto his back, and every muscle in his body protested the movement. If he'd wanted proof he wasn't as young as he used to be, his body was definitely letting him know he could no longer get away with a nonstop sexfest—not that he'd ever done anything quite like what he'd done with Janey during the night.

The scent of bacon and coffee wafted into the room while Joe stared up at the ceiling, reliving the most exquisite night of his life. He checked his watch. Six thirty. Still looking up at the cathedral ceiling and mesmerized by the movement of the fan, he made a decision and reached for the bedside phone.

"Leroy, it's Joe."

"What's up, Captain, my captain?"

"Can you take my runs today?"

"Love to."

Joe smiled. The older man had formally retired several years ago but maintained his license and remained on standby whenever Joe needed coverage. "Thanks, man. You're saving my life."

Leroy snickered. "You say that every time."

"My life is often in jeopardy. I'm on the nine to the island, ten thirty back, then one and two thirty."

"Got it. No problem."

Joe heard Janey whistling in the kitchen and hesitated only for a second. "Tomorrow, too?"

"Can do."

"Thanks, Leroy."

Joe's next call was to the office to let them know he was taking two days off. Family emergency, he said, and was grateful when they didn't ask any questions. Since he owned the business, he pretty much did as he pleased but rarely took a day off, especially this time of year when the ferries ran hourly.

He got out of bed, pulled on gym shorts and hit the bathroom to brush his teeth before he joined Janey in the kitchen, expecting this morning after to go one of two ways—major awkwardness or total avoidance. Joe didn't know which option he most preferred.

"Morning," he said.

"Oh, hi." She turned from the stove and greeted him with a shy smile.

Staggered, Joe halted in his tracks and stared at her. She wore an old T-shirt of his that fell to mid-thigh, her hair was in a high ponytail, and her face bore no signs of yesterday's misery. Rather, he detected a hint of razor burn on her neck and was oddly proud to know he'd left his mark on her. He suspected there were probably others.

"Joe?" She waved a hand in front of his face. "Everything okay?"

Shaking off the wonder that came with finding the woman of his dreams making breakfast in his kitchen, Joe moved to the coffeemaker. Anxious to keep his hands busy so he wouldn't give in to the urge to reach for her and have her again right there in the kitchen, Joe poured himself a cup of coffee and took the first sip.

She turned up her nose at him. "You take it black?"

"Uh-huh. Always have."

"Never noticed that before. Kinda gross."

Was it weird that he knew she took hers with cream and three healthy scoops of sugar? Probably. "I like to taste coffee, not milk and sugar." He glanced at the pan on the stove. "Whatcha making?"

"Oh, um, omelets. Hope that's okay."

"Sure it is."

"Joe—"

"Janey—"

Right before his eyes, Janey McCarthy blushed. If you'd asked him this time yesterday if she was capable of blushing, he would've scoffed. Seeing her like this, with morning-after shyness tinged with a hint of embarrassment, was almost like meeting her again for the very first time.

"What were you going to say?" he asked.

"I'm sure you'd like me out of your hair—"

"You're not in my hair."

"Well, I'm in your kitchen and your . . . bed." She blushed again, and he marveled at the way color crept from her chest to her neck and cheeks. Amazing.

Joe put down the mug and took a step closer to her. "I like having you in my kitchen." He brushed a kiss over lips still swollen from a night of passion. "And my bed." His hands found her hips and brought her in tight against his instant arousal. "Particularly in my bed."

She looked up at him, her pale blue eyes wide and astounded—or so it seemed to him. "What were you going to say? Before?"

"That you're beautiful in the morning."

"Oh."

He smiled. How could he not? She was so damned cute, and he loved her so damned much. He wished he could tell her . . .

"Don't you have to get to work?"

"I took the day off."

Her eyes got even wider. "You did?"

"Uh-huh."

"Can you do that during the busy season?"

He shrugged. "No biggie."

"Yes, I'm sure it is. Did you do that for me?"

"The truth?"

She nodded, and her hands skimming over his chest took his breath away.

"I did it for me." He kissed her forehead, nose and lips. "So I could spend more time with you."

"Joe," she said, "I've put you in an awful position."

He wrapped his arms around her. "I kinda liked the positions you put me in."

Janey giggled and nuzzled his chest. "You know what I mean."

"When are you due back to work?" he asked.

"Day after tomorrow."

"Then let's take today and tomorrow and not think about anything that happened yesterday or what comes next or what all this means. We'll just live in the bubble and keep the rest of the world outside until it's time to face it again."

"What if I'm not ready to face it when the bubble bursts?"

"You're stronger than you think. There's nothing you can't deal with. You just need some time to figure out your next move."

"It was grossly unfair of me to get involved with you . . . like this . . . right now, when I'm such a mess. I don't want you to think—"

He kissed whatever doubt she was about to express right off her lips. "Don't worry about me. I can take care of myself." But even as he said the words, Joe acknowledged he was setting himself up for a fall from which he might never recover.

Chapter Four

While Joe was at the store getting something to grill for dinner, Janey relaxed in a lounge chair on his back deck, watching the action in the harbor and doing her best to keep her mind clear of worries and fears and doubts and guilt. When she thought about how she'd all but begged Joe to have sex with her, she cringed. He'd said no. He'd offered her anything but that. And it wasn't like she didn't know why he'd been reluctant. But what had she done? Worked on him until he couldn't possibly say no and then had the very best sex of her life.

How was that even possible? In all her years with David, he'd never rocked her world the way Joe had. What was she to make of that? What did it mean?

She sighed and spun the dazzling, two-carat engagement ring around on her finger until it dawned on her that she should probably take it off—if for no other reason than Joe hardly needed the reminder that she was technically still committed to someone else.

Not that her *fiancé* had bothered to call for their

anniversary. Heck, he probably didn't even remember that they'd had their first date thirteen years ago yesterday, the summer before their sophomore year. Janey remembered every detail of every minute she'd spent with David. She knew the date of their first kiss, the date they finally had sex during their senior year, and the date of every momentous occasion over thirteen years together.

If pressed, David probably wouldn't even be able to recall the date they got engaged. Whereas Janey would never forget August 18 nearly two years ago, when he surprised her by proposing when they were sailing off Gansett.

She had to stop thinking about him. It was over. All the waiting and sacrificing and preparing had been for nothing. The life she'd thought she would have wasn't going to happen now. She laughed softly to herself, caught up in the fact that he didn't even know it was over between them. After what she'd witnessed in his apartment yesterday, she wondered if he would care.

Glancing down at the ring she'd loved so much, she braced herself for the onslaught of pain and slid it from her finger, then zipped it into the inside compartment of the tote she'd brought outside with her. She would give the ring back to him when she told him he had ruined everything and they were over. Or maybe she'd hold on to it and sell it. Why should she emerge with nothing after all the time and energy she'd invested in him?

The pealing ring of her cell phone sent her stomach plunging with nerves. She wasn't prepared to speak to

David. Not yet. A glance at the caller ID showed Mac's number, so she took the call.

"Hey." She made an effort to sound breezy and fine, as if her whole world hadn't been upended since she last saw her big brother yesterday afternoon.

"How ya doing, brat?"

Janey heard the concern in his voice and realized she should've known Joe would call him. "I'm fine. You?"

"Janey."

"What do you want me to say, Mac? I caught him in bed with another woman. I ran out of there, my car broke down, I called Joe and I'm staying with him for a couple of days until I get my head together."

"Saying I'm sorry doesn't seem sufficient. Am I allowed to beat the shit out of him?"

Janey laughed softly. Some things in her life were so predictable, and the oldest of her four big brothers was the most predictable of all. "As satisfying as that would be for both of us, it wouldn't change anything."

"It'd make me feel a whole lot better."

"Don't say anything to Mom and Dad. Please?"

"I won't. When are you coming home?"

"Tomorrow night. Probably the last boat."

"I'll meet you."

"You don't have to do that, Mac. I'm a big girl."

"You'll always be my baby sister, and don't forget it."

Her eyes filled for the first time that day. "How can I forget when you won't let me?"

He snickered. "How's Joe?"

A stab of something lodged in her belly. Guilt? Lust? Regret? All of the above? "Fine. Why?"

"Just wondering."

"He took the day off to babysit me, so you don't have to worry."

Silence.

"Mac? Are you still there?"

"Joe took a day off on Fourth of July week?"

Janey squirmed in her seat. Perhaps she should have kept that tidbit to herself. "Yeah. So?"

"It's just . . . unusual. That's all."

Janey couldn't help but wonder what Mac would think if he knew what else had happened between her and Joe. That was one thing her brother could never, *ever* find out about. "How are Maddie and Thomas?"

"Fine. We're worried about you."

"I'll get through it. Somehow."

"You're awfully calm. I would've expected hysterics."

"That was yesterday."

"Damn it, Janey, let me put a hurt on him, will you? *Please?*"

The screen door slid open, and Joe stepped onto the deck, his hazel eyes taking in every inch of her in one heated second.

Janey swallowed hard. "Um, I have to go."

"You never answered my question."

"Behave. I mean it. I'll deal with him in my own way. I don't need you fighting my battles for me."

"But, Janey—"

"Bye, Mac." She ended the call, turned off the phone and held it to her chest. Mac would do anything for her, but some things she had to do herself, even if she'd rather send her big brother to take care of it for her.

"I'm sorry," Joe said as he sat on the other lounge

chair. Instead of stretching out, he faced her, elbows on knees. Had she ever noticed before that the hair on his arms and the whiskers on his jaw sparkled gold in the sunlight? Or that he needed to shave twice a day? A sudden tingle between her legs took her by surprise. She couldn't believe she was reacting that way to *Joe*. Joe! The shock of her overwhelming attraction to him was almost as great as finding David in bed with another woman. "You asked me not to call him, but I thought someone should know you're here."

Crossing one leg over the other to address the tingling, Janey shrugged. "I figured you'd tell him."

"I didn't tell him what happened, just that you were here."

"It's fine, Joe. I don't mind that you called him. You saved me from having to do it."

"Is he all fired up?"

"Just a tad."

"He hates the idea of anyone hurting you. We both do."

Resting her head back against the cushion, she turned so she could see him. "I always felt so smug, you know?"

"How do you mean?"

"Here I was, the youngest of the five McCarthys, and my life was set. As you well know, my brothers were clueless in the romance department until recently when Mac met Maddie, and the others are still clueless. But I always knew exactly who I was going to marry, what my life would be like . . ." Her throat closed around a lump of emotion. Brushing at imaginary lint on her shorts, she glanced over to find him watching her intently.

"And now?"

"I have no idea what I'm going to do." A tear slid down her cheek, the first of the day, which was rather remarkable considering her life plan had been destroyed the day before. She swatted at it, refusing to go there again. Her eyes still ached from yesterday's performance.

He got up from his lounge and came over to hers, arranging himself so he was holding her from behind, her head cushioned by his shoulder. "Think of it this way—you can do anything you want now. Anything at all."

"All I've ever wanted was to marry David and have our four kids and live on the island."

"For a long while, you also wanted to be a vet," he reminded her.

"That was ages ago. I'm too old for that now."

"Who says?"

She snorted. "I've been out of school for six years. That ship has sailed."

"You can summon it back to port if that's what you want."

"Nice metaphor, Captain, but I can't imagine going back to the grind of school and studying and all that. I've gotten far too lazy."

"There's got to be something else you'd like to try, something you've never gotten the chance to do."

Sadness engulfed her, an ever-present reminder of her new reality. "Modern women everywhere would cringe to hear me say that what I wanted most was to

be his wife and a mother to our children. That's how
I've pictured my life since I was fifteen years old."

"You don't have to draw a new picture overnight."

"I know. What did you get at the store?"

"Salmon."

"That sounds good. After you left, I felt bad that
I'd forgotten to remind you."

"That you're a vegetarian? How could I forget the
scene you made when you found out steak and hamburger comes from cows?"

"I cried for a week."

"I remember." Joe reached for her hand and went
still behind her.

"What?" she asked, turning her head so she could
see him.

"You took it off."

"I couldn't stand to look at it."

He rubbed the groove the ring had left in her
finger. "You loved that ring."

"I loved what it stood for even more, but I guess I
was alone in that."

Joe held her gaze, his heated eyes sending ripples
of sensation darting over her skin. "It's his loss. He
had no idea how lucky he was to have you."

"Let's not talk about him anymore. I don't want to
think about him."

"Whatever you want."

She snuggled deeper into his embrace. "Could we
just stay here for a while?"

He tightened his hold on her and pressed a kiss to
the top of her head. "Absolutely."

* * *

As they worked in Joe's spacious kitchen to prepare dinner, Janey was struck by how comfortable he seemed there, as if cooking was more a hobby than a necessity. She added the discovery to the growing list of things she'd learned about him in the last two days.

"I never said how much I like your house. It's beautiful."

"Thanks. It was a work-in-progress for a lot of years. Sometimes I still feel like I should be painting or working on something, but it's finally done."

Astounded, Janey gazed around at the intricate tile backsplash, the granite countertop, the wood floor, the track lights over the center island. "You built this place *yourself?*"

"Every nail. Took me five years."

"Wow." Watching him proficiently slice and dice vegetables for a salad, Janey realized that even though she'd known him most of her life, she really didn't *know* him at all. "I had no idea." She laughed. "I never gave much thought to where you lived over here."

He shrugged. "Building this place kept me busy and off the streets."

She took a sip of chardonnay. "Why haven't you ever gotten married?"

The hand that had been rapidly chopping slowed. He glanced at her. "Just never got around to it."

"You've had no shortage of candidates," she said with a teasing smile.

"What's that supposed to mean?"

"Every time I turn around, you're dating someone new."

"I didn't realize you were keeping score."

"I'm not, but you know how it is on the island. People talk."

"About *me?*"

Janey giggled at the face he made. "Well, you are one of the more eligible bachelors in the area. A handsome, successful businessman. A *captain.*"

"What do they say about me?"

"Oh, you know, different day, different girl."

He put down the knife and wiped his hands on the towel he'd tossed over his shoulder. "For real?"

Janey shrugged, caught off guard by his dismay. "You know how it is over there. They've got nothing better to do than gossip."

"And you believe it? That I'm what? A man-whore?"

"*Whoa*, Joe! I never said that!"

He picked up the platter of marinating salmon and headed for the deck.

Unnerved by his reaction, Janey followed him. "I didn't mean to upset you."

He put the salmon on the grill and closed the lid. "You didn't."

Janey placed her hand on his shoulder, urging him to turn around. "Yes, I did. Talk to me."

He turned and rested his hands on his hips, his posture rigid.

"Joe?"

His face twisted into a hard-to-read expression. "It's just that . . ."

"What?"

"That's not how it is."

"You don't have to explain anything to me."

"I need you to know . . ."

"It's none of my business. I shouldn't have said anything."

"It is your business!" He ran his hands through his hair in a gesture of supreme frustration.

Janey watched him, baffled by the intensity of his reaction. "How is it my business?"

"God, Janey," he said softly as he gripped her shoulders. "How can you *not* know? Some days I feel as if I walk around with a neon sign strapped to my back."

"I don't understand," she said, unnerved by his torment.

He released her and moved to the rail that faced the harbor. Bending, he rested his elbows on the rail.

Janey went to him and put her hand on his back. "I'm sorry. I never meant to upset you." His shoulders were tight with tension she had caused.

"Janey," he sighed, dropping his head to his hands.

She didn't know what to say or do. Keeping her hand on his back, she gave him a minute. "Joe—"

He stood up straight, framed her face with his hands and captured her mouth in a deep, searing kiss. "I love you. I love you so much, and I have for as long as I can remember." Before she could say anything, he kissed her again. "I hated watching you care for a guy who didn't deserve you. I hated how he went weeks and sometimes *months* without visiting you. I hated watching you waste your time with him, *knowing* he would never love you like I do."

She'd suspected there was something . . . But never had she imagined that he'd spent *years* silently in love with her. Flabbergasted, she stared up at him. "I, um . . . I . . ."

"I shouldn't be saying these things to you, especially

right now. But I couldn't have you thinking I'm out whoring around or that I give a shit about any other woman. I date, I even have fun with some of them, and I've probably had more one-night stands than any guy alive. I'm not proud of that. Believe me. But not one of them has ever mattered."

Janey struggled free of him. "I shouldn't be here. I shouldn't have called you yesterday." Her hands began to shake as images from their erotic night together ran through her mind like a movie. "Oh, God, Joe. I didn't know. I didn't know it was like *that*." Sure, she'd figured out he had a little thing for her, but madly in love? For *years?* No, she hadn't known that. She hadn't had the first inkling.

"There's no way you could've known. I worked very, very hard to keep it hidden. Only one person has ever figured it out."

"Who?"

He smiled and tilted his head.

"Mac."

Nodding, Joe drew her back in close to him. "I don't want you to go."

"What happened between us . . ."

"Was the best thing to ever happen to me. Someday, when you're ready, maybe you'll see it was the best thing to ever happen to you, too."

Chapter Five

Janey lay in Joe's big bed that night, staring out at the harbor, trying not to think about all that had happened in the last two days and failing miserably. Since his profession of love earlier, they had bumbled awkwardly through dinner, unable to get back the easy groove they'd always shared. If she lost Joe's friendship on top of David's betrayal . . .

The thought of losing Joe made her ache with despair. Maybe she hadn't suspected the full depth of his feelings for her, but she'd always known he loved her. She couldn't lose that. She just couldn't.

Janey got up and padded into the living room, where he slept on the sofa. Squatting next to him, she reached out to toy with his hair.

He startled awake and stared at her for a long breathless moment.

"I'm sorry," she said. "I didn't mean to wake you."

He extended his arms, and as Janey sank into his embrace, the relief overwhelmed her. She stretched out next to him on the sofa, the heat of his body warming the chill that had descended upon them earlier.

"Janey," he whispered, smoothing a hand over her hair and down her back.

He trembled when she pressed her lips against his neck. His clean fresh scent invaded her senses, sending a surge of desire rippling through her. That she could feel so many conflicting emotions for this man she'd known for so long as a friend still took her by surprise.

His erection pressed against her belly, and his heart beat fast under her ear, reminding her they'd gone far beyond the simple bonds of friendship in the last few days.

Empowered by the effect she had on him, she raised her head and found his eyes in the darkness.

Earlier, he'd confessed to being wildly in love with her. Now, in his eyes, she saw the hunger and the need and the desire. She wondered how she'd missed it all these years—or rather, she conceded she hadn't allowed herself to look too closely for fear of finding exactly what she now saw in those hazel eyes.

Still holding his gaze, she lowered her head and kissed him, a sweet meeting of lips. A hum of awareness zipped between them. In all her time with David, Janey had never experienced anything quite like the raging desire Joe inspired in her. Over the years, her relationship with David had become comfortable, predictable, sturdy—or so she'd thought. Now, as she lay in Joe's arms wanting him so fiercely, she wondered if that easy comfort had led David to seek out another woman.

"What?" Joe asked.

Startled, Janey looked down at him. His nimble fingers massaged her shoulders. God, he was good at that!

"You just got all tense."

Since she couldn't tell Joe she'd been thinking of David and what might've driven him into the arms of another woman, Janey made an effort to relax under Joe's tender ministrations.

"What's going on in that pretty head of yours?" he asked.

Janey resisted the urge to purr as he worked his magic on her neck. "I just . . . ."

He kissed her softly. "What? Tell me."

"This," she said. "Whatever this is . . . It's surprising."

His handsome face lifted into a rakish grin. "Not to me. I've waited years for you to catch up."

Janey propped her chin on her fist and studied him. "It pains me to think I might've said or done something to hurt you when I didn't know how you felt."

"You didn't."

"I talked about him with you. I waved my ring around under your nose."

"You were happy, Janey. I never begrudged you that."

"But my happiness made you unhappy. I hate that."

"I'm happy right now. Holding you, kissing you . . ." He kissed her lips and chin before returning his attention to her neck. "It's everything I've ever wanted."

"I'm not ready for this to be anything more, Joe."

"I know." His tongue traced the line of her collarbone, setting off new shock waves of desire.

"I have things I need to resolve. I'm not sure how long it'll take . . ."

"I've already waited a long time." His hands coasted over her ribs and found her breasts through her thin tank top. "Whenever you're ready to find out what we might be together, you know where to find me."

"What if I'm never ready? After what happened with . . ." She stopped herself from saying David's name.

Joe ran his thumbs over her sensitive nipples.

Janey gasped.

"You'd never have to worry about me wanting someone else," he said, his tone fierce and heated. "If I had you, I'd have everything."

She smoothed his hair back from his forehead and combed her fingers through the thick strands. "Can I ask you something?"

He continued to tease her nipples. "Anything."

"Why me?"

"Ah, Janey, I don't know. I've asked myself that very question a million times. I don't even recall a time when it *wasn't* you. I see you, and I want you. Not just like this," he added, gently squeezing her breasts. "I want you in my life, in my home, sleeping next to me. I just want *you*."

Taken aback by his intensity, Janey wished she could give him even a fraction of what he so willingly gave to her. "I need some time."

"I'm not going anywhere."

Janey told herself she should get up and leave him while she still could, but it felt so good to be held in his strong arms, to be surrounded by his overwhelming love. Had David ever made her feel so treasured? Not that she could recall. "I should go back to bed."

"Take me with you."

They had this final night together before she returned to the disaster the rest of her life had become. He knew where they stood, that she had miles to go before she could consider anything more with him, and he wanted her anyway.

Janey got up and held out a hand to him.

He linked his fingers with hers and let her tug him up from the sofa. Holding hands, they walked through moonlit rooms to his bedroom.

Janey turned and wrapped her arms around him, pressing delicate kisses to his chest.

As if they had all the time in the world and not just, perhaps, this one night, Joe slowly undressed her, worshipping every inch of her fevered skin before he guided her onto the bed. He brought her to the edge of the mattress and kept his own feet on the floor as he entered her.

Janey floated on a cloud of sensation so exquisite and so devastating that she had no choice but to give herself over to him and let him take her where she'd never been before.

He bent to lave at her nipple and sent her soaring. She cried out, clutching his head to her chest as her body trembled with aftershocks. "Joe," she sighed. "God. What're you doing to me?"

"Loving you the way I've wanted to for so long." As his hips kept up a steady pace, Janey realized he wasn't done with her yet. "The way I want to forever."

While he made sweet love to her, Janey closed her eyes tight and tried to shut off the thoughts spiraling through her mind. But her best efforts couldn't stop one persistent realization from pressing to the forefront: it had taken just two days in the arms of her brother's best friend to make her wonder if she'd spent thirteen years with the wrong man.

Joe didn't sleep at all during that long night. He didn't want to miss a second of the simple joy of having Janey warm and soft and cuddled up to him. As she slept, he caressed her back and buried his nose in her fragrant hair. Committing each detail to memory, he had no idea when or if he'd ever get to hold her this way again. That thought sent a jolt of panic straight through him. After having her with him like this, how was he supposed to go back to a life that didn't include her? How was he supposed to go back to sleeping alone?

He tortured himself with questions. Had he done enough to show her how he felt about her? Had he made a mistake by telling her he'd been in love with her for years? Would he regret not giving her more time to recover from David's deception before stepping into the void? Over and over he replayed every minute they'd spent together since he rescued her on the highway. Over and over he came to the same conclusion: he had no regrets. Maybe the timing hadn't been ideal for her, but at least she'd leave here later today knowing exactly how he felt and what he wanted from her.

"Are you awake?" she whispered.

Instantly aroused by the sound of her voice, Joe wondered how it was possible that one tiny dynamo of a woman could have such an overwhelming effect on him. "Yeah."

"How come?"

"Couldn't sleep."

"Everything okay?"

"Everything's perfect." He kissed her forehead and then her lips. "Except that you have to go home tonight."

"We knew I'd have to face it all eventually."

"You could stay, you know. As long as you want to." In fact, forever would work just fine for him.

"I have to get back to work."

"You could call in sick and spend the holiday here." His heart filled with irrational hope. They'd just be prolonging the inevitable, but he'd have more time to show her what he already knew—they were meant to be together.

Janey surprised him when she raised herself up and started trailing kisses on his chest and then his belly. "That's a very tempting offer."

"And one you should consider very carefully before saying no."

She smiled at him and wrapped her hand around his throbbing erection.

Joe gasped and vowed right in that moment that no matter how long it took for Janey to see the light, he was done with other women in the meantime. He could never be with anyone else after her.

Bending her head, she dragged her tongue back and forth over his penis.

Joe clutched her hair and held on for dear life. If she was trying to kill him, she was doing it one stroke of her tongue at a time. He decided, as she drew him into the warmth of her mouth, that it was a hell of a way to go. "Janey. Oh, God. *Janey.*"

He kept his eyes open, watching her, wanting to absorb every detail as she loved him with her mouth. Despite the erotic visual, he managed to keep a firm grip on his control for several sexually charged minutes until she dragged a fingernail lightly over his balls, sending him over the edge. "Jesus," he muttered when he could finally speak again.

Kissing her way up, Janey rested her head on his chest. "I take it you liked that."

"Yeah," he said, gathering her in close to him. "You could say that."

"I can't stay, Joe. As much as I'd like to."

"I know." He decided to celebrate the half victory—at least she wanted to stay.

"We've got all day though," she said with a small smile, ever the optimist.

His heart skipped a crazy beat. "And what would you like to do?"

"This," she said as she kissed him. "Just this."

From his vantage point on the bridge, Joe looked down at Janey on the bow. She leaned against the rail lost in thought, the cool sea breeze blowing through the blond hair he'd shampooed in the shower earlier. He could only imagine her thoughts as she headed for home. Exhausted from the sleepless night, his body ached in a number of unique places thanks to a day of erotic pleasure.

After those amazing hours with her, he was more certain than ever that his life would never be complete without her by his side. But now he had to take a step back and let her do what she needed to do. Until she worked things out in her heart and mind, he could only wait and hope and pray that she'd come to the same conclusion he'd reached years ago.

His cell phone rang, jarring him out of his pensive thoughts. With a few words to the captain, Joe stepped outside the wheelhouse, extinguished the first clove cigarette he'd had in days and took the call from Mac.

"Hey, man," Mac said. "Where are you?"

"On the boat."

"Is Janey with you?"

Joe's eyes were riveted to her. Even though he wasn't working this trip, he'd insisted on seeing her home. "Uh-huh."

"David's looking for her. He tried her cell a bunch of times, but I guess it was off, so he called my mother. Of course she told him she thought Janey was with him. Now she's all up in arms about where Janey has been the last few days." Joe wondered if it was also possible that David had figured out what Janey might've witnessed in his apartment.

He suppressed a groan. The last thing Janey would want was Linda McCarthy all over her about what had happened during her eventful trip to the mainland. "Do me a favor," Joe said. "Don't let your mom swoop down on her tonight. Janey is kinda fragile right now."

"I'll do what I can, but you know how my mother can be."

"Which is exactly why she's the last thing Janey needs tonight."

"I hear ya. I'll talk to her."

"Are you meeting the boat?"

"Yep."

"Mac . . ."

"Yeah?"

Joe cleared the huge lump of emotion that lodged in his throat. "Take good care of her, will you?"

"You know I will."

"Thanks." He hated the idea of turning her over to anyone else, even her doting older brother.

"Everything all right?"

"Everything's fine," Joe said with forced cheer. As much as he'd love to unload on his best friend, he couldn't. Not about this. Not if he wanted to live through the night. Mac would assume Joe had taken advantage of his sister at her lowest moment, and Joe couldn't deny that if the roles had been reversed, he'd probably see it the same way. He and Janey knew how it had happened, which was all that mattered.

"We'll see you at the party?" Mac asked.

Joe's heart did a small happy dance at the reminder that he'd see Janey later in the week at the Fourth of July cookout Mac and Maddie were hosting at their new house. "I'll be there."

"Thanks for everything," Mac said.

"It was my pleasure." Surely that had to be the understatement of the century, Joe thought as he ended the call and took the metal stairs to the lower deck. Approaching Janey, he noticed tears on her cheeks that could probably be blamed only in part on the brisk sea breeze. It pained him to think that her time with him might've added to her torment.

"Hey." He squeezed her shoulder and ran a hand down her back, aware of the watchful eyes of his employees. The second to last thing she needed was to be the brunt of the island's vicious gossip machine.

"Hi." Her wan smile said it all.

They stood together at the rail, watching the bluffs on the island's northern coast emerge from the fog.

Joe took a deep breath and told her about Mac's call.

Janey winced. "I can't believe David called my mother. That's *just* what I need."

"I guess he was worried when he couldn't reach you."

Her snort was loaded with sarcasm. "Should I feel honored he cares enough to worry?"

"You'll have to talk to him at some point."

"Not until I'm good and ready."

"I'm sure your mother told him you'd gone to surprise him. He may have figured out why you disappeared."

"Good. Let him wonder."

At some point in the last few days, her disappointment had turned to anger. Joe supposed that was healthy, but he wouldn't be satisfied until she'd officially ended it with David. He didn't expect her longtime fiancé to go without a fight and couldn't bear the idea of him causing her any more pain than he already had.

As the ferry steamed toward South Harbor, Joe wanted to stop time, to go back to this morning when he'd held her naked in his arms, to when they'd had a whole day to spend in bed together. A tremendous sense of foreboding came over him as they got closer to the island. He wanted to howl and rage and grab hold of her and never let her go.

"Janey."

She looked up at him with those bottomless blue eyes, and he lost the words he'd been prepared to say. All he could do was stare at her and drink her in.

Mindless of the prying eyes that surrounded them, she dropped her head to his chest and rested her hands on his hips. "I never would've survived this without you."

Joe ached. How could he tell her he'd never survive the rest of his life without *her*? He couldn't. It would be so unfair to add to her burden.

He drew her into his embrace. "You know where I am. You know how I feel. You know what I want."

He felt her nod.

"No time limit, no statute of limitations, no pressure."

She looked up at him again, slaying him with the array of emotions that danced across her expressive face. "Thank you."

Gratitude was the least of what he wanted from her, but being the needy fool he was, he took what he could get. He kissed her forehead, and even though it cost him more than he could bear, he let her go.

Chapter Six

With Joe's steady presence giving her courage, Janey stepped off the ferry onto Gansett Island. She immediately noticed her brother pacing back and forth, filled with restless energy.

He looked up, saw them coming and rushed over, stopping short in front of them, his hands opening and closing into fists.

Janey smiled at his restraint and uncertainty. No doubt he wanted to toss her over his shoulder, carry her off and hide her away until he'd disposed of David's dead body. She put him out of his misery by reaching for him.

Mac put his arms around her and lifted her right off her feet. "Hey, brat."

"Don't call me that," she said as she always did.

He set her back down and took a good long look at her face. "What can I do? Tell me what you need."

Joe placed her bag at her feet and took a step back.

Mac finally seemed to register that his friend was there, too. He reached out to shake Joe's hand. "Thanks, man."

Joe shook Mac's hand. "Sure."

Janey turned to Mac. "Will you give us a minute? Please?"

Mac's sharp eyes shifted from Janey to Joe and then back to his sister. "Okay. I'll wait for you in the truck." With one more wary glance at Joe, Mac picked up her bag and took it with him.

"You'll make him suspicious," Joe said when they were alone.

"Because I want to say a proper thank-you to my good friend?"

"He knows, Janey. Don't forget that."

"I won't forget anything. That's all I wanted to say."

His eyes went soft. "Neither will I. Take care of yourself, you hear me? It's all about you and whatever you want and need. That's the only thing that matters."

Overcome by his softly spoken words and the emotion behind them, Janey nodded and hugged him one last time.

"I'll send your car over as soon as it's ready."

"Thanks. Would it be okay if I called you?"

"Yes, Janey," he said with a laugh, "it would be okay if you called me."

"Well," she said, taking a deep breath, "here goes nothing."

"You'll get through this. You can do anything you put your mind to."

"I guess we'll find out."

Joe gave her a little nudge. "Go. Before I kidnap you and take you back home with me."

She gave him a last reassuring smile. "See ya around, sailor."

He returned her smile, but she noticed it was tinged with sadness and didn't engage his eyes. "See ya."

* * *

Janey slid into Mac's black SUV, preparing to answer a million questions. However, her brother surprised her with his silence.

"Where're we going?" she asked as he drove them out of town.

"My place. I figured you might not be ready to be alone just yet."

Janey appreciated his thoughtfulness. Her house was full of pictures of her with David that someone would have to get rid of before she could return there. "Thanks."

"So what was all that just now with Joe?"

Her stomach rippled with nerves. She should've known he'd tune right into any secret she tried to keep from him. He always had. Except for times like this when he stepped back into the role of overbearing big brother, the seven years between them had disappeared once she reached adulthood. "He was really great. I just wanted to thank him."

"And that's all?"

"What else would it be?"

Mac studied her for a long moment before accelerating through an intersection. "David called Mom again."

Janey was glad her brother had moved on from interrogating her about Joe. "What did he want?"

"Since he still can't reach you, he said he's coming over tomorrow."

"Fabulous." She'd hoped to have some more time to prepare for that confrontation, but at least this way she could get it over with sooner rather than later. "I have to work tomorrow."

"I saw Doc Potter at the liquor store earlier," he said, referring to the island's veterinarian. "I told him you were dealing with a situation, and he said to take the rest of the week off. It's slow because of the Fourth anyway."

"Oh. Okay."

"I hope you don't mind that I talked to him."

"It's fine." His interference, which would've irritated her under normal circumstances, was the least of her concerns at the moment. "What'd you do about Mom?"

"I told her you'd call when you're ready to talk about it."

Janey glanced over at her handsome brother. He was tanned from long hours at the marina, his dark hair was damp from an earlier shower and stubble sprinkled his jaw. Being in love clearly agreed with him. He'd never looked better. "What makes you suddenly so good at Mom management?"

He grimaced at the backhanded compliment. "Fighting with her over Maddie."

Their mother hadn't approved of his relationship with one of the housekeepers who worked at the family's hotel. Mac had knocked Maddie off her bike by accident and then insisted on caring for her and her infant son until she was recovered—including taking her shifts at the hotel until she could work again. Unlike their mother, who had since come around, Janey had been delighted to watch her stubbornly single brother fall flat on his face in love.

"How's it going at the marina?"

"Surprisingly well."

"I still can't believe you're really taking the place over and moving home to the island."

"Some days I can't believe it, either, but I seem to be exactly where I belong. Finally."

"I'm happy for you, Mac. I really am."

He reached over and squeezed her hand. "I know you are, brat. I'm sorry all this is happening to you, especially with our wedding just around the corner."

"I certainly don't want what's happening to me to detract from your happiness. Please don't give that a thought."

"Are you still up for being Maddie's maid of honor?"

"Absolutely! I'd be heartbroken if she asked someone else."

"Good," he said, sounding relieved. Clearly, they'd given that some thought since they heard about what had happened with David.

It occurred to her just then that Mac had asked Joe to be his best man, since he'd refused to choose one of their three brothers. Her stomach took a nervous dip at the thought of serving as maid of honor to his best man at the upcoming wedding. That ought to make for an interesting day. Fortunately, it was almost two weeks off, and a lot could happen in that amount of time.

Mac took the last turn onto Sweet Meadow Farm Road, to the house he and Maddie had only recently moved into.

"How's the unpacking going?"

"We're getting there. My stuff arrived from Miami the other day, so it's a bit of a disaster area," he said with a note of apology. "We're praying for clear skies on the Fourth so we can have the party outside."

"Even if it rains, everyone knows you just moved in." Janey didn't care if the place was a disaster area.

Even chaos would be better than stewing alone in her house full of memories from her long relationship with David.

"Thomas is all about the bubble wrap," Mac said, chuckling. The ten-month-old had captivated his new daddy from the instant they first met. "He goes crazy when it pops."

Janey smiled at Mac, appreciating his efforts to take her mind off her troubles. "I'd like to see that."

They pulled up to the house, and Mac killed the engine. "Hey."

Janey looked over to find him gazing intently at her. "Whatever you need, anything at all, just ask me—or Maddie. We'll do whatever we can to help you through this."

She leaned into his one-armed hug. "Thanks. I'm glad you're here. I couldn't have dealt with Mom tonight."

He planted a kiss on the top of her head. "That's what big brothers are for." Retrieving her bag from the back of the truck, he guided her to stairs that led to an expansive deck. "You're sure I'm not allowed to kill him?"

"May I put that offer on hold until after I hear his lame excuses?"

"By all means."

After Mac and Maddie had wined and dined her and allowed her the privilege of giving Thomas his bath and bottle, Maddie tucked Janey into the guest room. Her soon-to-be sister-in-law had fawned over her, surrounding her with love and friendship that touched Janey's battered heart.

"I'm sorry it's kind of blah in here," Maddie said of the unadorned walls and windows.

"Don't be. You're still settling in. I can't believe how much you've already gotten done."

Maddie flushed with pleasure at the compliment. "We're working on a tight deadline. Mac is determined to have the downstairs presentable in time for the wedding."

Janey held out a hand, encouraging Maddie to join her on the still new-smelling queen-size bed. Maddie had corralled her long, caramel-colored hair into a messy bun that Mac had teased her about earlier.

Keeping hold of Janey's hand, Maddie stretched out next to her.

"Thanks for everything tonight. It helped to come here rather than my empty place."

"Mac figured it might."

"With a little encouragement from you, I'm sure."

"Maybe just a little. You wanna talk about it?"

Janey shrugged. "Not much to say. He was with someone else."

"And you *saw* him?"

"With my own eyes."

Maddie shuddered. "I can't imagine."

"And you never have to. Mac would die before he'd ever do something like that to you." As she said the words, Janey knew all the way down to her bone marrow that she spoke the truth. Mac had waited forever to find the love of his life and was utterly devoted to her and her son. Janey wanted that kind of certainty for herself, too. Until this week, she'd never realized just how important it was.

Thoughts of Joe resurfaced all at once, infusing her with heat and desire as she remembered his passionate lovemaking. After two days with him, she knew without a doubt that he'd never do what David had done.

"What, Janey? What is it?"

She glanced at Maddie. "I need to tell someone . . ."

Maddie pushed herself up on one elbow. "What?"

"You have to promise you won't tell Mac."

Maddie's eyes narrowed, and she swallowed hard. "We have a rule about keeping things from each other, but I suppose I could make an exception this once. He'd want me to do anything I could to help you."

"It's big, Maddie. Huge, in fact, and you're going to want to tell him, but you can't."

Maddie groaned. "I should run out of here right now while I still can, but now I *have* to know."

Janey smiled at the torment on Maddie's face. "I was counting on your female need to know."

"Spill it. Right now before I change my mind."

Her eyes darting to the open door, Janey whispered, "I slept with Joe."

Maddie's mouth fell open and then closed just as quickly. "Are we talking slept or *slept?*"

"Both."

"Wow," Maddie said on a long exhale as she fell onto her back. "You weren't kidding. That is huge."

"And you're already trying to figure out how you'll keep it from Mac."

Maddie turned her head so she could see Janey. "He can't ever know that, Janey. He'd totally flip out at Joe."

"I know, and it wasn't even his doing." Janey's face heated with embarrassment. "At least not the first time."

"*It happened more than once?*"

Janey swatted at her. "*Shhh,* will you?"

"Answer the question!"

"It happened a lot, actually."

"Oh, my God! I can't believe it. How was it?"

A bolt of heat traveled through Janey's body as she thought of being with Joe. "*Amazing.* I had no idea it could be like that. No idea at all."

"So what now? Are you guys like together or something?"

"No, nothing like that. He knows I have a bunch of crap to deal with."

"And then?"

"I don't know." Janey's stomach ached with dismay. She'd made a huge mess of things by getting involved with Joe, but somehow she couldn't bring herself to call what they'd shared a mistake.

"He's very . . . you know . . . devoted to you," Maddie said.

"It's much more than that, and you know it."

Maddie at least had the good grace to look guilty.

"You weren't kidding when you said you tell each other everything."

"Mac was worried about you both when he heard you were staying there."

"I was in such a fog after what I saw at David's. Then my car broke down. I probably shouldn't have called Joe, but he was the first person I thought of. And he was on the mainland while the rest of you were out here."

"And he came running."

"Yes." Janey filled her in on how they'd ended up in bed together. "I'm not proud of how I acted that first night, but he was so *there*. And even though I knew it was probably a mistake, somehow it helped."

"Wow."

"I know you must be thinking I'm a heartless slut."

"That's not at all what I was thinking."

"Then what?"

"I was wondering about Joe and how he's coping with all of this."

"He said he'd wait until I got myself together. However long it takes."

"That's good of him."

"It's probably far more than I deserve after he waited years for me to get a clue about how he felt about me."

"How do *you* feel, Janey? About both of them?"

She thought about that for a moment. "When I saw David under her while she rode him hard and fast—just the way he likes it—it was like something in me shut down. Everything I'd ever felt for him went away in that moment, and I don't think I can ever get it back."

"That's understandable. Anyone would feel the same way after seeing that. What about Joe?"

Janey glanced at Maddie. "When I said good-bye to him tonight at the ferry?"

Maddie nodded.

"All I could think about was how long I had to wait until I could see him again."

Chapter Seven

Reeling from everything Janey had told her, Maddie checked on Thomas one last time in his big new room before heading to the master suite she shared with Mac. She still wanted to pinch herself to make sure she wasn't dreaming about living with her own handsome prince in what could only be called a palace compared to the tiny apartment she used to call home.

Mac was already in bed, but he sat up when she came in. The covers fell to his waist, and Maddie took a moment to appreciate his splendid chest. She never got tired of looking at him.

"How is she?"

"Okay." Maddie released her hair from the bun and shook it loose. "Don't forget she's already had a few days to absorb the blow." In the gorgeous new dresser that matched the king-size bed he'd insisted on, Maddie found one of the half-dozen silk nightgowns he'd bought for her the same day they'd gone to the mainland to order furniture.

After a quick trip to their spacious bathroom to change and brush her teeth, she shut off the light and slid into bed next to him. Like he had every night since the huge bed was delivered, he met her in the middle and wrapped his naked body around her. Maddie had never known bliss like that which came from sleeping in Mac's arms every night. "Can you tell me again why we needed this massive bed when we only use about three feet of it?"

He kissed her bare shoulder, sending goose bumps all the way to her ankles. "When we wake up some morning in the near future surrounded by kids, you'll know why." His big hand found her flat stomach and branded her with its heat.

She knew exactly what he was thinking. They'd come close a few times recently to disregarding caution, but so far, caution had prevailed. Maddie turned so she could see him, wishing she could share with him what Janey had told her.

"You're not going to tell me what my sister said, are you?"

Startled, Maddie met his gaze, astounded as always by how easily he read her. "I . . . ah . . ."

Mac laughed and kissed her. "It's okay. You girls are allowed to have your secrets."

"We are?"

"Sure. I know you wouldn't keep anything monumental from me. We have rules."

Guilt pinged through her. Yes, they had rules—rules *she'd* insisted on. But telling Mac what had happened between Janey and Joe would set off an explosion that could ruin a lifelong friendship, not to mention what it might mean for their wedding.

Mac would never understand that Janey had been

the aggressor. He would only see that his best friend had betrayed his trust and taken advantage of his baby sister when she was vulnerable. She knew him well enough to be certain of how he'd react. So she said nothing. Instead, she reached for him and kissed him, hoping to get her mind—and his—off what she wasn't telling him.

"Mmm," he said against her lips. "I wait all day for this."

"Me, too. I don't know how I ever lived without it."

That seemed to fire his passion as he devoured her with heated kisses, shifted her under him and settled into the valley of her legs. "All this stuff with Janey," he said, kissing a path from her mouth to her neck to her breasts, "makes me realize how incredibly lucky we are."

Her fingers burrowed into his soft dark hair, and her legs curled around his hips in encouragement. "We're *so* lucky. So very, very lucky." And she hoped against hope that she wasn't risking everything by keeping a huge secret from him.

Using both hands, he brushed the hair back from her face and gazed down at her in the milky darkness. "I love you, Madeleine."

Her heart still tripped over itself whenever he looked at her that particular way. "I love you, too."

He started to reach for a condom, but she stopped him. She told herself it wasn't guilt that had her wiggling out of the nightgown while keeping him trapped between her legs.

"What're we doing?" he asked with a bemused expression.

"Throwing caution to the wind."

"Really?"

She crooked an eyebrow at him. "Are you saying no?"

He started all over again with deep, heated kisses. "I am most definitely not saying no."

Maddie smiled at him, loving him so desperately.

He threw his head back and moaned. "Oh, *man*."

"Good?"

"I won't last long like this," he said through gritted teeth.

She slid her hands over his back to clutch his backside. "Then you'd better make it count."

Mac proceeded to do just that.

Janey lay in bed in Mac's guest room trying to decide whether or not she should check the messages David had left in the last few days.

A soft giggle came from the room at the other end of the hallway, and Janey realized her brother was probably making love to his fiancée. For the first time, Janey had reason to envy her brother's romantic harmony. He was happily settled, and she was in the midst of an uproar. Avoiding it wouldn't make it go away.

With great reluctance, she powered up her phone and dialed into voice mail. "Hey, babe, it's me. I'm between patients, but I wanted to totally shock you by saying happy anniversary." Janey laughed to herself that he had called her the day *after* their anniversary. "You're shocked, right? I knew it. Thirteen years, can you believe it? Time flies when you're having fun. This time next year, we can celebrate together.

Anyway, I just wanted to say I love you, so call me so I can say I love you."

The sound of his familiar voice had tears spilling from her eyes. By "between patients," had he really meant he was between bouts of passionate sex?

She listened to the rest of his messages—increasing concern about where she was, why he couldn't reach her, and finally, irritation. "I'm going to call your mother if I don't hear from you within the hour. *Where are you?*"

Janey had never realized before just how available she'd been to him. Whenever *he* had time to call, she'd always been there. Well, not anymore. Curling into a ball in the comfortable bed, she clutched the pillow tight against the pain of David's betrayal. Even days later, the images ran through her mind like a horror movie she could never escape. If only she hadn't seen it. But if she hadn't, he might've gotten away with it, and she might've married a cheating scumbag.

"Not my David," she sobbed into the pillow. "How could you do this to me? How could you do this to *us?*"

In the midst of unbearable pain, Janey longed for Joe's strong arms, his soft words of comfort, his steady presence. With the phone still clutched in her fist, she considered calling him, if only to hear his voice. She thought about it for several minutes before she dismissed the idea as patently unfair. Before she could consider spending another minute with Joe, she had to put David in the past—literally and emotionally.

She cared for Joe far too much to risk hurting him any further by dragging him onto the roller coaster she faced in the immediate future.

Her stomach ached at the thought of seeing David tomorrow, of confronting him with proof of his infidelity, of calling off their engagement, of canceling their long-planned wedding.

As if she had conjured him straight out of a dream, she heard Joe's deep, sexy voice telling her she could get through anything, that she was strong and capable and resilient. He believed in her, and knowing that made it possible to believe in herself. She *would* get through this, if for no other reason than he was waiting for her, and she couldn't wait to find out what they might be together.

Joe tapped on the bar at the Beachcomber, signaling the bartender to bring him another round. He'd lost count of how many boilermakers he'd already consumed. However many, it hadn't been enough to dull the throbbing ache in his chest that had started the minute Janey walked away from him earlier.

The sexy bartender who always flirted with him quirked a questioning eyebrow. "What's up with you tonight? You're hitting it hard."

"Just supporting the local economy." He heard the slight slur in his speech and didn't care.

She poured him a new shot of whiskey and opened another bottle of beer.

He tried to remember her name. Charley. No. Katie. *Chelsea!* That was it. They'd spent a memorable night together upstairs three or four summers ago, and ever since then, she'd angled for a repeat performance. Those days were over, he reminded himself. Janey had ruined him for other women.

Thinking about her soft skin, her fragrant hair, the small but firm breasts that fit perfectly in the palms of his hands, the exquisite joy of being inside her when she came . . . Joe moaned.

"You okay, Joe?" Chelsea asked, looking at him now with concern etched into her pretty face.

Looking up at her, he was startled to realize he'd moaned out loud. It wouldn't do for the owner of the Gansett Island Ferry Company to be seen falling-down drunk at the island's landmark hotel. He knew that, of course, but it didn't stop him from downing the new shot in one giant gulp that burned all the way through him. What sweet relief it was to feel something other than desperate fear that he'd never spend another night with Janey.

After years of wishing and hoping and praying, all his dreams had come true in an unexpected interlude that would haunt him for the rest of his days if it was all he ever had of her. His heart raced with anxiety at the thought of never being with her again, and his stomach lurched. If he didn't get out of there immediately, he was going to be sick all over the bar. With a gesture for Chelsea to put the drinks on his tab, he tossed a twenty on the bar for her and ran out to the back alley where he was violently ill.

Sweaty and chilled, he leaned against the clapboard building and decided he'd been stupid to think booze would cure what ailed him. Only one thing could cure him, but he couldn't have her tonight. Wiping his mouth with the back of his hand, Joe staggered back inside and up the stairs to the room he kept on the third floor for nights he spent on the island. This wasn't one of his regular nights, but he'd missed the last boat back to the mainland.

In his room, Joe studied his haggard reflection in the mirror before splashing cold water on his face and brushing the sour taste from his mouth. Without bothering to undress, he landed facedown in the lumpy bed and slipped into tortured dreams about the one he loved but couldn't have. Every time he managed to get his arms around her, she somehow slipped away. The horrible dance went on all night until he woke with a start to blinding morning sun.

Rolling onto his side, Joe groaned at the inhuman pain in his skull. Surely agony like this meant that someone had stabbed knives into his forehead and temples while he slept. He gripped his head to keep it on his neck as he sat up and tried to shake off the horrible dreams. A new surge of nausea had him rushing for the bathroom, where he discovered that whiskey burned even more coming back up than it had on the way down.

He couldn't remember the last time he'd drunk himself into such a stupor—or the last time he'd had better reason. A freezing shower snapped him back to life, which also brought him right back to why he'd turned to alcohol in the first place. Leaning his head against the cool tiles, he yearned for her and called himself six kinds of fool for being so stupid as to make love to her when she wasn't really his. He should never have let that happen until she was free and clear to love him the way he loved her. The one thing the whiskey couldn't change was the irrefutable fact that he had only himself to blame for his misery.

He turned off the shower, grabbed a towel and

scrounged for some clean clothes. Dressed in khaki shorts, a green Gansett Island Ferry Co. polo shirt and Top-Siders, Joe made his way—painfully—down to the gift shop, where he bought three packets of Advil and downed every one of the six pills. Normally, he'd be face-first in coffee at that hour, but he didn't think his fragile stomach could handle it.

He gave himself a few minutes to make sure the Advil would stay down before he took the hotel's front steps to the sidewalk and crossed the street to the ferry landing. The first boat of the day had just arrived from the mainland, and his staff was hard at work unloading cargo and preparing the next boat. Off to the side, two of his younger employees engaged in good-natured horseplay while they waited to supervise the loading of the passenger vehicles that were lined up to drive onto the next ferry.

"Hey!" Joe called to the two young men, who immediately froze at the sound of his voice. "I'm not paying you to fool around. Knock it off!"

His unusual outburst caught the attention of all the employees working in the area, but Joe pretended not to notice as he headed for the office. Screw it, he thought. Even the best of bosses was allowed a foul mood every now and then.

"Hey, Joe!"

At the sound of a familiar voice, Joe turned, giving his aching head time to catch up to the sudden movement. His bleary eyes cleared to find David Lawrence coming off the ferry. Joe's hands rolled into fists.

"I thought that was you." David extended a hand. "How's it going?"

Joe in his right mind would've reluctantly shaken

David's hand and gone on with his life. Joe in love with the woman who had cried her heart out over this guy didn't shake the proffered hand or go on with his life. Rather, he raised one of those fists and plowed it into the good doctor's handsome, smiling face.

Now that, Joe thought as David collapsed to the pavement, had been worth getting up for.

Chapter Eight

They'd let him make one phone call, so naturally Joe called Mac, knowing his friend would approve of the so-called crime that had landed him in the island's only jail cell. A woman at the marina reported that Mac was out on the Salt Pond. She promised to give him the message as soon as he returned. In the meantime, Joe was left to cool his heels on a stiff cot with an ice pack wrapped around his swelling knuckles.

Images of David's bloody face and girlish shrieks ran through his mind. Joe grunted out a laugh. It'd been worth it. *So totally worth it.* Getting arrested for assault was a small price to pay for seeing that pompous ass taken down a few notches. Joe's satisfaction in exacting a tiny bit of revenge on Janey's behalf was tempered by the pounding in his head and the lingering nausea.

Right at that moment, it occurred to him—for the first time—that Janey might not appreciate what he'd done. An odd twinge of anxiety danced up his spine as the rustling of footsteps outside the cell had him sitting up straighter on the cot.

Along with Joe's high school classmate, Gansett Island Police Chief Blaine Taylor, Big Mac McCarthy came around the corner and stood outside the cell, hands on hips, his usually amiable face set into an expression of supreme displeasure.

Oh, shit.

Joe stared at the man he'd loved like a father since he'd been a newly fatherless seven-year-old transported from the frenetic energy of New York City to his grandparents' home on a tiny island with fewer than a thousand year-round residents. One of the more important residents, at least to Joe, was currently giving him the once-over and apparently not liking what he saw. Disappointing Big Mac had never been high on Joe's to-do list.

"What's the meaning of this, my friend?"

"Call it an act of impulse."

"You broke his nose."

"He broke her heart!"

Big Mac's lips tightened. "So I hear."

Joe crossed his arms and winced when his abused knuckles made contact with his shirt. "He had it coming."

"Perhaps, but to my thinking, it was her punch to throw, not yours." Big Mac ran a huge hand through wiry gray hair. "Do you know I haven't been in here since you and Mac decided to flatten half the mailboxes on the island with my truck?"

Blaine snickered, and Joe sent him a dirty look.

Joe swallowed hard as memories of a long-ago night came flooding back. That had been the first time he'd disappointed Big Mac, and Joe had gone to great lengths to make it the only time—until today.

"Remember what I did then?" Big Mac asked.

He and Mac had never forgotten the endless night in jail when they were just sixteen. And that, of course, had been Big Mac's goal. While they'd still gotten into their share of mischief, they'd never gone near another mailbox. Joe stared at the older man, incredulous. "You're not planning to leave me in here overnight."

"That's up to you," Big Mac said.

"What do you mean?"

"You need to apologize and kiss some serious ass so he'll drop the charges."

Joe released a humorless laugh. *As if!* "Not in this or any other lifetime."

"Then you'd better get comfortable. I hear the judge isn't due back until next Friday. Isn't that right, Blaine?"

"Sure is. He'll arraign you then on felony assault charges."

"That ought to be real good for business," Big Mac added.

Joe swore under his breath. Stuck in here for *six days*? That hadn't been part of the plan—not that he'd had much of a plan before the sight of David's smarmy face sent him over a cliff he hadn't realized he'd been teetering on. No, he didn't regret flattening the bastard, and he'd be damned if he would apologize.

"Does Janey know about this?" Joe forced himself to ask. His gut clenched with guilt and his mouth went dry as sand when it dawned on him that since he last saw Big Mac McCarthy, he'd made mad, crazy love to the man's beloved only daughter. The same daughter he'd called Princess until she turned nineteen and begged him not to.

"I reckon most of the island knows by now. The good doctor put on quite a show."

"Fucking baby," Joe muttered. "It's the least of what he deserves."

"Lucky for you, I happen to agree, even if I don't approve of you taking it upon yourself to even the score."

Oh, if only he knew . . .

"You're a respected businessman, a pillar of this community," Big Mac continued. "You've got no place resorting to violence in front of your employees and customers."

No one had ever been better at building Joe up or cutting him down to size when necessary. Apparently, not much had changed in the nearly twenty years since he and Mac had become adults.

"I'm sorry to disappoint you."

"I have a feeling I'm going to be the least of your worries." Big Mac nodded to Blaine who opened the cell.

Before Big Mac could change his mind, Joe made for the open door. "I thought you said I'd have to apologize first."

Big Mac's eyes twinkled with mirth. "I just wanted to see what you'd have to say to that."

Blaine laughed at the expression on Joe's face. "Well played, Mr. McCarthy."

"Glad I'm available to amuse you both," Joe said.

Laughing, Big Mac put an arm around Joe's shoulders. "While you know damned well I don't condone violence, after hearing about what he did, I probably would've been tempted to punch him myself. You saved me the trouble."

Even though he was usually taller than most men, Joe had to look up at Big Mac. "Did I really break his nose?"

Big Mac squeezed his shoulder. "Sure did."

"Good."

Joe had punched David. Joe had punched David *in the face*, breaking his nose. Thirty minutes after hearing about the incident at the ferry landing, Janey was still trying to get her head around it—and trying to decide where she wanted to go first, to the jail to bail out Joe or to the clinic to confront her wayward fiancé.

"I'll take you anywhere you want to go," Maddie said after Janey vocalized her dilemma. "Mac left us the truck."

"Don't you have to work?"

"I took a few weeks off to get ready for the wedding." Her cheeks flushed with color. "Your brother insisted I enjoy every minute of it."

"That's awesome. He's right. It's a once-in-a-lifetime event, and you should enjoy it." Janey ached, thinking about the plans for her once-in-a-lifetime day that wasn't going to happen now.

"What do you want to do, Janey?"

"What do *you* think I should do?"

Before Maddie could state her opinion, Janey's cell phone rang, and she took the call from her father.

"I've bailed out Joe," he said without preamble. "He's coming to the marina to have lunch with me."

Her insides churned with indecision. She needed to see Joe, to find out what had driven him to *punch* David, and mostly to see if he was all right. The Joe she knew and loved wouldn't do such a thing. So what had happened? Did David say something he shouldn't have? Janey wouldn't put it past him.

"Did he say anything about what happened?" she asked her father.

"Not much."

"I'll come by the marina after a while."

"Is there anything I can do, Princess?" he asked in a soft voice that brought tears to her eyes.

"I could use a big hug from my daddy."

"You got it," he said gruffly. "I'll see you soon."

Ending the call, she turned back to Maddie. "I need to see David. Can you take me to the clinic?"

"Of course."

Twenty minutes later, they arrived at the entrance to the Emergency Room. Janey reached for the handle to open the car door but was hit with a sudden bout of paralysis. Waiting inside was the man she'd loved all her life, the same man who had betrayed her and didn't have a clue that she knew what he'd been up to while continuing to profess his undying love for her.

"Janey? Are you all right?"

"I don't know if I can do this. How do I go in there and play the role of the concerned fiancée when I *know* what he's done?"

"Just take it a step at a time. Deal with the injury and what happened with Joe this morning. Later, when you're alone, you can talk to him about the rest."

Janey rested a hand on her aching belly. "I don't

want to be alone with him. The thought of it makes me sick."

"Then you don't have to be. Mac and I meant it when we told you we'll do anything we can to get you through this in one piece."

Janey continued to stare at the entrance to the ER. "It's funny, you know? A week ago, if I'd heard he was hurt, I would've dropped everything and gone running."

Maddie rested a hand on Janey's, infusing it with much-needed warmth. "That was before you discovered he'd been unfaithful to you. You don't owe him anything. If you'd rather not go in there, you certainly don't have to."

"If I don't, then the whole island will be talking about why I didn't show. Joe has already given them enough cause for speculation."

"Are you angry with him? With Joe?"

"I'm shocked, to be honest. It's so unlike him. I just keep wondering what David could've said to set him off."

"You'll find out soon enough."

"Yeah, well . . . First things first."

"Want me to come in with you?"

"Oh! Would you? That'd be great."

"Let's go."

Inside, they asked for David and were shown to a curtained cubicle at the end of a long hallway. Glancing at Maddie for courage, Janey stuck her head inside and gasped at the sight of David bruised and bloody and swollen. Damn! Joe had done quite a number on him!

"Well, look who it is," David said with a bitter edge to his voice. "My missing fiancée." His face was so distorted he didn't even sound like himself. "Where the heck have you been, Janey? I've been trying to call you for days!"

As if she was meeting him for the first time, she studied the thick dark hair she'd so loved running her fingers through, the piercing blue eyes, the strong jaw and sensuous lips. David Lawrence had always made her heart race, but looking at him now, she felt dead inside. "I had . . . um . . . some stuff to take care of."

"What kind of stuff? And what the hell's wrong with Joe?"

"Did you say something to him?"

"I said hello. That was it. Next thing I know, I'm on my ass with a broken nose that hurts like a mother." Under each eye was the start of what would no doubt be colorful shiners—the least of what he deserved. "What'd I ever do to him?"

Since Janey couldn't very well answer that question, she said nothing. He didn't seem to notice as he continued to rant.

"You didn't tell me what 'things' you had to take care of that kept you from calling me back for three days."

He sounded sulky and petulant. Did she dare remind him of the many times over their years together that she'd waited sometimes a week for a return call from him while he was doing who knows what with other women? As she studied him, she decided it wasn't worth the bother of the argument. What did it matter now?

"We need to talk—"

"Where's your ring?"

Her brain froze on the image of the buxom blonde riding him hard.

"*What the hell is going on here, Janey?*"

"It's over," she said softly. Thirteen years of her life. Gone. Done. Over. And she had absolutely nothing to show for them.

"What is?"

"We are."

"What are you—"

"I saw you."

His eyebrows knitted with confusion, which apparently pained him. Tears flooded his eyes, but Janey wasn't naive enough to think they were for her. Not anymore. "You saw me? Where?"

Janey felt like she was floating above herself, looking down at someone who looked like her and sounded like her but wasn't her at all. "In bed."

"You're talking in riddles," he said, exasperated. "When did you see me in bed?"

"I came to your apartment on our anniversary to surprise you, but the surprise was on me. You should really lock your doors when you're 'entertaining.'"

All the remaining color drained from his face when he finally got what she was telling him. "You don't understand."

"You're goddamned right I don't." Janey gave herself credit for keeping her voice down when she really wanted to shriek and rail and punch him until he hurt as much as she did. "And guess what? I really don't want to understand."

"Wait. Janey, listen—"

"There's nothing you can say and nothing you can *ever* do to get the image of you having sex with another woman out of my head."

"It's not what you think."

Janey laughed when she wanted to cry. "You're

probably going to tell me you were conducting medical research or some other lame story that you'll expect me to believe."

"It only happened once."

"I don't believe you."

"I swear to God!"

"Don't swear to God and then lie to my face. You'll go to hell."

He touched his wounded face and winced. "Already there."

"You don't *know* hell!" She no longer cared about keeping her voice down. "You didn't have to see me *writhing around in bed with another guy!*"

"You don't get it, Janey. Work is so stressful, I miss you so much, and there's this other thing going on . . . I just needed to take the edge off."

She stared at him, incredulous. "I offered to move to Boston so I could 'take the edge off' anytime you wanted, but you said I should stay on the island. At least now I know why you were so anxious to keep me tucked away where I couldn't 'surprise' you anytime *I* needed to take the edge off."

"Janey—"

"You've made a fool of me and a mockery of all the years I spent waiting for you. I was *always* faithful to you."

"She means nothing to me. You're the one I love. I've always loved you, and you know that."

Images of Joe making sweet love to her chose that moment to pop into her overworked brain. "If you really loved me, you wouldn't have 'taken the edge off' with other women while you were engaged to me." Deciding she wanted nothing to remind her of all the years she'd spent so foolishly devoted to him, Janey dug the ring out of her bag.

She dropped it on the bed and took one last long look at the man she'd loved all her life. "Don't get any ideas about pressing charges against Joe. You're lucky he *only* broke your nose. He and Mac were quite prepared to kill you after they heard what you'd done. I told them you weren't worth the trouble. Turns out I was right about that. Have a nice life."

Turning, she battled her way through the curtain to the hallway, where Maddie leaned against the wall looking embarrassed to have overheard the exchange.

"Janey!" David called. "Wait!"

"Get me out of here," she muttered to Maddie. Her legs suddenly felt like spaghetti, and Janey wasn't sure they'd support her weight for much longer. "Please just get me out of here."

"I've got you." As Maddie put an arm around her and hustled her through the waiting room, Janey felt every eye in the place on her. She and David hadn't been quiet. News of their broken engagement was probably already burning up the island phone lines.

"Oh, God, my parents," Janey whispered. "They should hear this from me, not the gossips."

"I'll take you to them. Just hang in there. The worst part is over."

"How'd I do?"

"Better than I would have. You held yourself together and got through it with your dignity intact."

That might be true, Janey thought, but hearing him casually confess to being unfaithful had broken what was left of her heart.

Chapter Nine

Maddie called ahead to let Janey's mother know they were coming, so Janey wasn't surprised to find both her parents, Mac, and Joe waiting for her at "The White House," the nickname the locals had given the McCarthys' two-story colonial that overlooked North Harbor. Down the hill from the house was McCarthy's Gansett Inn and McCarthy's Marina.

The first thing she noticed when she and Maddie stepped into the kitchen was Joe's swollen right hand. Before she could say anything about it, however, her mother rushed her. Janey could see her mother had been crying, which made her mad all over again at David.

"Oh, sweetie! I don't know what to say."

"I'm sorry you heard it from someone other than me."

"Don't worry about that," Linda said, stroking a hand over Janey's back. "All we care about is that you're okay."

"I suppose I will be. Eventually."

"These things take time, honey," Big Mac said.

Janey absorbed the comfort of her mother's embrace for a long, quiet moment. When she opened her eyes, she found Joe watching her intently. An odd current of awareness zipped through her, reminding her once again of the connection they'd shared during their time together.

She wanted a moment alone with him but knew it couldn't happen now.

Big Mac was next in line for a hug, and he lifted Janey off her feet. Surrounded by her father's familiar scent and overwhelming love, Janey finally broke. "Aww, baby," he said, holding her tight against him. "It's gonna be all right. I promise you'll be just fine. We'll see to that, won't we, Lin?"

"You bet we will."

Her parents guided her to a sofa in the family room and sat on either side of her. The others followed, hovering on the perimeter of her disaster.

"So will we," Mac said, standing with his arm around Maddie, who nodded in agreement.

Joe remained a quiet observer, but upon another quick glance, Janey noticed a tick of tension at work in his cheek. She looked away, unable to process all the emotion she felt coming from him. He no doubt wanted to scoop her up and take her away somewhere until she stopped hurting so badly.

"What happened at the clinic, honey?" Linda asked.

As Janey relayed as much of the conversation with David as she could bear to repeat, she watched Joe slip from the room and wished she could go after him. She hated that he was hurting, too.

Mac kissed Maddie's forehead and followed his friend.

Janey swiped at the tears on her cheeks. "We'll

have to cancel the wedding. You've spent all that money—"

"Don't give it a thought," Linda said. "We'll worry about that when you're ready to."

"I hate him for doing this to me," Janey whispered. "For ruining everything."

"So do we, honey," Big Mac said, squeezing her shoulder. "So do we."

Joe couldn't take another minute of listening to Janey's heartbreak. He'd already endured more than he could handle. Flexing his bruised hand, he winced at the shaft of pain that greeted the movement.

"Takes about a week," Mac said.

Turning to his friend, Joe said, "What does?"

"The hand. It took about a week for mine to heal after I flattened Darren Tuttle."

Joe smiled. "Ah, yes. I remember now. Another broken nose to our credit."

"Both times, they had it coming."

Darren, the loser who'd already ruined Maddie's reputation with false rumors in high school, had made an off-color comment about her voluptuous figure that Mac hadn't appreciated.

"Except you're not known as the hothead of this duo," Mac reminded him. "In fact, I suspect this might be the first broken nose to your credit."

"You suspect correctly."

"What gives, man?"

Joe stared out over the expansive view of North Harbor. "I saw his smug, smiling face and something snapped."

"So he didn't even say anything?"

"I believe he said hello."

Mac laughed. "Goddamn him."

"Exactly."

"So much for being subtle."

Joe looked over at his friend. "Where has that gotten me?"

"Joe—"

He held up a hand to stop Mac from saying any more. "I don't want to talk about it."

"You just need to bide your time," Mac said softly. "Give her a couple of months to get past this, and then maybe . . ."

"A couple of months." To Joe that sounded like a lifetime. One night without her and he'd managed to get drunk, throw up and punch someone. What would he look like after sixty nights without her?

"It seems like forever right now, but you've already waited forever. What's a little while longer?"

Joe's laugh was tight with irony.

Mac rested a hand on his shoulder. "What can I do for you? I hate to see you so spun up."

"Nothing. Like you said, I just have to bide my time. Somehow." In a perfect world, Janey would realize on her own that they were meant to be together and come to him, ready to plan their future. However, Joe had no illusions that he lived in a perfect world.

"Just think about what might be waiting for you on the other end."

That was the problem—Joe already knew *exactly* what was waiting for him, and he had no idea how to live without her for even a couple of weeks. "Yeah." He'd never before felt so out of sorts, like he was coming out of his own skin. "I need to get out of here."

"Where do you want to go? I've got the bike." Mac referred to his old motorcycle. "I can take you."

"Back to work, I guess. I've taken enough time off, and I can only imagine how they're all buzzing after watching me get carted off by the cops."

"They'll forget about it in a day or two. Come on, I'll give you a lift."

Joe followed Mac inside where Linda was forcing some soup on Janey. She glanced up, and their eyes met. A current of electricity crackled between them, and Joe wondered how it was possible everyone in the room didn't feel it. Before he succeeded in broadcasting his utter misery to her entire family, Joe mumbled a quick good-bye and thank-you on his way to the front door. He was surprised when Janey, rather than Mac, followed him.

"Joe! Wait!"

"Go back inside, Janey. I can't do this right now."

She grabbed his arm, forcing him to stop. "Please."

Oh, God, this woman was his *kryptonite*! He turned, took a breath, and put his hands on his hips. It took all his fortitude to make contact with those pale blue eyes. "What do you want me to say?"

"Why did you hit him?"

"Because he was there." Joe looked down at the ground, his eyes connecting with her delicate feet in flip-flops. A heated memory of pressing kisses to her sensitive arches came rushing back like a punch to the gut.

"Joe," she whispered, resting a hand on his arm. "You're so tense. I hate seeing you like this." She reached for his bruised hand.

He pulled it back and cast an uneasy gaze at the house, certain he'd find faces in every window. But no one was watching. Bringing his eyes back to her and absorbing the familiar burst of longing that occurred every time he saw her, he steeled himself to do what he knew he had to do, even if it killed him. "What happened between us was a mistake, Janey."

The flash of hurt that crossed her expressive face was the first nail in his coffin. "How can you say that?"

"Your father and Mac would kill me if they knew—"

"*Why* did you hit him?"

"Because he was smiling and smug and satisfied, coming to see you like nothing was wrong after what he'd done to you!" Joe's head felt like it might explode. He needed to get out of there, to get away from her. Now. "I have to go."

She clutched his arm. "Not like this."

"I can't do this! It's like I'm losing my mind! I hit someone! I got thrown in jail. Last night I got so drunk I puked outside the Beachcomber. I can't deal with it!"

"What can't you deal with?"

He stared at her, incredulous. As he became more agitated, she seemed to get calmer. "Any of it. You, him, us."

"It's over between me and him."

"On paper, maybe." In a jerky motion, he ran his hands through his hair, which served to dislodge her warm hand from his arm. "We both know you have a long way to go before you'll be over it."

"Maybe not so long. There's something about seeing your fiancé having sex with someone else that speeds up the process."

"You were just crying your eyes out over him ten minutes ago."

"I'm much more sad about losing the dream than

I am about losing him." She quirked her head as the realization settled over her. "Hmm, I didn't get that until I said it out loud."

"You don't have to lose the dream, Janey." As the words fell from his mouth, he wanted to take them back. Hadn't he just called what'd happened between them a mistake?

"I don't?"

Even though everything in him was urging him to run, he couldn't look away. He shook his head. "No," he said softly. "You can still have anything and everything you want with someone who would never betray you the way he did."

"Come to my place tonight. After work."

Joe finally tore his eyes off her and looked to the heavens for guidance. "That's not a good idea."

"Please?"

"This isn't how I want it to go. We should wait until you're ready, until the time is right." *Yeah, Joe,* he thought, *great ideas. Too bad you didn't have them before you slept with her.*

"I know you'll think I'm in shock or denial or something, but what I feel is very calm inside. If someone had told me, 'David is cheating on you,' I probably wouldn't have believed it. But I saw him . . . with her . . . I have no choice but to believe what would've been unbelievable to me only a few days ago. I'm not in denial, Joe. I promise you that. And I don't want to think about him anymore." She looked up and turned those potent eyes on him. "I felt good when I was with you. I want to feel that way again."

His entire body was riddled with tension as he studied her and fought a silent war with himself.

"Will you come?" she asked.

Who was he kidding? Like he could really say no to her. "Yeah." He uttered the single word and walked away while he still had a shred of sanity left. Funny how he'd thought loving her from afar had made him crazy. That was nothing compared to this.

Chapter Ten

Calling himself five kinds of idiot as he watched the last boat of the day depart the island, Joe returned to the Beachcomber to shower, shave and change out of the clothes he'd worn to clean one of the boats. Upon returning to the ferry landing earlier, he'd refused to answer any of the questions his employees were burning to ask about his arrest and had thrown himself into the demanding physical work in an effort to take his mind off everything that had happened. Too bad it hadn't helped.

Staring at his reflection in the mirror, he had to admit he looked like shit. The lingering effects of too much booze, not enough sleep and a couple of hours in jail had left him looking haggard, and his hand hurt like a bastard. "You absolutely should *not* go over there tonight. Do you hear me?" he said to the mirror. "Are you listening?"

Turning away, he muttered, "I didn't think so." He pulled on a clean shirt and buttoned khaki cargo shorts. "You're just going to talk to her. You have to convince her we need to wait until the dust settles with David. We can't blow our chance. We have to do it right. And no matter what, *no touching.* No matter what!" Marshalling all his defenses, he grabbed his wallet and keys, left the room and headed downstairs, where he ran into Luke Harris, their high school classmate and Mac's right hand at the marina. "Hey, Luke, how's it going?"

The two men shook hands, and Joe winced at the pain that caused him.

"Joe." Never one to be chatty, Luke sized him up with an amused expression. "Good day?"

"Screw you."

Luke's tanned face lifted into a small smile. "Never have liked that guy. Something not right about him."

Appreciating the other man's support, Joe grinned. "Couldn't agree more. So, hey, I guess I'm supposed to throw a bachelor party for Mac. You in?"

"Sure thing. What do you have in mind?"

Joe hadn't given it a thought. "Um . . ."

"How about poker and beer after work one night at the marina? We can take over the restaurant after it closes. Day after the Fourth? Mac's brothers are due to arrive that day for the wedding."

"That's perfect. I'll get Mario's to do the food. Will you spread the word on the docks?"

"Yep."

"Appreciate that. You have a good night."

"You, too."

At least this day hadn't been a total loss, Joe decided as he set out for Janey's small saltbox house, which was set back off Ocean Road, within walking distance of the veterinarian's office. Like her mother, Janey had filled her front yard with fragrant rose-bushes that grew through the slats of the white picket fence. Joe let himself in through the gate and took a quick look around to make sure no one was seeing him approach her front door.

She must've been watching for him, because she swung open the door and ushered him into her world for the first time. He'd been invited to cook-outs and other parties there in the past but had used work as an excuse to decline. He had gone out of his way to keep his feelings for her hidden from every-one, and had always suspected stepping into her private space would be too difficult for him. Now he wanted to take in every detail, every nuance. On first glance, he decided her tiny home was warm and cozy, everything he'd expect from her. Rich colors, shelves full of books, comfortable. Welcoming.

"Janey—" Joe forgot what he was going to say when she wrapped her arms around him and rested her face against his chest. He wondered if she could hear his heart hammering in response to her. All his good intentions were shot to hell when the scent of jasmine invaded his senses and soft hair brushed against his jaw.

What choice did he have but to put his arms around her? Once again, he was struck by the perfect fit, the click of two halves becoming a whole. Did she feel it, too? *There wasn't supposed to be any touching*, his conscience reminded him. *Shut up. Just shut up.*

"Thanks for coming," she whispered.

"We have to talk, Janey."

She tightened her hold on him. "I know, but can we just do this for a minute first?"

Even though a burst of emotion closed his throat, he managed to say, "Sure." Joe told himself they were going to talk. They *needed* to talk, but then her hands found their way under his shirt and all rational thought left his head in a tsunami of desire. Her hands were warm and soft on his back, and all he could think about was how soft the rest of her had felt under him, wrapped around him.

"I missed you last night," she said. "How is that possible when we only spent two nights together?"

His heart staggered, and his resolve disappeared. Drawing back from her, he caressed her face and brought his mouth down on hers for a kiss that was equal parts desperation and urgency, as if it had been years rather than days since their last kiss. As he feasted on her, a sense of calm came over him. This was what he needed. All the anxiety and despair he'd carried around since their return to the island faded away. He lifted her, felt her legs curl around his hips and her arms tighten around his neck.

"Bedroom," he mumbled against her lips.

She directed him through the one-level house to a room at the end of the hallway.

Joe couldn't have described the room. All he saw was the bed. Locked in another sensuous kiss, they landed hard.

A shriek from beneath them stopped his heart. "What the hell?"

"Trio," Janey said breathlessly, raising herself up. A large three-legged cat darted out from under her and bolted from the room.

"Jesus." Joe leaned his forehead on hers, still breathing hard. "That took five years off my life."

Janey laughed and ran her fingers through his hair. "Where were we?"

"Here," he said with a soft caress of lips touching lips. "And here." He ran his tongue over her bottom lip, and she responded by pressing her hips against his erection. Through the haze of desire and emotion, he became aware of other noises in the house. Scratching, moaning, more scratching. "What is that?"

"Dogs."

He raised his head so he could see her face. "How many?"

"Five," she said with a sheepish grin.

"You have *five* dogs in this little house?"

"And three cats."

Joe chuckled and fell even further into a love so deep it knew no boundaries or limits. "Do you know that one of my favorite memories of you was when you were about six? You had adorable pigtail braids and no front teeth. You had rescued a squirrel that had been hit by a car in front of your house. You carried him around in a shoe box. Remember?"

"Rocky." Sadness radiated from her as if it had been minutes rather than years. "I tried so hard to save him."

"Your mother was freaking about the germs, but you didn't care."

"I wasn't allowed to bring him in the house, so I snuck downstairs after everyone went to bed and brought him up to my room. She still doesn't know that."

"Probably just as well." He ran a finger over her soft cheek. "You had those overalls with strawberries on them."

She stared at him, amazed. "Strawberry Shortcake."

"Huh?"

"My favorite doll. I loved those matching overalls. I can't believe you remember that."

"I remember everything." Joe made a trail of kisses

on her face. "I think I might've started loving you that long ago. You were something else, even at six." More kisses, drawing soft sighs from her as the whining coming from the other room grew louder. "Could I meet your friends?"

"Now?"

"Sure, why not?"

"I thought you wanted to . . ." Pushing her soft center against his hardness, she reminded him of why they'd come to her bedroom.

As badly as he wanted her, he knew they needed to talk more than they needed to have sex again. "I'll still want to later."

"Promise?"

"Mmm," he said against her lips. "Always."

With what seemed to be great reluctance, Janey released him and sat up to run her fingers through her hair. She sat next to him for a long moment, studying him.

"What?" he finally asked.

"I'm still trying to figure out how everything changed between us so quickly. I look at you and I see Joe, my friend forever."

He swallowed hard. "Is that all you see?" His heart pounded as he awaited her reply.

"No," she said softly, "and that's the part I'm trying to understand. I see all this other stuff now."

Joe wanted to weep with gratitude and relief and amazement. Finally. Finally. *Finally.* "You're seeing all the stuff I've always seen when I look at you."

"I feel like I've just met you for the very first time and anything is possible."

Moved, he took her hand and linked their fingers. Bringing her hand to his lips, he said, "Anything *is* possible, Janey. You just have to be sure you're ready for it."

"I know you're worried, and I don't blame you for that, but I *am* ready for this. For you. I want this, Joe. When I see you, now, since we, you know . . ."

"Screwed each other's brains out?" he said with a grin.

She shoulder-bumped him. "Stop making fun of me."

"What happens when you see me now, honey?"

"I want to be alone with you. Even today, when I was so upset about the confrontation with David, all I could think about after I saw you at my parents' house was getting rid of them so I could be alone with you. I used the dogs as an excuse to come back here tonight. I told them my dog sitter had plans, and I needed to take care of my guys. Maddie wanted to stay with me, but I sent her home." Her face flushed to a rosy red that he found utterly captivating. "I can't stop thinking about how good it was. How good *we* were."

Joe let out a low groan. As if he hadn't relived every second, every nuance, a thousand times in the last few days.

"It was never like that for me before."

"Janey . . ."

"Hmm?" She leaned her head on his shoulder, and Joe experienced a wave of contentment unlike anything he'd ever known. Her hand wrapped around his, her head on his shoulder. Everything he wanted, right here. He cleared his throat, hoping the words would come. "You were going to introduce me to your pets."

"Oh, right." She got up but kept her firm grip on his hand as she led him across the hall to the other bedroom. "I put them in here earlier so they wouldn't rush you when you came in." Janey opened the door to a room outfitted for pets. Each one had a bed with his or her name embroidered on the cover, and the beds circled the small room. Right away he noticed they were all special-needs animals. One had no ears, and another was missing a tail. A third sat stoically, watching Joe with an intimidating intensity. The dog's wise eyes zeroed in on the firm hold Janey had on Joe's hand, and right away, Joe understood that he needed to win over the German shepherd if he had any hope of a future with her.

"This is Sam." Janey released Joe's hand so she could pick up and cuddle a white ball of fluff. "She's blind, but you'd never know it. She gets herself around using all her other senses." Janey lowered herself to the floor, and the others rushed in to vie for a spot on her lap. Except the German shepherd. He continued to stare at Joe. "We found Dexter," she said of the cocker spaniel, "missing his ears. I don't even like to think about how he lost them."

Joe sat down next to her. "Why didn't they bark when they heard me come in?"

"Since they've all been abused, they tend to keep quiet so as not to attract any attention until they know the visitor is friendly."

Sam, the white fur ball, left Janey's lap to take up residence in Joe's, giving him a thorough sniff and a friendly lick.

"I'll never understand how anyone could harm a helpless animal," Joe said.

"Neither will I. We see far too much of it, even out here on the island where you wouldn't think people would be capable. The summer folks have been known to leave their dogs behind when they go home. I found Muttley starving and malnourished by the side of the road up at the Northeast Light about a year ago. His tail was all bloody and infected." Shuddering at the memory, she stroked the brown-and-black mongrel.

Joe noticed how the dog shied away from her first tentative stroke before settling into the caress.

"He still thinks he's going to be hit. He prepares himself for the blow and seems surprised when it doesn't happen."

"Poor baby." Joe reached out to pat him, but the dog turned away from him.

"He might take a while to warm up to you, so don't be hurt by that."

Joe smiled. Could she be any more adorable? "I won't. What's the story with the general over there?"

"Oh, that's Riley. He's large and in charge."

"No kidding." Joe was quite certain the dog hadn't blinked once since they came into the room. "He looks like he wants to rip my heart out."

Janey laughed. "He's probably a little jealous. He never did care for David."

"I like him already."

She smiled at him, warming him all the way to his bones. "Riley, come say hi to Joe."

As the dog dragged himself forward using only his front legs, Joe realized he didn't have any back legs. "Oh, God, what happened to him?"

"He was hit by a car and left for dead. Doc Potter was able to save him, but no one wanted a two-legged dog."

"So of course you brought him home."

"I had cared for him for weeks by then. He was already mine."

"How can you afford them all?"

"Well, Doc squares me on vet care and meds, so it's really just food. I worry about what I'll do when Doc retires and a new vet comes to town. They need a lot of care, especially Pixie." The Jack Russell terrier licked her hand and plopped down in her lap, bumping Muttley onto the floor. "She has a persistent skin infection that makes her itchy and miserable, but it doesn't stop her from acting like she's queen of the roost."

Joe reached for Muttley and was honored when the dog gave him his belly to scratch. "You could always go to vet school and then you wouldn't have to worry about affording their care when a new vet comes to town."

"I told you," she said, "that ship has sailed."

"No, it hasn't. And don't tell me you're too old. You're only twenty-eight. Give me a break."

"But—"

Riley edged closer to Joe and sniffed his leg. "You won't know if you don't apply."

"How would I ever afford it?"

The question proved she'd at least considered the possibility. "Didn't your parents offer to give you the money? I believe David convinced you that the two of you shouldn't be so in debt to them, which was flat-out ridiculous, if you ask me."

A black cat with one eye wandered into the room and rubbed against Janey, vying for some attention, which of course Janey gave her. "None of you like him, do you?" she asked in the small voice that rattled him. It was *so* not her, and it pained him to see her questioning herself in the wake of the David disaster.

"We often didn't like the way he treated you."

"Why did it take seeing him with another woman to open my eyes?"

"You loved him, Janey. You don't have to apologize for that. Not to me, anyway."

"Was he always bad? Deep inside where it matters most, do you think he's always been a bad person, and I never knew?"

"Aww, honey, I can't answer that. All I can say is if I'd been fortunate enough to spend years with you, I would've considered myself the luckiest guy in the world."

"You really mean that, don't you?"

"Of course I do."

"How did I not see that you felt that way about me? It's like I've been walking around with blinders on all these years, and when they were finally ripped off this week, I found out that David's a scumbag and you're . . ."

"What? What am I?"

Her clear blue eyes shifted to meet his. "I'm not sure yet, but I want to find out."

Joe reached over to tip up her chin to receive his kiss.

Riley growled a low warning.

Janey laughed and patted the dog. "Easy, boy. It's okay. He's one of the good guys."

Joe decided that was, without a doubt, the best compliment he'd ever received.

Chapter Eleven

Janey raised Joe's right hand to her lips and pressed gentle kisses to each of his abused knuckles. She ached when she thought about how he'd injured his hand and how out of character it was for him to hit someone. "I wanted to do this earlier when I got to my parents' house and saw your hand all swollen and bruised."

"That would've shocked them, huh?"

"Just a little. Well, except for Maddie. She knows. About us."

Joe gasped. "Oh, my God, Janey! If she tells Mac—"

"She won't. She promised me."

He released a long, rattling deep breath. "He'd kill me. You know that."

"After everything that happened, I had to talk to someone."

"And it had to be *her*? Your insanely protective older brother's fiancée?"

"We've become very good friends, and I knew she'd understand."

"I don't like it, Janey. I don't want any trouble with

him. We go back too far, and with his wedding right around the corner . . ."

Anxious to quell his worries, Janey straddled him, pressing him into the back of the sofa. "I trust her to keep it quiet, or I wouldn't have told her."

"People will think I took advantage of you—"

She silenced him with a kiss that, like most kisses with him, quickly spun out of control. "If anything, *I* took advantage of *you*, and we both know that."

"That's not how it'll look to other people, especially Mac, because he knows how I've felt about you for years. He'll think I jumped you the first chance I got."

"When it was quite the other way around."

"He'll never believe that, Janey. Never."

"Then let's keep this between us for now. No one else needs to know until we're ready for them to know."

"And what is this that we're keeping between us? What would you call it?"

"Fun." She kissed him. "Exciting." Another kiss. "Passionate." This time, she ran her tongue between his lips. "Delicious."

Joe's fingers combed through her hair, anchoring her for another desperate kiss. Tongues tangled in a violent, exhilarating battle that sent pleasure darting from her breasts to her core.

Janey pulled her lips free and pressed them to the pulsating nerve in his cheek. "Is it later yet?" she asked as she turned her attention to his neck. The tremble that rippled through his big frame filled her with a sense of her own power.

His fingers ventured beneath the hem of her tank top. "Mmm, definitely."

"And have we talked about everything we need to talk about?"

"Not even close."

She rolled the tendon that joined his neck to his shoulder between her teeth.

He jolted, gasped and his fingers dug into her hips, holding her tight against his erection.

"Will it keep?" she whispered.

"I suppose it'll have to." He shifted his hands to her bottom and stood, accommodating her weight effortlessly. "Because this won't."

In a cacophony of claws on hard wood, her menagerie followed them to the bedroom.

"Are we going to have an audience?" he asked, setting her down next to the bed.

"Come on, guys." She shooed the animals from the room, closed the door and turned to him. "Alone at last."

The whining protests from the hallway reminded them they weren't completely alone.

"Whatever do you plan to do with me?" he asked.

Smiling at his playfulness, she sashayed over to him, shedding her top on the way. There was something about knowing he'd loved her from afar for so long that had Janey also shedding inhibitions that had plagued her relationship with David. She'd often found it difficult to be free and unguarded around him because she never seemed to have his undivided attention. That wasn't a problem with Joe.

His hands slid from her ribs to cover the lacy bra she'd worn with him in mind. Judging by the hot gaze he directed at her breasts, the bra had done the trick. "You're so beautiful, Janey. So incredibly sexy."

She raised his shirt and trailed her fingers over the ridges of muscles on his abdomen. "So are you. I can't believe you cover this six-pack with a shirt. That ought to be a crime."

He snorted with laughter. "I'll keep that in mind."

"Just keep your shirt off, and I'll be happy."

"Mmm, I want you to be happy." Lowering her to the bed, he kissed the plump flesh that spilled from the top of the push-up bra.

"I'm feeling very happy at the moment." Janey squirmed under him, itchy with desire and need and something else that tightened in her chest, demanding she not ignore what he made her feel. She tugged the shirt over his head and massaged his shoulders as he worshipped her breasts through the bra. He got rid of her shorts, leaving her in just the bra and a matching thong.

Watching his eyes darken with awareness when he saw the thong made her laugh.

"You're out to give me a heart attack, aren't you?"

She fluttered her eyelashes at him. "Would I do that to you?"

"Uh-huh. I do believe you would." His talented lips went to work on her belly, and as his tongue flicked into her belly button, Janey discovered a new erogenous zone.

She clutched his hair, her heart hammering when she realized where he was heading. That he *liked* to do that was still a bit of a shock to her, and he seemed to *really* like it. Just the thought of it made her skin heat with embarrassment and nervousness. "Joe . . ."

"Relax, honey."

Despite his softly spoken words, Janey trembled as he spread her legs and settled between them.

She closed her eyes and tried to control the trembling, but it only intensified when he tongued her through the silky thong. A low moan exploded from her chest as the sensations became almost painfully intense. Keeping up the pressure with his tongue, he slid a finger into her. After just a few more strokes of his finger and tongue, a scorching orgasm stole her breath.

"So beautiful," he whispered as he kissed his way to her lips. "So very, very beautiful."

Janey focused on drawing air into her heaving lungs as aftershocks reverberated through her body.

While she recovered, he got rid of the rest of their clothes and came back to join her, covering her body with his. Infused by his warmth, Janey floated on a cloud of satisfaction.

"You aren't going to sleep on me, are you?" he asked. She could hear the laughter in his voice as he throbbed against her leg, letting her know he was very much awake.

"I wouldn't do *that* to you," she said, even though she was having trouble opening her eyes. She curled her legs around his hips, urging him to take what she offered.

"Look at me."

Janey forced her eyes open to find him looking down at her, his gaze full of love and awe. Overwhelmed by everything she saw in his eyes, she put her hands on his face and drew him into a sweet kiss as he entered her in one swift stroke that made her cry out from the sheer amazement of how good he felt inside her.

"God, Janey," he muttered through gritted teeth. Something in him seemed to snap as he abandoned his tightly held control and hammered into her. With both hands, he clutched her bottom, holding her right where he wanted her for his fierce possession.

Janey had never experienced anything even close to Joe out of control, crazy in love and lost in passion. She could only hold on for the ride until a second orgasm, even more powerful than the last, ripped through her, drawing an equally turbulent finish from him.

Gasping for air, he clutched her close to him. "I'm sorry. I didn't mean to be so rough."

She brushed the hair back from his damp forehead. "Please don't apologize. I loved it."

"I've never lost my mind like that before."

Janey loved knowing she had done that to him. "No?"

His eyes locked on hers, he shook his head, brushing soft kisses on her lips. "Never."

"Did you like it?"

"If I liked it any more, it might've killed me."

She laughed and tightened her legs around him, keeping him from shifting off her. "Stay."

He rested his head on her chest and continued to take deep breaths. "I'm not going anywhere, sweetheart."

Janey held him tight against her and closed her eyes, wallowing in the contentment of being exactly where she belonged.

She woke up before dawn the next morning to Joe placing soft kisses on her back. Arching into his embrace, she wanted to purr like a kitten. Janey clung to the pillow as he reawakened her body, working his way down her spine. It occurred to her that if she hadn't walked in on David with another woman, she might never have known this kind of passion existed. She would've married him and gone on with her life, thinking she understood desire. What she would've missed . . .

Joe reached her bottom and paid homage to each cheek, kissing, licking, biting. He had her on the verge of another climax within seconds. Raising her to her knees, he entered her from behind. Whereas before he'd taken her fast and hard, this time was all about slow and sensual—and still, he hadn't said a word.

He kept up the slow, easy pace until Janey thought she'd go mad from the sensations storming through her body. Cupping her breasts, he tweaked her nipples, sending a jolt of shocking desire straight down to where they were joined. As he was always so in tune with her, he sensed she was close, so he reached down and stroked her to climax. They collapsed into a heap on the bed.

"I love you," he whispered in her ear.

Janey clutched his hand to her chest. She loved him, too. Of course she did. But was she *in love* with him? She could be. Absolutely. However, until she was sure, she couldn't say the words she knew he needed to hear.

"Joe, I—"

"Don't, honey. Don't say anything."

How well he understood her, and how grateful Janey was to be so in sync with him.

"I need to go."

"Not yet."

"If we're going to keep this just between us, I shouldn't be seen leaving here in the morning."

Janey turned to face him. "Are you sure you're okay with keeping it a secret for a while?"

He combed his fingers through her hair. "I used to imagine sometimes how it would be if we got together. I have to admit, I never pictured having to sneak around."

"I know this isn't what you want."

Joe rested a finger over her lips. "I didn't say that. I want *you*. That's all I've ever wanted. If this is how it has to be for now, then we'll deal with it."

"Do you know what I was thinking before?"

"What's that?"

"I'm glad I didn't get married without knowing it was possible to feel this way."

"He didn't . . . satisfy you . . . in bed?"

"Not like this. The sad thing is, I didn't even know it should be different. Until you showed me. I thought I had a good thing with him, but now I see it was mediocre at best. It probably was for him, too, which is why he did what he did."

"Those are the things I want you to work through before you make any kind of commitment to me, Janey. I don't want to look back and have regrets because we rushed into something before you were ready. That's what worries me most." He gathered her in close to him. "I waited a really long time to be able to hold you like this. I don't want to blow it."

"We won't blow it." She pressed her lips to his chest and ran her hand over his back. "It's too good."

"Yes," he said, his voice heavy with emotion. "It is. I don't want anything to screw it up."

"When will I see you again?"

"I got a call yesterday that your car is ready to be

picked up. If you want to come over with me tonight, we can get it in the morning."

Janey thought about that for a minute. She'd have to explain spending another night at Joe's, but no one other than Maddie would think to question it. Except for maybe Mac.

"Could you get someone to watch the dogs?"

"My usual sitter is off-island. I suppose I could get Maddie to come by and let them out."

"I'd rather that Mac not know you're coming with me again."

"I'll ask her not to tell him."

"Janey," he sighed, "you're playing with fire. He's going to blow when he finds out about this."

"So then let's make sure he finds out about it *after* his wedding, when he'll be all dumb with happiness, wanting everyone else to be happy, too."

"Maybe then he'll cut me a break and let me live."

Janey laughed and peppered his chest with kisses, working her way up to his scruffy chin. "We can get through ten days, right?"

He captured her wandering mouth and devoured her once again. "I suppose if I've already survived years, I can get through another ten days."

"Mmm," she said, encouraging more heated kisses.

"I have to go to work."

"I know." But she didn't let him go. Rather, she straddled him and took him deep inside her.

"*Janey.*"

"You do own the company."

"And I am required to actually work once in a while."

She slid off him and flopped onto her back. "All right. Never mind. If you've got better things to do . . ."

Growling, he rolled on top of her and set out to finish what she'd started. Just as she'd known he would.

After, she unearthed a razor and toothbrush for him, and he showered while she made coffee. It all felt so domestic—waking up with him, making love, listening to him in her shower while she made coffee before sending him off for the day. This was how it could be if they were together all the time.

After shooing the dogs into the backyard, she carried her "Doctors Make Better Lovers" coffee cup to the window to watch a cardinal foraging for seeds in one of her feeders. The stained-glass dream catcher David had given her for her birthday years ago sparkled in the morning sun, reminding her that just a week ago, all her dreams had been tied up in him, not the man in her shower.

Although she'd done a quick trip through her house the night before to remove photos and other obvious mementos of David before Joe arrived, the mug and dream catcher were reminders it would take far longer to remove thirteen years of memories from her home and her heart. That didn't mean there wasn't room in her home and her heart for something new in the meantime, or so she told herself.

A knock on the front door had her tying her robe tighter around her naked body. She glanced at the closed bathroom door to make sure Joe was still in the shower. Janey opened the door to David's bruised and battered face. She suppressed a gasp. "What're you doing here?"

"We need to talk, Janey." He sounded like he had a bad cold. A bandage covered his nose and both eyes were black and swollen. His dark hair was standing on end, as if he'd spent hours running his fingers through it, and exhaustion clung to him. Janey was satisfied to realize he'd been up all night while she'd slept peacefully in Joe's arms. A few sleepless nights were the least of what he deserved.

"I said everything I have to say yesterday," she replied, anxious for him to be gone.

"*You* said everything. I didn't get to tell you what I need you to know."

"And what's that?" she asked, even though she didn't really care. Not anymore.

He opened the screen door and caressed her cheek, but Janey jerked her head out of his reach and pulled the screen closed. She prayed Joe would hear their voices and stay out of sight until she got rid of David.

"She means *nothing* to me, Janey. It was just sex. It has nothing to do with you and me."

Janey stared at him, incredulous. "You really think you can separate what does and does not involve us? *Everything* you do—or I should say everything you *did*—involved me. You were *engaged* to me, David. You can't just sleep with someone else because you're bored or stressed or lonely. It doesn't work that way."

"I can't lose you over this, Janey. We've been through so much, and we're *so* close to having everything we've waited so long for. You know I love you. You *know* that."

"I thought I knew that until I saw you having sex in our bed with someone else. Let me ask you some- thing, David."

"Anything."

"Why'd you bring her there? Why would you do that in the bed you shared with me?"

He glanced down at his feet and then winced at

the pain the movement caused him. "She works at the hospital, and she . . . she has roommates."

Janey released a harsh laugh. "Ahh, I see. And you couldn't let the people at work find out that the honorable Dr. Lawrence is really a cheating pig."

"I'm sorry, Janey. What can I do to make this up to you?" He took a step forward, but Janey pulled on the handle to the screen door to keep him out. "I'll do anything."

"There's nothing you can do or say that will ever scrub that image from my memory. I *saw* you, David." She hated how her throat closed and her eyes burned with tears. "I saw you."

"I'd give everything I have to take back what happened that night. If only I'd known you were coming—"

"*What?* You wouldn't have screwed someone else because your oh-so-willing fiancée was coming to town? You make me sick!"

"That's not what I meant! I would've been thrilled you were coming! I miss you all the time, Janey. I hate living like this. I can't wait for our wedding."

"There isn't going to be a wedding. It's over."

"It's not over. You can't just walk away from thirteen years like they never happened over one mistake. That's all it was. *One* mistake."

"Go back to Boston, David."

"I can't go back there looking like this. I told them I was in an accident, so I'll be sticking around for a few more days."

"Great. Have a nice visit with your mother. Just leave me alone." She started to close the inside door, but he moved quickly to push open the screen door to stop her.

"Janey, honey, *please*. Let me come in. Let's talk

about this. There's nothing we can't get through. Look at all we've already survived to get to this point."

A low growl came from behind her. "It's okay, Riley. David was just leaving." With a hand to his chest, she pushed him out of the way, closed the door, flipped the lock into place and rested her forehead against the cool wood.

"Janey!" David called from outside. "Come on! You can't do this!"

"Please go or I'll call the police, David. I mean it."

"Fine. I'll go. But I'll be back. This is *not* over. Far from it."

Janey didn't breathe until she heard him stomp down the front stairs and slam the gate behind him.

Whimpering, Riley nudged at her leg, and she reached down to stroke his silky ears. "He's gone now, boy."

"Everything all right?" Joe asked.

Chapter Twelve

Janey spun around to find Joe standing outside the bathroom door, a towel wrapped around his waist. Just the sight of his sculpted chest and abs and the light dusting of blond hair that trailed into the towel was enough to stir the hum of desire she was coming to expect in his presence.

Tipping his head, he urged her over to him.

Janey crossed the room and let him envelop her in his warm, welcoming embrace. "How much did you hear?"

"Enough to get that he's not planning to go quietly."

"No," she sighed.

Joe smoothed a hand over her hair. "You're shaking, baby."

"He caught me off guard." Janey looked up at him. "I hope you understand why I asked him about bringing her to his house."

"That's exactly the kind of stuff I was talking about when I said you need to work your way through it all. Naturally, you have questions. Anyone would."

Janey returned her head to his chest. "I don't know

if I'd be able to deal with this quite so well without you to lean on."

"I'm here."

She nuzzled her lips into the curve of his neck. "I'm glad for that, Joe. I really am."

"I need to get to work. Will you be okay today?"

Reluctantly, Janey let him go, followed him into the bedroom and sat on the bed. "I have a few things I need to do. Keeping busy will help." When he dropped the towel, she let her eyes take a leisurely stroll from muscular shoulders to sculpted chest to belly and below. Licking her lips, she took her gaze back up to find him watching her, his own eyes blazing.

He pulled on his shirt. "What?"

"I'm just wondering how I never noticed the supreme hotness you've got going on over there."

He stopped in the midst of buttoning his shorts. "Is that so?"

"Uh-huh."

Keeping his eyes fixed on her, he came over to the bed, bending at the waist to bring his face level with hers.

Janey smiled, looped her arms around his neck and dragged him down on top of her.

"Listen, you sex-crazed vixen, I have to go or I'll get fired."

She rubbed her lips back and forth over his, reveling in the moan that rumbled from deep inside him. "You can't get fired. You own the place." Her hands traveled over his back to cup his ass.

"Could you hold that thought for twelve or so hours?"

"*That* long?"

He pressed hot, open-mouth kisses to her neck

and trailed his tongue over her collarbone. "Mmm, I'll make it well worth the wait. I promise."

Janey ran her fingers through his hair. "Is this real, Joe? Is it really happening?"

"It's real and it's happening and it's magic. Do you feel it, too? Even just a little?"

"I feel a lot of magic, and that's what I can't believe. We've been friends forever. And now this."

"And now this." Holding her gaze, he linked their fingers and stretched her arms over her head, aligning their bodies.

Janey wrapped her legs around his, marveling at the emotion, the desire, the overwhelming passion. "You have to go."

"I know." But he made no move to leave. Rather, he devastated her with kisses that quickly had her craving more.

She ran her tongue over his bottom lip, and he pulled away.

"No," he said, once again capturing her mouth with just soft lips on lips.

Janey groaned with frustration. "You're being mean!"

Chuckling, he said, "I'm just making sure you'll think about me today."

"Oh, I will."

Another soul-stirring kiss. "Promise?"

"Yes, Joe," she said, laughing. "I promise I'll think about you today."

"Then my work here is finished." With what appeared to be great reluctance, he pushed himself up and off her. "Meet me at the ferry landing at seven forty-five?"

She followed him into the kitchen and filled her

favorite travel mug with black coffee. "I'll be there. Want some cereal or something?"

"I'll grab something at the diner." He examined the mug she'd handed him. "Seriously? You expect me to walk through town carrying a cow full of coffee?"

"It's my favorite," she said with a playful pout. "It's a huge honor for me to bestow my cow upon you. I expect you to take very good care of Bessie."

Rolling his eyes, he kissed her once more, fast and far too brief, and headed for the door. "Thanks for the coffee. I think."

"Joe! Wait."

Turning, he raised an eyebrow in question.

"Just, you know, take a look before you go out."

A flash of hurt crossed his face and then vanished just as quickly. The sneaking around bothered him, and Janey hated that.

"Sure," he said. The lips that had teased her so sensuously a few minutes earlier were now tight with tension. "We wouldn't want anyone to know, right?"

"Joe—"

"It's okay." He glanced back at her. "For now."

Linda McCarthy stepped into the South Harbor Diner and looked around. Kay Lawrence waved from one of the booths in the back. Feeling every eye in the bustling restaurant on her, she slid in across from Kay.

The other woman reached for Linda's hands. "Thank you so much for meeting me."

"It was no problem."

Kay released her hands and sat back in the booth. "You're angry."

"I'm furious. And with good reason."

"Believe me, I'm as angry as you are. I love Janey like my own. You know that."

"Yes."

"I just can't believe David would risk everything he and Janey have worked so hard for by acting so foolishly."

Linda nodded to the waitress who offered coffee. "And thoughtlessly."

"That, too." Kay took a sip from her mug. "I'm truly appalled by his behavior, Linda."

"I have no doubt. You've always been so proud of him."

"Which makes this so much harder to understand." She dabbed at her eyes. "How's Janey? I can't stop thinking about her."

"She seems to be holding up okay. She insisted on going home last night so she could be with her pets. They make her happy."

"David loves her so much. He's beside himself."

"He has an odd way of showing his love."

"He swears it was a one-time thing, and he deeply regrets it. If you could've seen how stirred up he was last night, you wouldn't doubt his sincerity."

"I'm not sure what you think I can do about it," Linda said. In the mirror, she watched Mac come through the door, holding Maddie's son, Thomas. Joe followed them into the diner. Linda waved to them as they took over a table inside the door.

"Oh, that Joe Cantrell," Kay whispered. "He broke my David's nose! Can you imagine?"

"He's like a brother to Janey. My husband or son might've done worse if they'd gotten to David first."

"It's no way to handle a disagreement."

"This is far more than a disagreement, Kay. He *cheated* on her, and she *saw* him."

Kay's brown eyes filled with tears. "Surely there has to be *something* we can do to help them find their way back to each other. All those years . . . I can't imagine either of them without the other."

"I don't know if I want her back with him. Not if that's the kind of husband he plans to be."

"He's having some challenges right now," Kay said tentatively. "Things he needs to discuss with Janey."

"She has no interest in discussing anything with him."

"Once they're married and living together, everything will be perfect—the way it was always meant to be since they were kids. If we can just help them get there, I'm sure they'll be so happy. It's meant to be. We both know that."

"I used to think so, but now . . ." Linda recalled how upset she and her husband had been when David discouraged Janey from going to vet school. Other than that fiasco and the current one, however, Linda had to acknowledge that their relationship had always seemed solid.

"We have to do something, Linda. We can't let them lose their way now, not when the wedding is just a year away."

"I don't know."

"Can you imagine Janey being happy, truly happy, without David?"

"She's amazingly resilient. I'm sure she'll bounce back in no time at all."

"She's never been tested like this before. You can't know that for sure." Kay again reached for Linda's hand. "How can we not at least try to help them figure this out? That way, if they decide in the end to part, at least we know we did all we could for them."

Linda had to acknowledge the other woman made a good point. "What do you suggest we do?"

Kay leaned in and lowered her voice. "Okay, here's what I'm thinking."

Sitting across from Mac and Thomas, as he did most mornings lately, Joe tried to focus on the conversation, but what he really wanted to know was why Linda McCarthy was engaged in an intense conversation with Kay Lawrence.

"Luke said you guys have big plans for a bachelor party," Mac said.

Joe tore his eyes off the table in the corner and returned his attention to Mac. "Oh, yeah, I was going to talk to you about that today. You up for some poker and beer on the fifth?"

"Sure. My brothers are due in that morning, so that's perfect."

Joe took a sip from the cow mug Janey had given him.

"Where'd you get that goofy mug?" Mac asked.

"Oh, um, a friend gave it to me." He cleared his throat, anxious to steer the conversation in any other direction. "So, it's starting to look like this whole wedding thing is really going to happen, huh?"

Mac uttered an ironic laugh. "Hard to believe." He glanced down at Thomas. "But I wouldn't have it any other way."

Thomas flashed a gummy grin. "Dada, dada, dada."

Joe smiled at the soft look of love his friend bestowed

upon the blond, blue-eyed baby. "If you ask me, you fell for him even before you fell for his mama."

"I sure did. He's the frosting on a very nice cake."

"I give you credit, man. Raising someone else's kid isn't the easiest thing to take on."

"He'll never know me as anything other than his father. I have a feeling it'll be the easiest thing I ever do."

"I'm happy for you, Mac. You've got it all worked out."

"All except for one thing: Maddie's mom. She doesn't know yet."

"About you?"

"About any of it." Mac's brow furrowed with worry. "She has no idea she's coming home to a wedding, and something tells me she won't be thrilled to learn her daughter is marrying a McCarthy."

"You're crazy in love with Maddie *and* Thomas. What's there not to be thrilled about?"

"For one thing, my mother helped to land her in prison. She won't soon forget that."

"*She* landed herself in prison by passing bad checks all over the island for years. Hell, I wrote off more than five hundred bucks in bad debt with her name on it."

"You didn't press charges?" Mac asked, incredulous.

Joe shrugged. "Would've just been piling on at that point, and I wouldn't have gotten the money back."

"Sometimes I wish my mother could've seen it that way, too," Mac said.

"She had no way to know you'd end up marrying the woman's daughter."

"Still . . ." Mac's face was set in a pensive expression that Joe didn't often see from his usually confident friend. "I just hope she doesn't cause any trouble. Maddie is so happy, and after everything she's been through, she deserves a beautiful wedding with no complications."

"You both deserve that. Leave it to your best man and your brothers to run interference."

Mac smiled. "Gladly."

Kay Lawrence rushed by them, casting a menacing scowl at Joe before she left the diner.

"Whoo," Mac said, whistling. "Mama Bear is *not* happy with you."

"Her baby bear got *exactly* what he deserved."

"You won't hear me arguing."

Linda approached their table. "Scoot over, you two," she said to Mac and Thomas.

Pretending to be put out by her, Mac made room for his mother.

"Now, give me that baby."

Smiling, Mac handed Thomas over to his new grandmother. Joe marveled at how far they'd all come, from Linda not approving of Mac's relationship with a woman unfairly branded the town tramp to Linda holding the woman's child like he was her own flesh and blood.

"How's my little man today?" Linda cooed, kissing the baby until he giggled with delight.

"I'm here, too, Mom," Mac said with a petulant pout.

Never taking her focus off the baby, she said, "Yeah, yeah. Good morning, my darling Malcolm. Better?"

Mac scowled at her use of his dreaded first name. "Go back to ignoring me. Please."

Joe laughed at their banter. "So," he couldn't help but ask, "what were you and Kay up to over there?"

"She thinks we need to try to get Janey and David back together."

The news hit Joe like a punch to the gut, and it was all he could do to refrain from sucking in a sharp deep breath.

Apparently tuning in to his dismay, Mac met his gaze and rolled his eyes. "Tell me you didn't agree to be part of that, Mom."

"I agreed to think about it."

Mac's eyes bugged out of his head. "You gotta be kidding me! The guy *cheated* on your daughter! You can't still want to see her married to him!"

Linda sighed and seemed to sag a bit. "Kay makes a good point about how long they've been together. I don't want Janey to have any regrets."

Mac snorted. "The only regret she would've had is if she'd married him and *then* found out he's a cheating scumbag."

"He swears it only happened once."

"And you *believe* that? Come on, Mom. Get real."

Paralyzed, Joe listened to their back-and-forth with a growing sense of dismay.

"Is that Janey's mug?" Linda asked Joe. "She has one just like it."

He looked up to find Mac zeroed in on him, but before he could say anything, Thomas let out a lusty wail, demanding his new daddy's full attention.

Joe took that as his cue to escape. "Gotta run, folks. I'm on the nine."

Distracted by the baby, Mac and Linda uttered hasty good-byes.

Outside, Joe took deep, gulping breaths of fresh air, hoping to slow his charging heart. Here they were trying to keep their relationship a secret, and a stupid cow mug had nearly undone the whole thing. Mac might've been distracted by Thomas, but later, when he had time to think about it, he'd wonder what Joe was doing with an odd mug that was exactly like one his sister owned.

"Shit," Joe muttered as he made his way to the ferry landing. And Kay Lawrence, determined to fix things for her creep of a son . . . That news didn't exactly make Joe's day, either. "You gotta have faith in Janey. She knows what he is. It'll take more than a couple of scheming mothers to undo the damage he did."

"Having a nice chat with yerself?"

The voice startled Joe out of his musings. Big Mac McCarthy's best friend, cab driver Ned Saunders, leaned against his battered woody station wagon waiting for his next fare.

Joe shook his hand. "How goes it, Ned?" The grizzled old man wore tattered khaki shorts with a T-shirt that read SQUEEZE YOUR LEMONS ON A LOBSTA.

"Getting tossed in jail and talking to yerself. What's going on with ya, boy?"

Joe released a huff of laughter. "You wouldn't believe me if I told you."

"Never known ya to be one to take care of things with ya fists."

"Your buddy Big Mac has already given me the same lecture."

"I heard he didn't make ya spend the night this time," Ned said, chortling with laughter.

"Now that you've had your entertainment for the day, I gotta boat to catch."

Ned went back to perusing a copy of the *Gansett Gazette*. "Give her some time, boy. She'll come round."

Startled, Joe stopped and turned back to stare at the older man. "What'd you say?"

"Ya heard me right the first time." Ned nodded to the ferry landing. "Looks like they're gonna leave without ya."

Questions cycled through Joe's mind: How did Ned know? *What* did Ned know? Who else knew? But the questions had to wait, because the ferry wouldn't, and Joe needed to get back to his office on the mainland. As much as he hated to leave the island—especially with David still in town—Joe had a business to run, and last time he checked, it didn't run itself.

Jogging down the hill to the ferry landing, Joe felt torn in a thousand different directions. His love for Janey had always been one of the simple truths in his life. How, then, he wondered as he dashed aboard the boat just as the final warning horn sounded, had the simplest thing become so damned complicated?

Chapter Thirteen

After Joe left, Janey resisted the urge to go back to bed and instead took a shower and got dressed. She was out in the yard enjoying the warm sun and playing with the dogs when Maddie arrived.

"Hey," Maddie said as she came through the house to the backyard. "The door was open, so I let myself in. Hope that's okay."

Janey smiled at her. They were still working out the boundaries of their new friendship. "Of course it is. You don't have to knock here."

"Oh, I'll still knock. I wouldn't want to *interrupt* anything."

Janey felt heat creep into her cheeks when she thought of waking up with Joe.

Maddie laughed. "Your face gives away your every thought."

"I know! I hate that."

"Do I take that to mean you had a *friend* over last night?"

"Perhaps."

Maddie lowered herself to the grass next to Janey. "Do tell."

Janey fell back onto the lawn, which the dogs took as an open invite to lie on top of her. Running her fingers through Muttley's soft fur, she tried to find the words. "Everything with him is so *easy*, you know?"

"That's the way it should be. It wasn't like that with David?"

"I thought it was, but it wasn't like this. Joe is just so . . ."

"Perfect for you?"

"In many ways, yes."

"Why do I sense a 'but' coming here?"

"Everything that's happened with David has me questioning my judgment. If you'd asked me last week if I ever imagined he'd cheat, I'd say not in a million years. I was that sure of him. And look at what he was doing."

"Janey, you can't let what he did cause you to doubt yourself. You loved him. You thought he loved you. Why in the world would you think he'd cheat on you? The failing is in him, not you."

"And I know that, but I can't get past the idea that I must've missed something. There had to have been signs, right?"

"You guys have lived apart a long time. It's not as easy to see the signs when you aren't with him every day."

Janey stroked Muttley's ears. "Still . . . When I look back now, I can see there were things I either chose not to see or chose not to question. Like why it took him days sometimes to call me back or how plans would get canceled at the last minute. I always chalked that up to his job and didn't think a thing of it. But now . . ."

"Now you're questioning everything."

Janey nodded. "It's making me nuts."

"I don't want to say the wrong thing or overstep," Maddie said tentatively.

Janey smiled at her. "It's not possible for you to say the wrong thing to me. I want us to be the best of friends. You should feel free to speak your mind."

Maddie's eyes flooded with tears, which made her laugh. "I'm like an emotional disaster area these days. Everything makes me cry."

"They're happy tears."

"Absolutely. Not only did I get Mac, but you and all your family. I feel so incredibly lucky."

"Wait till our other brothers get here. *Lucky* might not be the word you're using when you see how crazy Mac gets with them."

"Don't try to scare me off. Nothing could keep me from marrying him."

Janey grinned at her. "What were you going to say? Before?"

"Just that I hope you won't hold what David did against Joe. That wouldn't be fair to Joe."

"No, it wouldn't, but let's face it, none of this is fair to Joe. He's in love with me, and I'm a mess. I know I shouldn't be encouraging what's happening between us, especially right now, and I have all these good intentions to stay away from him. But then he walks in the room and all my good intentions disappear. I can't keep my hands off him."

"You're in major lust—and I can see why. He's adorable and sexy."

"Definitely *major* lust, but what if that's all it is?

That would crush him. He hasn't said anything, but I know where he's hoping this is heading."

"How do you feel about him?"

"It's hard to tell. Everything is so jumbled. If you're asking if I love him, of course I do. I've always loved him."

"But as a friend."

"Right, and that's the problem. It's hard to tell if I suddenly love him as more than that, or if I'm under the influence of great sex."

"If you start to feel like it's only a rebound, you need to end it. Immediately."

"I know," Janey said. "I'm so afraid I'm going to hurt him."

"He's a big boy, and his eyes are wide open. You can't take responsibility for him. You have to think about yourself and what you want."

"I'm trying, but it's hard."

"Just take it a day at a time and don't feel that you have to figure anything out right away."

"That's good advice, and you should know after all you went through with Mac."

"When I think about how close I came to losing him . . ." Maddie shuddered.

"You two are meant to be. You would've ended up together one way or the other."

"I agree, but my mother won't. I'm picking her up in the morning, and I can only imagine what she'll have to say when she finds out I'm marrying Mac McCarthy next week."

"You need to take your own advice and do what's best for *you*. I can't imagine why anyone wouldn't want to see their daughter married to my fabulous brother. But if she gives you grief about it, just let her know if she forces you to choose, you won't choose her."

"That's exactly what I plan to do."

"Just remember what's waiting for you in a week's time, and you'll find the courage you need to deal with her."

"I can't wait to be married to him, but I just keep worrying that something's going to happen to mess it up before we say I do."

"Nothing's going to happen."

Right on cue, Mac walked into the yard with Thomas on his shoulders. Talk about meant to be . . . Janey couldn't get over how easily her stubbornly single brother had slipped into life as a family man.

"There're my guys," Maddie said, glowing at the sight of them.

"I got your text that you'd be here, so we're making the transfer." He hugged and kissed Thomas and lowered him to his mother. "See you later, buddy."

Thomas let out a wail of protest.

"It's so not fair," Maddie said with a pout. "You carry him for nine months, you practically kill yourself giving birth to him and then he picks his new daddy over you every time."

Thomas squealed with delight when the dogs sniffed and licked his outstretched hands.

Mac squatted down to kiss the pout off Maddie's lips. "Daddy picks Mommy *every* time."

"Well, I guess that's *something*," Maddie said with a teasing glint in her eye.

Chuckling, Mac kissed her again before he stood. "Got any coffee, brat?"

"Sure. Help yourself."

"I need a travel mug."

"Oh, I, um, left mine at work."

Mac studied her for a long moment before he said, "Never mind, then. I'll get some more at the marina. Oh, by the way, Mom was powwowing with Kay Lawrence at the diner just now. I think they're conspiring to get you and David back together."

"Fabulous."

"I reminded Mom that the guy cheated on you, and you're better off without him."

"Thanks."

"Still, watch out for them. They're up to something. And, oh, *man*, is Kay pissed at Joe! If looks could kill!"

"Joe was there, too?" Janey asked, making a supreme effort to sound casual and unconcerned.

Mac gave her a knowing look that set her nerves on edge. "Uh-huh. Well, I'd better get to work. You ladies have a nice day."

"Love you," Maddie said.

"You, too, babe." He waggled his fingers at Thomas and walked around the side of the house to the street.

"What was that all about with the coffee?" Maddie asked.

"He might be on to me and Joe. I gave Joe my cow mug this morning, and I'll bet my mother said something about it."

"You might want to tell Mac the truth now rather than letting him find out later."

"Not until after the wedding. We all know Mac is going to be pissed with Joe over this, so let's get through the wedding before we go there."

"If he finds out I kept this from him, there might not be a wedding."

"Oh, there'll be a wedding. Neither lying sisters

nor disapproving mothers nor wild horses nor randy best men could keep my brother from marrying you."

"Let's hope you're right."

Janey decided to call on Doc Potter to take care of the animals, rather than give Maddie anything more to keep from Mac. She did, however, let her future sister-in-law know where she'd be in case of emergency. As she packed for her night with Joe, Janey's hands trembled with excitement and anticipation. She might not be certain how she felt about him, but she was damned sure she couldn't wait to see him again.

Her conversation with Maddie kept running through her mind. Was she in love with Joe? Had she ever really loved David? Did she even know what it meant to be in love? It worried her that she'd gotten over David so quickly. She knew that was probably due to the shock of seeing him with someone else, but still . . . Thirteen years was a long time, and whatever love she'd felt for him had died a quick and sudden death.

She spent a last minute with each of her beloved pets, grabbed her bag and skipped out of the house.

"Going somewhere?"

Janey about jumped out of her skin. "Jesus, David. You scared the heck out of me."

"You're looking awfully excited for a woman who just called off her engagement."

"I'm in a hurry. I can't talk right now."

"Where're you going?"

"That's none of your business. You lost the right to

ask me things like that when I saw you in bed with another woman."

He winced. "I wish you'd believe me when I tell you how sorry I am about that."

"You're just sorry you got caught."

"That's not true! If you'd just talk to me—"

"I have nothing to say. Now, I've got a boat to catch. Please let me by."

"Why are you going to the mainland?"

Janey decided she had to humor him if she was going to make the boat. "To get my car. It broke down after I saw you in bed with another woman."

"Where are you staying tonight?" he asked through gritted teeth.

"With a friend."

"What *friend?*"

"I'm not telling you that!"

He grabbed her arm and held it tighter than he should have. "Have you got someone else, Janey? This whole time you're making me feel like shit, and you're probably doing the same thing. *Who is it?*"

Infuriated, she shook him off. "I was never unfaithful to you," she spat at him. "*Never.* Just like our relationship, this conversation is *over.*" Pushing past him, she made her way down the sidewalk, resisting the urge to look back. Her future was in front of her, not behind her. Joe was expecting her, and she couldn't wait to see him.

Joe paced back and forth on the ferry landing. *Where was she?* The boat was minutes from departure, and because he was the captain on this trip, he had to go with or without her. After waiting hours to see her,

Joe couldn't imagine what was keeping her. A deep fog had descended upon the island, and the hours he'd spent navigating the boats through the soup had left him tired and tense.

The final warning horn sounded just as he saw her come dashing through the parking lot, her blond ponytail streaming behind her.

"Janey," he whispered.

Since the landing was crowded with people, he couldn't greet her the way he wanted to. Instead, he grabbed her hand and all but dragged her onboard the ferry.

"I'm sorry," she said, panting from exertion. "I had an unwelcome visitor just as I was leaving."

"*Again?*"

"I wish he'd go back to Boston."

"Me, too."

Janey squeezed his hand. "We don't have to think about him tonight."

"That's right."

"Will we be okay in this fog?"

He glanced down at her, feigning indignation. "You doubt me?"

"Never." She looked up at him with those captivating blue eyes. "I trust you with my life."

"Thank you," he whispered, stealing a kiss in one of the darkened passageways. Just when he thought she couldn't move him any more than she had before, she managed to top herself. "Since you're such a major distraction, I can't have you up top with me tonight. I'll come find you when we get in."

She smiled as if being called a major distraction was a compliment. "I'll be waiting."

"You'd better be."

"Be careful, Captain."

"Always, but especially with such precious cargo onboard." He kissed her once more. "See you in a bit." He watched her choose a table and withdraw a book and her phone from her tote bag. Like any native islander, she'd come ready to kill an hour on the ferry.

With seconds to spare before departure, he bolted up the stairs to the wheelhouse. Since he'd completed a safety check earlier, he ignored the raised eyebrow of his first mate, Rob. "Ready?"

"Whenever you are, Cap."

"Then let's do it."

By the time Joe backed the ferry into its berth in Point Judith, his head was pounding and his shoulders were stiff with stress. Following their usual protocols for zero visibility, Joe had stationed two deckhands on the bow as lookouts and had sounded the horn every thirty seconds. They'd relied on radar to scan for other vessels in the area and GPS to lead them to port. No matter how many times he safely guided a ferry full of passengers through the fog, however, it never became routine.

"Nice job, Cap," Rob said when Joe returned to the wheelhouse after locking up the aft controls he'd used to back the ferry into port.

"A team effort as always." Joe shut down the electronics and secured the wheelhouse. "See you tomorrow."

He parted with Rob on the second level and went to find Janey. At some point during the trip, she had curled up on the bench and gone to sleep with her overnight bag tucked under her head. Before waking her, he took a moment to just take her in. Sometimes it was hard to believe that she was real—that *they* were real. At least they were for right now. He tried not to think about how it might end, but that sense of doom hovered just above his head at all times, waiting to swoop down and take her away from him. Well, now that was a pleasant thought . . .

Determined to not let gloom or doom ruin their precious time together, he leaned over to kiss her awake. "Hey, baby. We're there."

She smiled up at him, a sleepy, sexy smile that stopped his heart. "Mmm," she said, stretching. "My hero."

"Nothing to it."

"Somehow I doubt that." Sitting up, she combed her fingers through her hair and retied her ponytail.

Joe took her bag and reached for her hand. He was so anxious to be alone with her that he didn't bother to make his usual stop in the office before leading her to his truck.

Janey shivered. "The fog makes it so chilly. It's hard to believe it's July."

"I have just the thing for that at home."

She smiled at him. "I can't wait to see what it is."

In the truck, Joe took her hand again, needing to touch her, wanting her close to him. This, he decided, was heaven. Taking her home with him, talking to her at the end of a long day, anticipating a night of passion and love. If this were all he ever had—if *she* was all he ever had—his life would be more than complete.

"What are you thinking over there?" she asked.

He glanced at her. "That I like having you here with me."

"I like being here."

He told himself that her pleasure had nothing to do with escaping from David and all her troubles on the island. It had to do with him, with what was happening between them. Of course it did.

They reached his house within minutes. "Damn it," he said as he killed the engine. "I just realized you must be starving. I know I am." He'd been so focused on getting her home that he hadn't given dinner a thought.

"How about we order a pizza?"

"We can do that. A veggie for my veggie?"

Janey cracked up as she followed him inside. "If that's what you like. I can do plain cheese, too."

"I like veggie."

"No olives, though," she said, wrinkling her cute nose.

"You got it." While she stashed her stuff in his room, Joe called in the pizza and wondered how long it would take for her family to come looking for her if he kidnapped her and kept her here forever.

As he ended the call to the pizza place, she returned to the kitchen and slipped her arms around him from behind. "I'm freezing. Warm me up?"

"Right this way." He took her hand and led her into the family room that overlooked the deck and harbor, but the view tonight consisted of pea-soup fog. Squatting before the stone hearth, he had a roaring fire going in no time.

"Mmm," Janey said from the sofa. "Perfect."

"Told you you'd like it. Come down here with me."

Janey crawled over to him.

Joe put his arm around her and breathed in her sweet scent.

When she leaned into his embrace and released a sigh of contentment, all the tension of the day seemed to leave his body.

"The heat feels so good," she said.

He kissed the top of her head. "So do you."

Tilting her face up, she studied him intently.

"What?"

"I couldn't wait to see you tonight," she said softly.

Joe's heart turned right over in his chest. Did she have any idea what she did to him when she looked at him that way or said such amazing things to him? "I couldn't wait, either. Today was a bitch with the fog. You start to feel like you're hallucinating after staring at it for hours."

"I can't imagine. It's so cool how you can get the ferry from point A to point B without being able to see a thing."

"It's stressful."

"It's *very* sexy."

Joe laughed. "Is that so?"

"Uh-huh."

"I need to take you out in the fog more often, then."

Janey raised a hand to his face, sliding it over the stubble on his jaw.

"I should shave," he said, staring down at her.

"I like it." She followed her hand with her lips. "Also very sexy."

A tremble rippled through him. "Janey—"

The doorbell interrupted the intense moment.

While she chuckled at his distress, he groaned and

got up to greet the pizza man. Joe unearthed a bottle of merlot, and they ate picnic-style in front of the fire.

"I look at you sitting here in my house with the firelight dancing on your beautiful face, and I think I have to be dreaming. Tell me I'm not dreaming."

Rising to her knees, she pushed the empty pizza box out of the way and closed the distance between them, resting her hands on his shoulders. "If it's a dream, don't wake me up, okay?"

He reached for her and fell backward, bringing her with him. "Deal."

The hair she'd let down from the ponytail made a curtain around them, sealing them off from the world as she lowered her head and captured his mouth in a soft, sensual kiss.

Even though he wanted to devour her, Joe cupped her face and let her take the lead. She seemed freer tonight, less concerned about where all this might be leading and more interested in seizing the moment— *their* moment. Her tongue traced a trail from bottom lip to top before dipping inside to flirt with his.

Joe couldn't seem to draw a breath as he responded to her gentle strokes. And then she was gone, shifting her attention to his jaw before rolling his earlobe between her teeth. He sucked in a sharp deep breath as the sensation traveled from his ear straight to his cock. "*Janey.*"

"Hmm?" Now she was at his neck on her way to his chest. She worked his shirt up and over his head without missing a beat in her game of sensual torture. "You're so tense. Relax, Joe. Let me take care of you for a change."

Would he survive her brand of caretaking? Her lips were soft and smooth on his chest, and he had to remind himself to keep breathing. She shifted lower, pressing her belly against his straining erection.

"Baby, you're driving me crazy," he whispered, running his fingers through fine strands of golden hair.

Massaging his shoulders, she licked his nipple. The sensation zipped through him like an electrical charge he felt in every cell. Then she was at his belly, teasing and tempting him with her tongue and lips.

Joe hadn't been this close to an embarrassing accident since high school—and that was before he felt his zipper travel down over his straining shaft. He bit his lip—hard—hoping to regain some control.

"You smell so good," she whispered against his belly, causing an outbreak of goose bumps on his overly sensitive skin.

"What do I smell like?"

"The sea and fresh air and sexy man."

"All that?"

"Mmm-hmm." This she muttered against the head of his penis, which had somehow found its way to her mouth.

"Janey, honey, wait . . ."

She looked up at him with innocent blue eyes that were mocking him. "Why?"

"You're a vixen, aren't you?" he asked, laughing softly. "You know exactly what you're doing to me."

The gentle strokes of her hand quickly had him on the verge of explosion.

"Are you complaining?"

Joe released a ragged breath. "No." He broke out in a sweat when she took him deep into her mouth while using her tongue and hand to caress him. "Janey . . . honey . . . *God.*"

She laughed, and the vibration almost finished him off.

"Baby, come up here. Let's do this together."

Joe got a second lease on life when she released him to shimmy out of her skirt and panties. Watching her pull her top over her head and remove her bra, however, had him right back at the brink. He reached for her, certain he'd never been more turned on in his life.

With her hand on his chest, she eased him back, letting him know she was still in charge. She strad-dled him and rubbed her moist heat over him.

He grabbed her hips, desperate to be inside her, but she wasn't done playing with him.

Apparently, she didn't care that she was making him crazy, because she tossed her head back and laughed. Sliding his hands from her hips to her ribs, he cupped her breasts and ran his thumbs over her nipples. That finally seemed to get her attention. She stopped tormenting him and took him in.

"Ahhh," she sighed, gazing down at him through half-lidded eyes. "That feels *so* good."

Joe linked their fingers and held on tight, expecting her to ride him hard. But once again she surprised him by stilling the movement of her hips. He groaned. "*Janey!*"

"Tell me something about you that I don't know."

He stared up at her, incredulous. "*Now?*"

She bit her lip and nodded. "You know me so well. You know how I take my coffee and that I'm a vege-tarian. You even remember my injured pet squirrel and the Strawberry Shortcake overalls. I need to catch up."

His fingers traveled over her back to cup her

bottom, bringing her in tighter against him. "And we have to play get-to-know-you right this minute?"

Tilting her hips ever so provocatively, she nodded again. "Just *one thing*, Joe. That's all I'm asking for."

"I can't believe you expect me to think right now."

She squeezed his shoulders. "You can do it, and when you do, you'll be *richly* rewarded."

"Well, when you put it that way . . ." He squirmed beneath her, needing more and needing it now. Somehow, he managed to say, "I like to paint."

"Walls?"

"Canvas." He gasped when she rolled her hips and bent to drag her breasts over his chest. "Landscapes."

"Oh! You mean paint *paint*."

"Right. Can we have sex now?"

"We *are* having sex."

"Can we do it my way?"

Her lip came out in a pretty pout. "You don't like my way?"

"I love your way." He sat up and curled her legs around his hips. "But I'm about to explode. You wanna come with me?"

"Will you show me your paintings? After we explode?"

He bit back a smile. Had she ever been more adorable? "*Yes!*"

She wrapped her arms around his neck, pressing her breasts against him. "Then I wanna go with you. Take me with you, Joe."

"Gladly, my love."

Chapter Fourteen

Whoa, Janey thought. When he said explode, he meant *explode.* The aftershocks tingled through her body, reminding her of the amazing moment of intense connection and utter harmony. Not once, in all the years she'd spent with David, had they ever come even close to achieving such a moment.

Lying on top of Joe, feeling him throb between her legs as he caressed her back, Janey couldn't have moved if she had to. In the back of her mind, however, were nagging questions that refused to be quieted in the aftermath of amazing sex. What was happening between them? Why did it feel so important? Did she really want to go from something long-term and serious to something even more serious?

Joe was so free with the "L" word. Did it hurt him that she didn't say it back? How had Joe become so vital to her in just a few days? And, most important of all, she had been so terribly wrong about David. How could she trust herself and her judgment in the wake of that spectacular failure?

"There's an awful lot going on in that pretty little head of yours," he muttered.

How did he know? How did he *always* know?

"Want to talk about it?"

"No."

"All righty, then, want to see my etchings?"

Janey laughed. "Mmm-hmm."

"Then you'll have to get your big old self off me."

But rather than move, she burrowed in closer.

Joe's arms tightened around her. "Or we could just stay right here all night."

"I do want to see your paintings."

"They'll keep."

Janey rested on top of him, reveling in his scent, in the tender way he held her, in the certainty that he loved her. But always, under the surface of her contentment, were those blasted questions with no answers.

"I wish you would tell me what has you so worried."

"I should be worried about how well you know me," she said with a nervous laugh.

"Is that a bad thing?"

"It's unnerving at times."

"Want to talk unnerving? How about when you suddenly decide, in the middle of having sex, that you don't know me as well as I know you?"

She winced. "Sorry."

"Don't be. It was cute." Joe turned them so he could look down at her. "I'm a pretty simple guy, Janey. What you see is more or less what you get."

"That is *so* not true! That's what you want people to think."

He raised a questioning eyebrow. "Why do you say that?"

"You have all kinds of talents besides steering a hundred-foot ferry through pea-soup fog."

"Such as?"

"Look at this awesome house you built with your own hands or how you whip up your own salmon marinade. And now I find out you're also an artist!"

He laughed. "I wouldn't say *that*."

"I'll be the judge." She flashed a coy smile. "Of course, there's also that thing you do with your tongue. Mmm. That's *quite* a talent."

His face lifted into the smile she was growing to love in ways she never could've imagined a few days ago. He bent to kiss her. "You know me, Janey. You know all the important stuff."

She reached up to push the hair off his forehead. "I'm only just beginning to figure out the important stuff."

"I hope you see yourself at the top of the what's-important-to-Joe list."

Even though she knew it was cowardly, Janey looked away from the intensity and the longing she saw on his face.

"You don't like being at the top of my list?"

"It scares me."

With his finger on her chin, he forced her to look at him. "Why?"

"I'm so afraid I'm going to hurt you, Joe. I don't want to, but I'm afraid I will anyway."

"You're not responsible for me, honey. I'd never want you to feel that way. I knew what I was getting into. I knew the timing sucked, and I let it happen anyway."

"If this doesn't work out, if *we* don't work out, will you be okay?"

"I won't lie to you. I really want it to work out."

"But if it doesn't? I need to know you'd be okay. I *need* that."

"I have a great life. I get to do what I love every day. I have awesome friends and a home I like returning to every night. Is it perfect? No, but it works for me. If you were waiting for me when I got home every night? Now *that* would be perfect."

Janey rolled her lip between her teeth. "You really think so?"

He nudged at her until she yielded her abused lip to him. "I know so. But the only way I want you with me is if it's where *you* want to be. No questions, no doubts, no reservations."

"You didn't answer my question."

"Yes, Janey," he said. "I'll be okay."

"Promise?"

"Yeah." The single word was full of sadness, but then she watched him try to rally. "So you like that tongue trick, huh?"

"Oh, *yeah.*"

He kissed his way down the front of her. "They say practice makes perfect."

"Is that what they say?"

"Uh-huh."

Steeped in the incredible pleasure, Janey decided the worries would have to wait. They had this night together, and she didn't want to spoil it. Tomorrow would have to take care of itself.

By the time they got around to looking at his paintings, it was nearly three in the morning. Kneeling on the floor of his studio, Janey wore a T-shirt of his that showed off her shapely legs. He'd pulled on boxers when she insisted on dragging him into the studio. Watching her flip through canvases that few people had ever seen made Joe feel vulnerable and exposed—an uncomfortable feeling he was becoming accustomed to lately.

"These are *amazing*! Why haven't you ever done anything with them?"

Embarrassed by her effusiveness, he ran his fingers through his hair. "It's just something I do for fun."

She turned those potent blue eyes on him. "You're incredibly talented, Joe."

God, she just *tore him up* when she looked at him that way. "Thanks."

Standing, she reached for the canvas that depicted the island's Northeast Light. "Look at this! It's exquisite. The colors and the passion! How do you get the water to look like it's moving?"

"I don't know," he said, laughing. "I just paint what I see."

"I'm astounded that you've kept such a huge talent hidden for so long."

"It's a *hobby*, Janey."

"It's amazing."

"You can have that one if you like it so much."

"I couldn't! You could get good money for it!"

"I don't want good money. If you love it, you can have it."

"I can't possibly take it. You need to show them and sell them and make tons of money!"

He smiled at her foolishness. "That's not me, hon. I'm a ferryboat captain, not an artist."

"Why couldn't you be both? Aren't you the one trying to convince me I need to go to vet school?"

Damn, the girl could argue! He'd always admired the way she more than held her own with four older brothers. "That's different."

The hand on her hip and the saucy tilt to her chin made him want her all over again, as if he hadn't just spent hours trying to sate a need he was beginning to understand would never be fully sated.

"How's it different?" she asked.

Cornered, Joe took the canvas from her and grabbed her hand to lead her from the room. "Put this with your stuff. It's yours now."

"You're not going to tell me how you pursuing your artistic talent is different from me going to vet school?"

In the kitchen, Joe got a glass and filled it with ice and water. After he took a drink, he passed the glass to her and watched the way her lips and throat worked on the glass. It was official: everything she did turned him on.

"I have a job I love, one that fulfills me in every possible way. I get to be on the water all day. I regularly see whales and dolphins and have to use my brain and my instincts and years of hard-won know-how every day. It's enough for me."

She handed the glass back to him. "But it doesn't have to be everything. Why couldn't you have that and your art, too?"

"I already have both. The painting is something I do to relax, to blow off steam. It's no big deal."

"I took an oil class in college." Her eyes were locked on the painting he'd given her, which she had propped against the wall. "I know what it takes to make the water appear to be moving, and I didn't have it. In fact, no one in my class did. I don't even think the teacher could do it. You're incredibly talented, and you don't even know it."

"I don't *care*," he said, laughing softly with exasperation. "That's what you're not getting. The whole world could see my paintings and declare them masterpieces, and that wouldn't add anything to my life that I don't already have."

Fixated now on the cabinet behind him, she bit her thumbnail. "And yet . . ."

He put down the glass, went to her and rested his hands on her hips. "And yet what?"

"You said that having me here with you, all the time, would add something you don't have."

"Yes," he said, his voice hoarse with the emotion she aroused in him without even trying. "It absolutely would."

"You have this amazing talent that means nothing to you, but I—"

"You," he said, kissing her nose, "mean *everything* to me."

"How can that be?"

"It just *is*, baby. Damned if I can explain it."

She reached for him, brought him down to her and kissed him so sweetly, so gently, that Joe wondered how he managed to remain standing.

"Let's go to bed." She took his hands, linked their fingers and walked backward, leading him to what could be his ruination. Even knowing that, he willingly followed her.

On the first boat off the island the next morning, Maddie stood at the rail, holding a cup of coffee and pondering the coincidence of her mother being released from prison on Independence Day. "Let freedom ring," she whispered as butterflies stormed about in her belly. After tangling with Linda over bad checks written to the hotel bar, her mother had a low opinion of all things McCarthy. What would she say when she found out her eldest daughter planned to marry their eldest son in a week's time?

Maddie shuddered when she imagined her mother's reaction. Over and over she had practiced what she would say, how she would break the news. Each time she pictured the scene, she saw her mother's face turn red with rage.

Mac had wanted to come with her today, but she'd insisted on doing this alone. Besides, they were having people over later, and one of them needed to stay back to finish the preparations. Their new house had a fantastic view of the fireworks, and they wanted to share it with the people they loved.

She remembered the way he'd held her so close during the night and made sweet love to her at dawn, as if to fortify her to fight for them against what would no doubt be her mother's strong objections. In the brisk breeze, tears stung her eyes. She shouldn't have to fight for anything. He was a kind and decent man who loved her and her son with everything he had. Her mother had never even met Mac, yet she would judge him because his family was one of the "haves" on an island in which she and her family had always been one of the "have-nots."

That wasn't his fault any more than it was hers. Just as it wasn't their fault that her mother had written enough bad checks to establishments such as the bar at McCarthy's Gansett Inn that the proprietors had had no choice but to report her. *She* had landed *herself* in jail, and if the McCarthys could see fit to separate Maddie from her mother's sins, then perhaps her mother could find it in her heart to judge Mac for himself.

"Wishful thinking, girl," she whispered to herself. "She's going to freak, and there's nothing you can do to stop it." But nothing her mother could possibly say, Maddie reminded herself, would stop her from marrying the love of her life—with or without her mother's blessing. It sure would be sweeter, however, if her mother could find a way to accept that her daughter was happy with Mac, and that she didn't give two figs about his last name or his money.

With that thought at the forefront of her mind, Maddie drove off the ferry in the black SUV Mac had bought to get their little family around the island. Her mother's first question would be about where she had gotten the money for such an extravagant vehicle.

During the hour-long drive to the state prison in Cranston, Maddie focused on happy thoughts of Mac and Thomas, on wedding plans and blissful nights in the arms of the man she loved. Nothing and no one would ever come between them again. She was almost to the prison when her phone rang, and Mac's number popped up on the caller ID. Even though she knew he was calling to offer his support, she chose not to take the call for fear that hearing his voice would cause her to fall apart in these last crucial minutes.

No, she would wait until they were back on the ferry home before she returned his call. "Please," she whispered as she pulled into the parking lot and turned off the truck. "Please, for once, be happy for

me. Just this once." As fortified as she was going to
get, Maddie opened the door and stepped into the
July sunshine. Inside, she signed in and was assigned
to an air-conditioned waiting room.

Thirty minutes passed in which Maddie shivered in
the chill before the door opened and Francine Chester
appeared, wearing the release-day outfit Maddie had
sent her and carrying a plastic bag of other belongings.
Gray roots had overtaken her mother's cap of dyed red
hair. No doubt her first stop on the island would be
at the beauty shop, which would sneak her in as long
as she paid cash.

"Get me out of here." Francine brushed past her
daughter as if they had just seen each other yesterday
rather than three months ago.

Nice to see you, too, Maddie thought as she followed
her mother to the exit and directed her to the parking lot.

Francine tilted her head into the sunshine and
took deep breaths of fresh air. "About damned time
they let me out of that hellhole. Was your sister too
busy to come with you?"

"Ashleigh wasn't feeling well," Maddie said of her
infant niece. "Tiffany said they'll see you when you
get home. She has the apartment all ready for you."

"What apartment?"

"My old place at Tiff's house. We figured you could
stay there until you get back on your feet."

Francine eyed her with cagey green eyes that didn't
miss a trick. "And where will you be?"

"I wanted to talk to you about that." Maddie clicked
the button on her key fob to unlock the truck and
watched as her mother's eyes widened with predictable questions.

"Did you hit the lottery while I was gone?"

In a way, Maddie thought. Here goes nothing . . . "It belongs to my fiancé."

Francine turned to her, incredulous. "What *fiancé?*"

Maddie swallowed the fear, the worries and the sense of impending doom and looked her mother dead in the eye. "The one I plan to marry a week from today."

"You're getting *married,* and you haven't seen fit to mention this to me until now? You could've sent a letter or mentioned it during one of the calls."

"I wanted to tell you in person."

"So tell me. Who is he?"

Once again, Maddie refused to blink. She refused to be ashamed or to cower under her mother's intense scrutiny. "Mac McCarthy. Junior."

Francine released a harsh bark of laughter. "Like hell you're marrying a McCarthy."

"I am *absolutely* marrying a McCarthy, and I'm proud of it." She held open the door to the truck.

Francine crossed her arms and tilted her chin defiantly. "I will not ride in a vehicle owned by a McCarthy."

"Fine," Maddie said. "Then you can find your own way home." She walked around the truck to get in the driver's side and started the engine. Her stomach ached, and her eyes burned with tears. Did she really have the nerve to drive off and leave her mother there with no money and no other way home?

In the brief span of silence that stretched into tense minutes, Maddie realized her entire life had come down to this moment—and if she had to choose between a past full of heartache and disappointment and a future with Mac that promised to be filled with love and joy, then she chose the future. With him.

She glanced at the open passenger door. "I love him, he loves me, he adores Thomas, and I'm going to marry him, with you or without you. I'd prefer to do it with you, but if you force me to choose, I choose him."

Since she had no alternative, Francine got in the truck and slammed the door. "You'll marry him over my dead body."

Maddie shrugged. "If that's what it takes." Despite her show of bravado, her hands shook so badly she wondered how she would drive.

Chapter Fifteen

Janey was thrilled to find Maddie and the SUV in the line for the three o'clock ferry. After checking her fresh-from-the-shop car into the line, Janey skipped over to where Maddie leaned against the black truck, her arms crossed and her face set in an unreadable expression.

"Hey!"

Maddie looked up, startled. "Oh. Hi."

Janey studied her friend. "What's wrong?"

"My mother."

"*Ohhh.*" Janey leaned back against the truck, next to Maddie. "I take it the pickup didn't go well?"

"Let me quote, shall I? 'You'll marry a McCarthy over my dead body.'"

"Ouch. I resemble that remark. What did you say?"

"If that's what it takes."

"Good for you." Janey snorted. "Where is she now?"

"On the boat. She took the ticket I bought her and stalked off." Maddie slid her slender foot in and out of her flip-flop, an aura of weary resignation clinging to her every movement. "I knew it was too much to hope that she might be supportive, but still . . ."

"You hoped anyway."

"I never learn. That's my problem. I expect people to change, but they don't."

Janey linked her arm with Maddie's and rested her head on her friend's shoulder. "Do you know what I love best about you?"

Maddie tilted her head to lean it on Janey's. "What's that?"

"You're always upbeat, even when you have good reason not to be. I admire that quality in you, and I know Mac does, too."

"Thank you. That's sweet of you to say."

"I know she's your mom, but I'd hate to see her take anything away from your happiness. Not when you and Mac waited so long to find each other."

"You're right. You're *absolutely* right."

"She can't ruin it for you unless you let her."

Maddie stood upright and turned to Janey, a brilliant smile lighting up her pretty face. "I can't wait until you're officially my sister-in-law."

Janey hugged her. "I can't, either."

"So where's Joe?"

"On the island. He was on the one thirty. I stayed over here to do a few errands after I picked up my car."

"How was last night?" Maddie asked with a salacious smile.

"*Amazing.*"

Maddie laughed. "That good, huh?"

"It's incredible. We just have this unbelievable connection."

"So why don't you look happy?"

"I am happy. I'm *so* happy. That's the problem."

"You've lost me."

"Not even a week ago, I was engaged to David. I had my whole life planned. I was in love, content, settled, you know?"

"Uh-huh. And now?"

"Now, it's like David's dead to me, everything I ever felt for him is gone, and I can't be in the same room with Joe and not want to jump him."

Maddie giggled behind her hand.

"What's so funny?"

"You are. You're madly in love with *Joe,* and you don't even see it."

Janey stared at her, wondering if Maddie had lost her mind. "How can you say that? I was in love with David a week ago! When did I become this fickle fannie who loves a different boy every week?"

"You're *not* a fickle fannie. You were with the same guy all your life, Janey. He did a despicable thing that you had the misfortune—or fortune, depending on how you look at it—to witness."

"Fortune." She shuddered, imagining what she might never have known about him if she hadn't seen it with her own eyes. "Definitely fortune."

"Is it any wonder that you instantly fell out of love with him?"

"I guess not. But how do you explain that I managed to fall halfway in love with Joe in just a few days?"

"Maybe you were already halfway there but never admitted it to yourself because you couldn't."

Janey sucked in a sharp deep breath. "Jeez, you don't pull any punches, do you?"

Maddie shrugged with playful indifference. "Just calling it the way I see it."

Janey found the insight truly astounding. "You really think that's possible?"

"He's always been good old Joe, there when you need him, to lend an ear or a shoulder to lean on, to make you feel good about yourself because he had something nice to say about your hair or your outfit or your smile. What girl wouldn't be halfway in love with a guy who always gave her his full attention—especially when her fiancé was never around?"

Janey stared at Maddie. "How do you *know* all that? You just met us recently!"

Maddie snickered with laughter. "I was guessing, but judging by the expression on your face, it looks like I hit a bull's-eye."

"You've certainly given me something to think about."

"Don't think too hard, Janey. He's a good guy, and he loves you. He really loves you. Why does it have to be any more complicated than that?"

"I don't know, but I'm sure I'll think of a reason."

Maddie laughed and hip-checked her. "Just run with it and don't ask any questions." Her cell phone rang, and she tugged it out of her back pocket. "It's Mac," she whispered to Janey. "Hey, babe. About like I thought it would. I know. You don't have to do that." Maddie laughed softly. "Okay. I'll see you then. Love you, too." She ended the call and turned back to Janey. "He's meeting the boat so she can see Thomas."

"That's good of him."

"It's more than she deserves."

One of Joe's employees signaled that it was time to back their cars onto the ferry.

Janey started toward her car but turned back.

"When we get on the boat, how'd you like to introduce your future sister-in-law to your mother?"

"You know what?" Maddie said with a big grin. "I think that would make my day."

"Mine, too," Janey said.

After receiving the deep chill from Maddie's mother, Janey felt sad for Mac and the reception he'd no doubt receive from his future mother-in-law. Why couldn't people just be nice and get along? She tried to imagine a scenario whereby she wouldn't at least *try* to be happy for her daughter if she was marrying the man she loved.

The entire situation saddened her, and she suddenly couldn't wait to see Joe. He always made her feel better. Maddie had been right about that much. The rest of their conversation kept replaying in her mind. Had she been halfway in love with Joe even when she was still with David? Was that even possible?

With her thoughts continuing to churn, Janey drove off the ferry and parked in the thirty-minute lot next to Maddie. When her friend stepped out of the truck, Janey went over to her, squeezed her shoulder and walked with her to where Mac waited with Thomas.

Maddie stepped into his embrace, and they whispered softly to each other.

Janey stood back to give them a moment alone.

"What's going on?" Joe whispered.

Janey startled and turned to him. "Maddie's mom." She nodded to the bitter-looking woman walking off the ferry. "Not good."

Joe scowled. "What's her problem?"

"God only knows."

As if she owned the island and everything on it, Francine strolled over to them. "There's my grandson! Oh, look how *big* you've gotten!"

"Mom, this is my fiancé, Mac McCarthy."

As if Maddie hadn't spoken, Francine reached for the baby.

Maddie stepped between them. "If you can't be civil and say hello to the man I intend to marry, then I'm afraid your grandson isn't available to spend any time with you."

"Don't be ridiculous!" Francine sputtered. "I haven't seen him in three months!"

"Then I would think you'd do the polite thing and say hello to the man I just introduced you to." Maddie crossed her arms, but Janey could see she was trembling.

Apparently, Mac saw it, too, because he reached out to rest a hand on her shoulder.

The two women stood locked in a standoff for a long moment before Francine rolled her eyes and looked up at Mac disdainfully. "Hello. Now, may I have my grandson?"

Maddie shook her head with disbelief, and her eyes shone with tears, but she stepped back to give her mother access to her son.

Mac handed the boy to his grandmother.

Francine hugged the baby close to her and walked away from them to get reacquainted.

"Well," Maddie said, her voice wavering, "that was pleasant."

"It's okay, babe." Mac drew her into a hug and stroked a hand over her hair. "It's okay."

"It's not okay. I'm sorry she was rude to you."

"You have nothing to be sorry about."

Feeling like she was intruding on an intensely private moment between her brother and his fiancée, Janey strolled away to lean on one of the wood pilings.

Joe followed her. "That was screwed up, huh?"

"I feel bad for Maddie."

"I feel bad for her mother. She's so busy being bitter that she's willing to risk missing out on what should be one of the happiest times in her life."

Janey studied his handsome face. "You're a good guy, Joe Cantrell. And a generous guy to feel bad for her after the way she just behaved."

He shrugged off her praise and glanced at the ferry preparing for departure. "I gotta go. See you at the party?"

"Yes, you will."

"I'll be there around eight thirty."

"Right in time for the fireworks," she said suggestively.

He groaned under his breath. "I really, really want to kiss you right now," he whispered.

Janey smiled up at him. "Really?"

"*Really.*"

She chuckled at his tortured expression. "I'll make it up to you."

"Mmm, you sure will."

The burst of heat that traveled through her body took Janey by surprise. "Hurry back." When he walked away without touching her, Janey felt the loss just as acutely as she'd felt the desire. *Oh, my.*

* * *

Janey spent the few hours until the party making potato salad, taking a bath and blow-drying her hair. As she applied jasmine-scented lotion, she told herself she was *not* putting it on because Joe loved it so much. He went kind of nuts over it, to be honest. She couldn't wait to be with him again.

Maybe she was in love with him. Maybe she had been for a long time but didn't allow herself to acknowledge it while she was with David. Maybe it was time to just run with it, to throw herself wholeheartedly into a relationship with him, to tell the world and let it happen.

Then she thought of Mac and what he would have to say about her involvement with Joe.

Maybe the world didn't need to know quite yet.

After slipping on a red sundress, she contemplated going over to Mac and Maddie's early to help them finish getting ready but dismissed that idea. They needed some time alone after the day's drama. With an hour to kill, she sat down at her computer workstation and thumbed through the files in the drawer. Finding the one she wanted, she pulled it out and opened it on the desktop.

Memories came flooding back. Transcripts and letters of recommendation and applications and essays. Her professors in the school of animal science at the University of Connecticut had written glowing letters. Enclosed in the folder was the rejection letter from the top-ranked Cornell University College of Veterinary Medicine. But she had gotten into number two Colorado State and number five Ohio State. She'd all but settled on Doc Potter's alma mater, Ohio State, when David convinced her they couldn't possibly both go to medical school.

"What an idiot I was," she whispered as she read over the letters from her professors. Remembering her trip to Columbus, Ohio, Janey smiled and thumbed through the catalog of courses. A zing of anticipation raised goose bumps on her arms. She'd been so excited, so certain of her calling in life. And then David had stepped in and changed her plans.

"Never again," she vowed. "I will never again allow a man to make decisions for me." She skimmed through the catalog twice more. "But if I'm in Ohio, how can I start a relationship with Joe?"

"Why not?" she heard him say as if he was right there in the room with her. "Why couldn't we have it all, baby?"

Janey smiled. That's exactly what he'd say. Encouraged by his imaginary support, she fired up her laptop and, before she could lose her nerve, sent off e-mails to the three UConn professors who'd recommended her, asking if they'd be willing to endorse a better-late-than-never applicant.

She couldn't wait to tell Joe.

As she was getting ready to leave, her cell phone rang. Kay Lawrence. Again. Reluctantly, Janey took the call from the woman who'd been like a second mother to her.

"Hi, Kay."

"Oh, Janey! Thank goodness you finally picked up. I've been really anxious to talk to you."

"I know. I'm sorry. I've just needed some time."

"Please don't apologize to me. I should be apologizing to you."

"It's no reflection on you."

"Could we get together, honey? I'd love to see you."

"Things are so crazy this week with Mac's wedding."

"You need to talk to David, Janey. He has something he has to tell you."

"I have nothing to say to him."

"You can't mean that—"

"I mean it, Kay." Janey regretted taking the call when she'd been in such a good mood. "I know that's not what you want to hear, but I can't possibly marry him now."

"Would you please wait until you talk to him before you make any decisions?"

"I've already made my decision, and I won't change my mind."

"You might when you hear what he has to tell you."

Janey's stomach began to hurt. "I have to run now, Kay. I'm due over to Mac's for a cookout."

"We both love you very much, Janey," Kay said, her voice thick with tears. "Please let David tell you what he needs you to know."

"Bye, Kay."

By the time Janey arrived at Mac's, the setting sun had cast a warm glow on the yard and the meadow that stood between Mac's property and the coast. Sitting in chairs sprinkled around the yard were her parents, Luke Harris from the marina, her dad's friend Ned, Maddie's sister Tiffany and her family, Maddie's coworkers from the hotel, and some of the other guys from the docks, all of whom greeted Janey with hugs and words of encouragement that touched her heart.

She had to give Maddie credit. No one would ever know she'd been traumatized earlier by her mother's less-than-favorable reaction to her engagement.

Wearing a white top over red shorts, she flitted about making sure everyone had drinks and passing trays of hot and cold appetizers while Mac worked the grill. He looked so happy and content that Janey was almost tempted to tell him about her and Joe.

Almost.

Her father came up to her and slid a tree-trunk arm around her, tugging her in close to him. "How's my princess?"

"Hanging in there, Dad."

"I'm proud of you."

She glanced up at him. "For?"

"Holding your head up. The gossips on this island can be vicious when they get a bone to chew on. You're not hiding out."

"What else can I do?"

Big Mac kissed the top of her head. "That's my girl."

"Could I ask you something?"

"Anything."

"Remember a few years ago when I was thinking about going to vet school and David was worried we couldn't afford for both of us to go?"

Big Mac's normally amiable expression shifted to a scowl. "I don't like to think about that."

"I know it was upsetting to you."

"I would've given anything to see you in vet school. It's where you've always belonged."

"I was kind of hoping you'd say that."

A white brow lifted in question.

"Are you still willing to float me a loan?"

"Really?" he asked softly.

She bit her lip and nodded.

"Oh, baby." He enveloped her in a tight embrace. "No loans."

Surprised, she pulled back to look up at him. "I know you just retired—"

"Don't say another word," he said with a playful scowl. "I will not loan you the money. I will gladly and happily *give* it to you. It would give me great pleasure to see my daughter become a veterinarian. Allow me to do this for you. Please."

Janey smiled at him, knowing she could argue all day and he wouldn't budge. "You're sure you can swing it?"

"I might have to switch to hamburger instead of steak," he said with a teasing grin, "but I've got you covered, Princess."

She hugged him again. "Thank you."

"Now I'm even more proud than I was before. This is the best news since your brother's engagement."

"Don't say anything about it yet. I still have to get in."

"My lips are sealed."

Janey eyed him skeptically. The news would be all over the docks in the morning, and they both knew it. "Sure they are."

They shared a laugh, but Janey's smile faded when David strolled into the yard.

"What's he doing here?" Big Mac asked, scowling again.

"Good question." Janey squeezed her father's arm and went to stop David from progressing into the party.

Chapter Sixteen

"What do you think you're doing?"

"I need to see you, Janey."

In the faint twilight, she could see that his bruises had turned yellow overnight, and his face was even more swollen than it had been the day before. And was that alcohol she smelled on him? "You have no business here, David. This is my brother's home, and I'm asking you to leave."

"Not until I talk to you."

"I'm not talking to you. Not now, not ever." Even though her back was to the party, Janey sensed her father and brother approaching them. "Please leave."

"You are so full of it, you know that?" he hissed, staggering as he closed the distance between them. "I saw you, too."

"What are you talking about?" she asked, as a twinge of fear trickled down her spine.

"You and *Joe*. How long has he been keeping you warm at night while I was in Boston?"

Janey heard her father and Mac gasp but didn't

take her eyes off David. "Joe is my *friend*. You know that."

"Friend with *benefits*."

"Believe whatever you want. I'm done." She started to walk away, but he grabbed her arm.

"You're making me feel like shit when you're doing the same thing! No wonder why he hit me. He's always wanted you for himself! I'm sure he was more than happy to pick up the pieces of Janey's poor shattered heart."

Janey saw red, and somewhere deep inside, a switch was flipped. "So what? You're the only one who's allowed to have cheap, meaningless sex?" The instant the words were out of her mouth, she regretted them.

More gasps sounded from behind her, but one was different. One sounded an awful lot like . . . Janey broke free of David's grasp and spun around to find Joe staring at her, shock all but reverberating off him.

He turned and disappeared into the darkness.

"Joe!" Janey cried, intending to go after him.

As Mac followed his friend, David grabbed her arm again. "Janey, wait!"

She all but growled at him. "Let me go. *Now!*"

"I have cancer."

The world seemed to tilt on its axis as she stared at him. Later she would be ashamed that her first thought was that he would literally say anything to get her back.

Joe wanted to run as far away as he could get. Nothing in his life had ever hurt more than hearing Janey refer to what they'd shared as cheap and meaningless, even though he was fairly certain she didn't think of it that way. David had pushed her buttons, and she'd pushed back. But damn if those words hadn't hit Joe right where he lived.

"Joe! Wait!"

God, could this get any worse? Now he had to face Mac, too?

"Joe!"

Hands on hips, jaw set with tension, Joe turned, preparing himself for anything from a fist to the face to yet another arrow to the heart. "What do you want, Mac?"

"Is it true?"

Joe stared at his oldest friend and couldn't lie to him. He just couldn't. "Yes, but it was neither cheap nor meaningless."

Mac raised his hands, and for a second, Joe thought Mac was going to hit him. But instead Mac gripped his hair, as if he was trying to occupy his hands so he wouldn't punch Joe. "*Since when?*"

"Since the night she caught David with someone else."

"Are you *serious?* The *same day?* You told me I could trust you. 'Who better than me?' That's what you said!"

"It was entirely and completely consensual, Mac."

"She was crushed! Devastated! How could you take advantage of her like that?"

"I did *not* take advantage of her. I love her. You know I do."

"God, Joe, I can't *believe* this! Why didn't you tell me?"

Joe snorted. "Right. So you could accuse me of taking advantage of her? So you could freak out and run me out of your life right before I'm supposed to be the best man in your wedding? None of us thought that was a good idea."

"None of who?"

Oh, shit. "Janey and me."

"And who else?"

"No one."

"*Who else?*"

Joe sighed. "Maddie."

Mac recoiled in shock. "No way she knew this and kept it from me."

"Janey confided in her, but she didn't want to upset you any more than we did. We all knew how you'd see this, and it didn't happen the way you think."

"Great, so you all conspired to keep me in the dark."

"It wasn't like that. We were going to tell you after the wedding."

Shaking his head, Mac looked down at the ground. "Three of the people I'm closest to in the world decided to keep something this big from me. I have no idea how I'm supposed to take that."

"We were thinking about you."

"Were you? While you were screwing my devastated baby sister, were you really thinking of me?"

"That's not fair. It wasn't like that." Although after hearing Janey's description of what had transpired between them, he had cause to wonder.

"I can't believe this."

"To be honest, it's really none of your business."

"*None of my business?* She's my *sister*! It's absolutely my business! And you know that, which is why you didn't tell me."

"She's also a full-grown adult, in case you haven't noticed."

"She'll *always* be my baby sister."

As Mac growled those words, the first of the fireworks exploded overhead.

"I'm going," Joe said. "If you're still interested, I'll see you at the bachelor party tomorrow night." Without giving Mac a chance to reply, Joe turned and walked away, hoping he could grab a cab back to town. Whatever it took to get the hell out of there.

Janey had never been more torn in her life. As the fireworks lit up the night sky, she dodged her concerned parents and loaded David, half-drunk and sobbing, into her car to drive him to his mother's house. All she could think about was the look of utter shock on Joe's face when he'd heard her call what they'd shared cheap and meaningless. He had to know she didn't really think that, didn't he?

She wanted to go after him, to tell him she'd just been reacting to David, that she didn't mean it. But first she had to deal with David and the bomb he'd dropped on her.

"I'm sorry," he said as they drove away from Mac's. "I should've told you sooner. I know that, but it all happened so fast."

"How long have you known?"

"A month."

Janey gasped and looked over at him, wondering if she'd ever really known him. "And you didn't think your fiancée needed to know you have *cancer*?"

"There was never a good time to tell you. I didn't want to just call you out of the blue and drop it on you."

"Instead, you kept it from me. Were you hoping I wouldn't find out?"

"I was going to tell you, but I wanted to see how I responded to the first round of chemo."

"You've had chemo."

"Yes."

"Jesus, David."

"It's non-Hodgkin's lymphoma. Stage two. After I had strep last year, I had a raised node in my neck that never went away. I finally got around to getting it checked, and voilà. Cancer. But the prognosis is pretty good. The chemo seems to be working, but I feel like total shit."

As Janey tried to process what he was telling her, she felt strangely removed, as if none of this was happening to her. Only a few weeks ago, this news would have devastated her. It was further proof of just how separate their lives had become during the long years they'd spent apart. That he could keep something of this magnitude from her while they were engaged told her a lot about what kind of husband he might have been.

"I need you, Janey." He reached for her hand and held it between both of his. "I can't go through this without you."

She tugged her hand free. "That is so incredibly unfair! You keep this from me for weeks, you sleep with someone else and then you *still* expect me to support you?"

"I love you, Janey. That hasn't changed."

Her eyes flooded with tears, making it difficult to see, so she pulled the car off the road and turned to him. "I'm not in love with you anymore. I'm sorry if that hurts you, but it's the truth. I don't want you to be sick, and I hate that you have to go through this, but it doesn't change how I feel."

"We can get through it together, like we've gotten through everything."

She shook her head. "I can't. You have your mother, your sisters, your friends. You won't be alone."

"Janey, please. I'm begging you. *You're* the one I need. You can't do this to me in the midst of everything else I'm dealing with right now. I even had to take a leave from my internship while I'm in treatment."

"You should've thought about how much you needed me before you slept with someone else."

"She means nothing to me! She's an oncology nurse who I met during my treatment. It was a one-time thing. I was scared and freaked out. It was comfort. That's all."

Surely, Janey thought, her head would explode any minute. "I need you to listen to me. Can you do that?"

His eyes bright with new tears, he nodded.

"I loved you so much. There was absolutely nothing I wouldn't have done for you. I gave up my dreams of being a vet to accommodate you. I waited for you. I was faithful to you—always."

"Until recently," he muttered.

"I never went near another man until I saw you screwing a big-breasted blonde!"

"Janey—"

"Wait, I'm not finished. Anything and everything I ever felt for you died the minute I saw you with her. And now I find out that you've had this huge thing going on in your life and never saw fit to tell me. I should've been your first phone call, David. I should've been there when you got the diagnosis. I should've been there when you settled on a treatment plan and when you decided to take a leave of absence. That's what people in committed relationships do—they include each other in big decisions. But I was denied all that because you chose to keep me in the dark—about this and God knows what else."

"I didn't mean to."

"The minute you chose not to pick up the phone and tell me you were being tested for cancer is the minute you made a decision about our entire relationship. The minute you decided to bring that woman home to *our* bed, you made another decision. I suspect you've probably made a few others I don't know about. Either way, this isn't how I want to live."

"I'll make it up to you. This is just a bump in the road, honey. I've learned a valuable lesson, and it won't happen again. I promise you that. You were right all along. You should've moved to Boston to live with me while I was in school. If we'd done that, none of this would be happening now."

"Or it might've happened a lot sooner."

"I don't believe that."

"Here's what I think happened—we got complacent. We went along for years on autopilot and began to take each other for granted."

"That's not true!"

"If it wasn't true, David, you never would've felt the need to sleep with someone else."

He shook his head. "I never took you for granted."

"Yes, you did. And I did the same. We assumed our

relationship would be fine even if we never put any real effort into it."

"How can you say we didn't put effort into it when we were together for thirteen years?"

"Can I ask you something? And will you tell me the swear-to-God truth?"

"Yeah."

"Swear to God?"

"Yes!"

"When you . . . had sex . . . with her, was it better? Than it was with me?"

"You can't ask me that!"

"I just did, and you swore you'd tell me the truth."

"I'm not going to talk to you about that."

"You just answered my question," Janey said softly. "How?"

"If it wasn't better, you would've said so."

"Now you're just playing games with me."

"No, I'm not," she said. "It's over, David. We both know it, so let's not make a mockery of all we shared in the past by hanging on to something that died a long time ago. It's too bad we both refused to see that. We could've saved ourselves a lot of trouble."

"I thought for sure you would come back to me when I told you about the cancer," he said sadly.

"I wish I was a better person. I wish I could forget what I saw that day in your apartment and be there for you during your treatment. But I can't do that. The old Janey might've done that, but I've changed in the last week, and I can't go back to who I was before I saw you with her."

"I'd give anything to take that back."

She was on the verge of saying she would, too. "You know, you may not understand this, but in hindsight

I'm kind of glad I saw you. It probably stopped us from making a huge mistake."

"I'll never believe we would've made a mistake by getting married."

"We would have, and it would've been so much worse to find that out after the wedding."

He took her hand again, and she let him. "It's really over?"

"I'm afraid so. But I hope we can still be friends. I'll want to know how you're doing, how you're feeling, how the treatment is going. Will you keep me informed?"

He nodded. "I'd like for us to be friends, too," he said, reaching for her.

Engulfed in sadness, Janey leaned into his embrace.

David kissed the top of her head and held her tight against him. "I'm sorry I hurt you. After all the time we were together, you deserved much better from me."

Tears burned her eyes. Since she couldn't dispute that statement, she didn't try.

"Can I ask you something?"

Janey pulled back from him. "Sure."

"Is it better with him? With Joe?"

Her face heated under his scrutiny, and she was grateful for the dark. "I'm not answering that."

His face lifted into a sad half smile. "You just did."

Chapter Seventeen

After everyone left, Maddie cleaned up the kitchen while Mac carried items in from outside. They worked together for about fifteen minutes before she realized he was giving her one-word answers and otherwise not speaking to her. A cold ball of dread lodged in her belly. She'd seen him chase Joe after the confrontation between Janey and David but hadn't had a chance to ask him what had transpired. By now she had a pretty good idea.

"That's the last of it," he said as he put the grill utensils in the sink.

"It was a nice party."

"Uh-huh."

"Why don't we leave the rest for the morning and head up to bed?"

"I'm going for a run."

"*Now?*"

"Yeah."

"But it's so dark! You could get hit by a car."

"I'll wear a vest."

"Mac . . ."

He turned to her, and what she saw on his face stopped her heart.

"Why don't we just talk about it and get it over with?"

"Get what over with?" he asked.

"You're clearly mad at me."

"No, I'm disappointed."

"I couldn't tell you! You would've lost it, and Janey didn't need that when everything else was such a mess. She begged me not to tell you, and I agreed that was the best thing at the time."

"So you chose her over me."

"No." Her heart ached from the sadness she heard in his voice. "I'd never choose anyone over you or Thomas. You know that."

"We have a deal, Maddie—a deal *you* insisted on."

"I know, and I was so torn, but I thought you'd want me to do anything I could to help her. That's what I tried to do."

"I wish you had told me. I would've been cool about it."

She shot him a look full of skepticism.

"What? I would've been!"

Maddie went to him and curled her arms around his neck. "Do you know one of the things I love best about you?"

"No," he said, his body rigid and unyielding. His arms dangled loose at his sides, even as she tightened her hold on him.

"Your fierce love for your family. It's overwhelming and beautiful and it makes you you. As much as you love them all, though, Janey holds a special place in your heart. While you might wish to believe otherwise, you would *not* have understood Joe hooking up with her the same night she found David in bed with another woman. And you would *not* have believed Janey initiated it."

He tried to wiggle free of her embrace, but Maddie held on tight.

"I guess we'll never know how I would've reacted, because no one told me. Am I such a jerk that you guys got together and decided to keep this from me?"

"It wasn't like that at all. We were protecting you until some time had passed and you would've been more reasonable about it."

"So I'm not a jerk, but I *am* unreasonable?" He reached for her arms to draw them down and away from him.

"Mac, honey, come on. Try to understand."

"I need to get out of here for a while. I'll be back." With that he turned and dashed up the stairs to get changed.

Frozen, Maddie watched him go, her heart racing. He had never rebuffed her like that before, and she began to wonder if she might lose him over this. "No," she whispered. "That can't happen. It just can't."

But as she finished cleaning up her sparkling new kitchen and got ready for bed, the thought nagged at her. A life that had once been empty and difficult without him was now joyful and magnificent—or it was until today. First her mother's disapproval and now this . . . Just what they needed a week before their wedding.

Wearing one of the silk nightgowns he loved so much, Maddie got in bed and pretended to read a book while she waited for him. Her thoughts wandered back to the day she met him. He'd accidentally knocked her off her big clunker of a bike when she was on her way to a housekeeping shift at his parents' hotel. With her knee, elbow and hand bleeding, she'd been unable to work at the hotel or help out at her sister's daycare. Mac had stepped in for her, taking her place at both jobs so she wouldn't lose either of them, and taking care of her and Thomas until she recovered from her injuries. He'd been taking care of them ever since.

More than an hour passed before he finally returned, sweaty and breathing hard as he came into the bedroom and made a beeline for the shower without a word for her. He stayed in there long enough that Maddie deduced he was still avoiding her.

Slipping out of bed, she tugged the nightgown over her head on the way into the bathroom and stepped into the spacious, steamy shower.

He startled when she put her arms around him and hugged him from behind. "What are you doing?" he asked.

"Hugging you."

"I thought you were asleep."

"Were you hoping I'd fall asleep if you stayed gone long enough?"

"Maybe."

Maddie urged him to turn around. "I could never sleep knowing you're mad with me."

"I'm not mad."

"Disappointed. Same difference. You're not happy, so I'm not happy."

He shrugged. "It's all so screwed up. How could Joe let that happen, especially when she was such a mess?"

"It was all her. He tried to tell her it was a bad idea,

but she worked on him until he caved. I'll tell you what I told her earlier: I think she was halfway in love with him before any of this happened with David."

Mac shook his head. "I don't think so."

"I do."

"And what makes you so smart?" he asked with a hint of amusement that buoyed her sagging spirits. "You haven't known us that long."

"Janey said the same thing," Maddie said with a small smile and a lot of relief. At least they were talking. "I happen to know that when a man pays special attention to a woman, when he looks at her like she's the most beautiful creature in the world and hangs on every word she says, of course she starts to have a little crush on him. How can she not?" Reaching for his bottle of soap, she smoothed some over his chest and was gratified when his lower half sprang to life as she massaged him.

"And you have some experience with this, do you?"

"Mmm-hmm. *Recent* experience."

His face shifted into that devilish grin she so adored. "I know what you're doing."

"What am I doing?" she asked, full of innocence.

"You think if you get me all worked up that I'll forget you kept something rather important from me after we made a deal to never do that."

"It was wrong of me, Mac. I know that now, and I knew it then. But it was what Janey needed at the time, and I really, *really* want her to be my very best friend. Do you know how long it's been since I had a friend I like as much as I like her?"

He combed his fingers through her long wet hair. "How long?"

"Since my friend Sydney used to come for the summers with her family when we were in high school. We were so close, but we grew apart when she stopped coming out. I saw her a couple of years ago when she was here with her family."

"She's Luke's ex-girlfriend, the one who lost her husband and kids, right?"

Maddie nodded, still saddened by her friend's terrible tragedy. "Yes." Maddie had written to her after the accident but hadn't heard back from her.

"Well, you'll be glad to know I've decided to forgive you."

Maddie looked up at him, a smile tugging at her lips. "Is that so?"

"I asked you to help me take care of my sister, and that's what you did. I suppose I can't fault you for not breaking her confidence."

"She's all grown up, Mac, and she has to follow her own heart, even if it leads her to Joe."

"I know that," he said through gritted teeth.

"Wouldn't you love to see them together?"

"Of course I would. I just can't bear the idea of any guy—even him—taking advantage of her."

"He didn't, Mac. I promise you, he didn't. He tried to tell her it was a bad idea, but she convinced him it was what she wanted."

"Are they together now?"

"Not officially. They'd planned to keep it quiet until after the wedding. I'm not sure what'll happen now that David blasted them out of the closet."

"So what? Joe spent a couple of nights with her and that's that?"

"They've got a lot to work out." She squeezed out more soap and massaged her way down his back to his muscular backside.

He groaned. "Your evil plan seems to be working quite well," he said, glancing down at his erection.

Maddie giggled and ran soapy hands over his most sensitive parts.

"Mmm." He reached for her and pulled her in close, capturing her mouth in a deep, passionate kiss.

"Will you do something for me?" Maddie asked when they came up for air.

His hands moved over her, awakening her body. "Anything."

"Don't run away the next time you're mad or disappointed or upset. Stay with me and work it out?"

"I will." His hands coasted over her back. Suddenly, he lifted her and pressed her against the wall.

Maddie gasped when warm skin met cold tile. She ran her fingers through his wet hair and then skimmed them over the stubble on his jaw. "Promise?"

"I promise." He kissed his way up her neck and rolled her earlobe between his teeth.

Maddie arched her back, seeking him. "Mac . . ."

"Tell me what you want."

She clutched a handful of his hair and wrapped her legs around his hips. "You. Only you."

He entered her in one swift stroke that stole the breath from her lungs.

She held on tight as he took her hard and fast against the wall. "Oh, *God*, Mac . . ."

When he bent his head to suck on her nipple, they reached the finish line at the same exact instant.

Maddie came back down to find him gazing intently at her.

"I love you so much," she said.

He kissed her nose. "I love you, too."

"I was so afraid . . ."

Mac leaned into her, keeping her pressed tight against the wall. "Of what?"

"That I'd lose you over this. We had a deal, and I didn't keep my end of it."

"Let's make a new deal, okay?"

She nodded.

He moved the damp hair off her face and trailed his finger over her cheek. "No matter what happens, no matter how big a fight we have or how mad you make me or how crazy things get, I will never, ever leave you."

Her eyes filled with tears. "Never?"

He shook his head. "I couldn't possibly live without you. Or Thomas."

Maddie wrapped her arms around his neck and clung to him. "I could never live without you, either. Not for one day."

"Let's go to bed."

Janey drove David to his mother's house on the island's west side. He held her hand the entire way. Their intense conversation coupled with the alcohol he'd consumed earlier had made him more emotional than usual, which made this whole thing even harder on her.

She pulled into Kay's driveway and went around to open David's door. "Come on," she said, holding out a hand.

David took her hand, and they walked up the sidewalk.

Kay met them at the door, a big smile on her face as

she stepped out to hug them both. "Oh! You worked it out! I knew you would."

David turned to Janey and hugged her. "Thanks for the ride."

"No problem. You'll let me know how you are?"

"Sure." He caressed her face and brushed a light kiss over her lips. "Take care of yourself, Janey. You know where I am if you change your mind."

"Wait a minute," Kay said. "What's going on?"

"Come on inside, Mom, and I'll tell you."

"Wait, stop," Kay said. "Are you back together or not?"

"We're not," David said. "We've agreed our relationship is over."

"And she knows?" Kay turned to Janey. "You know he has cancer? That doesn't change anything?"

"Mom—"

"I'm sorry, Kay," Janey said. "This has to be a terrible time for you, and I'd give anything to spare you all that's ahead."

"But you won't be around? That's what you're saying, right?"

"I won't be around."

"You're not the person I thought you were, Janey."

"That's not fair, Mom. I'm the one who screwed it all up, not her."

With that, David earned back some of Janey's respect.

"Go inside, David," Kay said. "I'd like a word alone with Janey."

"Not if you're going to berate her for a decision we made together."

"I'd just like to talk to her. Will you please give us a minute?"

David glanced at Janey.

She nodded.

"I'll be in touch," he said.

"Okay."

After he'd gone inside, Kay turned to Janey. "I'm disappointed in you."

"Yes, ma'am, I can see that."

"Do you have any idea what he's facing in the next few months? After all the years you spent with him, how can you not have the compassion to give him a second chance when he has apologized to you?"

"It wasn't like he forgot my birthday. He *had sex* with another woman, and I *saw* it. How am I supposed to forgive that?"

"He's sick, Janey. He's not behaving like himself. It's not like him to drink and get into fights or have sex with strange women. You know that."

"I know what I saw, and I know I'll never forget it. There's no going back to before that. We've realized our relationship was probably over a long time ago, but we chose not to see the signs. If things were good between us, he would've told me about his diagnosis weeks ago, and he certainly wouldn't have sought out other women."

Kay folded her arms and blinked back tears. "None of that should matter. He's sick. How can you walk away from him now?"

Janey took a deep breath. "Because I know he has you and the rest of your family and his friends, and you'll take very good care of him."

"Do you have someone else? Is that what this is about?"

"I was faithful to David every day that we were together."

"And since then?"

"I've moved on with my life. He gave me no choice. I'm sorry if this hurts you, Kay."

"What about the wedding? All your plans?"

"There's not going to be a wedding, and I'm making different plans now."

"Maybe you just need some more time, to think—"

Janey rested a hand on the older woman's arm. "I'm not going to change my mind."

Kay's lips tightened with displeasure before she turned, walked into the house, closed the door and shut off the porch light.

"Well," Janey whispered. "I guess that's that."

Rattled by the disagreement with a woman she'd always loved and respected, Janey sat in her car for a long time before she drove home to where she was greeted by her pets. After she fed them and took them into the yard for a few minutes, they came back inside and settled on the floor to snuggle. Surrounded by their unconditional love, Janey finally broke down, overwhelmed by the day's events.

David has cancer. God. It was just so hard to believe, and it certainly explained a lot about his recent behavior. Even before she'd caught him in the act, he'd been putting out odd vibes that she hadn't bothered to question. If she'd been more connected to him, maybe she would've noticed something was wrong.

Riley dragged himself over to nudge at the tears on her cheeks.

He whimpered, and Janey hooked an arm around him. "I'm okay, boy. Or at least I will be."

Muttley crawled into her lap, bumping Sam onto the floor.

Despite the tears, Janey laughed softly as she scratched Sam's ears. "You guys are so funny. I don't know what I'd do without you."

As she hugged Riley and stroked Muttley's belly, she let her thoughts wander to Joe and the stricken expression on his face when he walked in on her argument with David. "I need to talk to Joe," she said.

She kissed Riley, got up from the floor and grabbed her purse. "I'll be back, guys. Don't wait up."

Chapter Eighteen

Joe stared up at the ceiling in his room at the Beachcomber. After the confrontation with Mac, he'd been tempted to spend another night bellied up to the bar. But since that hadn't helped anything the last time, he'd come to his room, where he'd stared at the ceiling for the last few hours, torturing himself with thoughts of what Janey might be doing.

Had David convinced her to give him another chance? Was their engagement back on? Would Mac ever forgive him for sleeping with his sister at her lowest moment? Was he still the best man in Mac's wedding, or would he ask one of his brothers to fill the role? What if Janey had meant what she said to David? What if she viewed all they had shared as cheap and meaningless, while he saw it as the answer to his every prayer?

Sadly, the ceiling had none of the answers he so desperately needed.

A knock on the door drew his attention off the ceiling. He got up to answer it.

Janey.

As he stared at her beautiful face, he had no idea what to say to her.

"May I come in?"

"Oh, um, sure." He stepped aside to let her go past him in a cloud of jasmine that awakened his every sense. Steeling himself for what he might hear, Joe closed the door and then turned to lean against it. He noticed right away that she was tightly wound, as if she too was nervous about what might transpire between them in the small hotel room.

"I'm sorry for what you heard me say. You have to know I don't feel that way about . . . us."

"I was hoping you didn't."

"He just . . . He pushed my buttons, and it was out of my mouth before I even took a second to think about what I was saying." She came over to stand in front of him, looking up at him with those eyes that ruined him every time she trained them on him. "I'm sorry if I hurt you."

He shrugged off her apology, as if she hadn't cut him to the quick with thoughtlessly spoken words.

"Are you back with him?"

"He has cancer."

They both spoke at once and then took a moment to absorb what the other had said.

Her words hit Joe like a blow to the gut. "So you're back with him?"

"No. I told him I can't go back after all that's happened. He's been sick for a month and never told me. It's further proof that we were over a long time ago but chose not to see it."

Joe held on tight to the doorknob behind him, as if it was an anchor keeping him from breaking into a million tiny pieces. "He must've tried to convince you to come back, in light of his . . . illness."

"He did, and so did his mother. I told them both the old Janey might've felt obligated to stand by him through his treatment, but the new Janey is thinking about her own life and what's best for her—for once."

"That's good. That's what you should be doing."

"It feels good. It's not that I don't have empathy for what he's about to endure or that I don't care about him, because I do. I just can't put my life on hold for him or anyone else anymore. I've done that long enough."

"It couldn't have been easy to walk away from him when he needs you."

"Seeing him in bed with another woman has made a lot of things easier than they would've been otherwise."

"I suppose so." Standing between them was the question Joe couldn't bring himself to ask, no matter how badly he needed to know. *Where does this leave us?*

"So, you talked to Mac?"

"Uh-huh."

"What did you tell him?"

"Since the cat was more or less out of the bag, I went with the truth."

"How did he take it?"

"About how you'd expect."

Janey chewed on her thumbnail, something he'd noticed she did when she was nervous or unsettled. "It's really none of his business."

"Which I told him. Didn't seem to matter, though. He's got a real blind spot where you're concerned, but of course you know that or you would've told him yourself."

"I can't talk to him about this stuff. He still sees me as a thirteen-year-old in braces."

"He probably always will. He loves you, Janey. You can't fault him for that."

"No, but I *can* fault him for being an unreasonable buttinsky."

Joe smiled. "He is that."

"I'll talk to him tomorrow. I'll make sure he knows how it all went down."

"You might want to choose different words."

Her cheeks flamed with the blush he loved so much. "That's very dirty, Joe. I'm surprised at you."

Smiling at her, he held out his arms. "No, you're not." When she stepped into his embrace, Joe was finally able to breathe again after torturous hours filled with uncertainty. He held her tight against him, brushing his lips over her fragrant hair. "Rough day, huh?"

"Yeah. Until now."

Joe breathed her in, steeped in the peace that came over him whenever he held her this way. "You're tired."

"Exhausted."

"Want me to walk you home?"

She drew back to look up at him. "Do you know what I'd really like?"

"What's that?"

"To sleep curled up next to you. I don't know what's going to happen with us, Joe. All I know is I feel better when I'm with you than I do when I'm not."

His throat tightened with emotion at her softly spoken words. "That's a good place to start."

"So it's okay if I stay?"

He took her hand and led her to his bed. Sitting

on the edge, he arranged her so she stood between his legs as he undressed her and helped her into one of his T-shirts. When she was settled into bed, he stripped down to boxers and joined her. Sure enough, she curled up to him, her face pressed to his chest, her hand resting on his belly and her leg between his. He tried to tell himself that tonight was all about peace and comfort, but as usual when she was around, certain parts of his anatomy had other ideas.

"This is what I needed," she whispered.

He tightened his hold on her. "Me, too."

"Were you upset earlier?"

"A little bit."

"Just a little?"

"Okay, a lot."

"I'm so sorry," she said, sprinkling kisses on his chest that intensified the problem brewing in his lap. "I would never intentionally hurt you."

His fingers tunneled into her thick hair. "I know that."

She kissed her way to his neck and jaw.

"I thought you wanted to sleep."

"I do. Eventually."

"Janey—"

She cut him off by pressing her lips to his in a chaste kiss. Somehow she ended up stretched out on top of him with his erection pulsing between them. "I keep telling myself that I need to leave you alone until I figure things out, but I can't seem to stay away."

"You don't hear me complaining."

She gazed down at him, and his heart ached with longing. He wanted her to be his. He wanted all their issues worked out and the future clear before them.

"I know the roller coaster ride is tough on you," she said.

"It was tougher watching you with someone who didn't deserve you." He cupped her cheek and guided her back to him for more of those sweet kisses. "That was unbearable."

She kept her kisses chaste, as if she intended to torment him.

Joe groaned and tightened his hold on her hair, to keep her where he wanted her. "You're being mean."

"I'm very, very sorry."

"You are *so* not sorry."

Janey laughed, and he released her hair to comb his fingers through it.

"I know we're not talking about the future or even tomorrow, but I want you to know that I really, really love you, Janey." The minute the words were out of his mouth, Joe regretted them, because her smile faded and the playfulness was gone. "I shouldn't have said that."

"It's okay."

He linked their hands and brought them to his chest. "You're not ready to talk about serious stuff."

"I love you, Joe. You have to know that."

"Sure. I know." Joe released her hands, helped her off him and sat up.

From behind him, Janey looped her arms around his shoulders and kissed his neck. "Then what's wrong?"

"I don't want you to love me, Janey. I want you to *love* me love me."

"I just need some more time."

"Maybe we should take a break until you're ready." The hand that had been caressing his chest went still.

"Is that what you want?"

"No, but it may be what I need."

"Oh. Okay. If that's how you feel." Janey got up and reached for her dress.

As he watched her take off the T-shirt he had loaned her, he called himself fifty different names for being so damned stupid. He started to tell her to stop, that he didn't want her to go, but the words wouldn't come.

She finished getting dressed and slid her slender feet into sexy silver sandals.

What are you doing? You're really going to let her leave? Are you out of your mind? "Wait. Janey. Wait."

On the way to the door, she turned back to him.

He got up and went to her. "I don't want you to go."

"But I probably should. I don't want to hurt you, Joe."

He took her hands. "Is it at all possible that down the road, at some point, you might maybe *love* me love me?"

"Yes!" She laughed and threw her arms around him. "Yes, yes, *yes.*"

Smiling, Joe lifted her off her feet. "I hate when you mince words that way."

She let her head fall back, laughter gripping her.

He took advantage of the opportunity to nibble on her exposed neck. "Can you give me an idea of how far down the road we're talking?"

Her fingers sifted through his hair, her eyes alight with amusement. "A block, maybe two."

"Wow. That close, huh?"

"Yep."

Setting her down, he kept his hands on her shoulders. "If we're that close to our destination, perhaps we should hold off on any more . . . how should I say this . . ."

"Hot sex?"

Just hearing her say the words made him want it. He swallowed hard. "As much as it pains me to even suggest it, maybe we should wait until we arrive?"

"That's probably not a *bad* idea."

"It's a truly terrible idea. Forget I ever said it. Let's go back to bed."

Still laughing, Janey resisted his efforts to drag her to bed. "You wouldn't have said it if you didn't think it was sort of a good idea."

"You're not going to forget this, are you?"

"Nope."

"And you won't have sex with me? Really?"

"Not until I'm very, very sure that I'm in love with you."

"But you're taking away one of my best weapons to make you fall in love with me!"

"I said we couldn't have sex." She pushed him onto the bed and straddled his lap. "I didn't say we couldn't do other stuff."

"What other stuff?" Intrigued, Joe ran his hands up her legs, pushing her skirt up as he went.

"Well, there's kissing," she said, pressing soft kisses to his face that made his heart race. "And touching." She massaged his shoulders and chest.

Joe closed his eyes as he realized it was possible that *not* having sex with her could be even more exciting than *having* sex. "What else?"

"Cuddling, snuggling, talking. Dating—like normal people."

"You want to date."

Her fingers danced over his skin, giving him goose

bumps—among other things. "Do you have a problem with that?"

"No, no problem. So let me get this straight. After we've done, well, everything, you want to go back to holding hands?"

She reached for his hand and brought it to her lips, pressing a kiss to his palm. "I love to hold hands. Don't you?"

"All depends on whose hand I'm holding."

"What do you think of mine?"

He loved this coy Janey, who was having so much fun playing with him. "Your hand," he said, nibbling on her fingers, "is my most favorite."

A smile lit up her face. "Wanna make out?"

"We're really going on a sex diet?"

"Yep."

"In that case, I'd love to make out."

Joe walked Janey home the next morning and headed to the South Harbor Diner where he met Mac and Thomas for coffee just about every morning he was on the island. Joe told himself it didn't mean anything that Mac didn't show. Perhaps he'd decided to sleep in or to make it an early morning at the marina. As Joe bought coffee and a blueberry muffin, he figured if Mac was still mad with him, he'd find out soon enough.

Feeling the first sting of coffee against his abused lips brought back memories of the night before. Making out with Janey for *hours* had turned out to be among the most exciting and frustrating experiences of his entire life. After having all of her, it was damned hard to settle for less. She'd allowed second base but nothing more, and Joe had gone nearly out of his mind with wanting her. In fact, long after she had fallen asleep in his arms, he'd lain awake vibrating with desire and dissatisfaction.

Janey had to work most of the day, and he had to take care of the final details for Mac's bachelor party that night, not knowing if the groom-to-be was even talking to him. "Fabulous," Joe muttered to himself as he left cash on the table and got up to leave the diner. With the bachelor party tonight and the bridal shower tomorrow, Joe didn't expect to see Janey again before tomorrow night at the earliest. Another reason to be in a foul mood.

How was he supposed to make her fall in love with him when they couldn't spend much time together? Just as he had that thought, he passed the florist shop. A bright yellow arrangement caught his eye. The sunny colors reminded him of Janey as he pushed open the door and stepped inside. Ten minutes later, he had arranged for delivery of the yellow bouquet to the vet clinic and was laboring over what to write on the card.

When the phone rang, the nosy florist left him to go answer it. Joe stared at the card. What to say? He chewed on the end of the pen for another minute, until he heard the florist wrapping up her call. He wrote quickly: "*Pick you up at 8 tomorrow night. Wear something sexy. Love, Joe.*" By the time the florist returned, he had sealed the note into the tiny envelope. "That'll do it." He figured the news would be all over the island within an hour that Joe Cantrell had sent flowers to Janey McCarthy.

"Very good, Mr. Cantrell. We'll deliver your order this afternoon."

"Thanks." Joe left the shop and whistled all the way to Mario's. He confirmed the bachelor party food order, which would be delivered to McCarthy's Marina at seven. Checking his watch, he was surprised to realize he had wasted so much time at the florist. He was captain on the eleven o'clock boat back to the mainland and returning on the two. While he was on the mainland, he had to run home to pick up a suit for tomorrow night.

Approaching the ferry landing, he smiled to himself. "She wants a date? I'll show her a date."

Chapter Nineteen

"There has to be something you can do," Mrs. Roberts said, tears streaming down her wrinkled face as she held the limp and listless Molly to her chest. The seventeen-year-old yellow mutt kept a watchful eye on the people in the room, but raising her head took more energy than she could summon.

"I'm sorry," Doc Potter said gently, resting a hand on the elderly woman's shoulder. "I'm afraid her time has come."

Watching the scene, Janey wiped a tear from her cheek. This was Doc at his very best, and she learned something from him every day she worked for him. She couldn't begin to imagine Mrs. Roberts's pain. The idea of losing any of her pets killed her, but at least she had a big, loving family all around her. Mrs. Roberts only had Molly, and she'd resisted their suggestions over the last year that she might want to think about getting another pet so that when Molly's time came, she wouldn't be all alone.

"Am I doing the wrong thing?" Mrs. Roberts asked between sobs. "Letting nature take its course?"

"She doesn't seem to be in any pain," Doc said.

"What do you think, Janey?" Mrs. Roberts asked.

"I think Molly wants to stay with you as long as she possibly can, but she hopes you'll know when it's time to help her along."

Doc nodded with approval. "That's right."

"Okay, then," Mrs. Roberts said. "That's what I'll do."

"Just keep her comfortable and try to get some liquids into her." Doc helped the elderly woman up and escorted her to the door. He scratched Molly's ears and kissed her sweet face. "I can come to the house if need be. You have all my numbers, right?"

"Yes. Thank you both so much. I wouldn't be able to get through this without you."

"That's what we're here for," Janey said, feeling bruised and battered by Mrs. Roberts's terrible grief.

"It's so sad," said Lisa, the receptionist, after the door closed behind Mrs. Roberts.

"I can't stand it," Janey said. "Seventeen years!"

"Molly doesn't want to leave her," Doc said. To Janey, he added, "You said just the right thing in there. Well done."

"My heart was breaking the whole time."

"Mine, too," he said with a frown. His bushy white eyebrows and mustache drooped with sorrow. He took these things hard. They all did. "I hope Molly goes on her own so we don't have to put her down. I don't want to have to do that."

"I hope so, too," Janey said. "Just the thought of that makes me ill."

"Something came for you when you were in with Mrs. Roberts, Janey," Lisa said, smiling. "I put it on your desk."

"Thanks." She wandered back to her office and gasped when she saw the huge bouquet of yellow flowers. Even before she found the card in the midst of all the bright blooms, she had broken into a smile. *Joe.* Tearing the envelope, she read the brief message over and over, her heart fluttering with anticipation. How would she stand to wait until tomorrow night to see him again? If he was out to make her fall in love with him, he was off to a great start. She couldn't remember the last time she'd received flowers.

"Oh, hey, nice flowers," Doc said from the hallway.

Janey leaned in to take a deep breath of fragrant lily. She loved picturing Joe going to the florist to buy flowers for her, even if it meant the whole island would know about them by sunset. "Aren't they?"

"From David?"

Janey held the card against her chest. "Nope." Doc had always been more like a beloved grandfather than a boss, and he loved to tease her about anything and everything.

"Well, who else would it be?"

Janey was surprised that news of their breakup hadn't reached him yet. "David and I broke up last week."

"Oh. Well. Mac said you had a situation, but I didn't imagine . . . Wow."

"It's okay, Doc. It was for the best."

"You're handling this quite admirably. Had to be a big disappointment."

"It was, but I've come to realize it was over a long time ago. We just chose not to see it."

"I'm glad you're okay."

"Thanks for all the time off. It really helped."

"Pshaw," he said. "It's been quiet this week with the

holiday and all. Besides, you hardly ever take time off."

Janey tucked the card from Joe into the pocket of her lab coat. "Do you have a minute? There's something I need to talk to you about."

"Only if you tell me who sent the flowers," he said, smiling as he came into her office and shut the door.

"You'll find out soon enough. Nothing stays a secret for long on this island." She'd been thinking about the conversation she needed to have with Doc for days, but now that the moment was upon her, she was struck with nerves.

"Is something wrong? Besides the thing with David?"

"Everything's fine. It's just that I've been, um, thinking . . ."

"About?"

"Vet school."

His eyes widened. "You don't say! That's wonderful news. I've been saying for years it was a travesty you didn't go after college."

"I know," she said. "I should have. I see that now."

"Have you applied?"

"I let Ohio State know I'm interested in taking them up on their six-year-old offer. I haven't heard back yet."

"What can I do?"

"Write me a new recommendation?"

"Done."

"Thank you so much," she said, relieved.

"You know I've been thinking about retiring," he said tentatively. "But if I thought you'd be ready to go in a couple of years, I'd be willing to wait."

"Wait? For *me*?"

"I'd love nothing more than to turn this practice over to you, Janey."

She sat back in her chair, flabbergasted. "Wow."

"You're a natural. You'll sail through vet school because of what you already know."

"Thanks to you."

"And you. You took advantage of every opportunity to learn and grow. I'll write you the most bang-up recommendation letter they've ever gotten." Full of fire, he got up to leave. "We'll get you in. Don't worry. Probably be next year, though."

"I know," Janey said. That was a long way off. "You're the best for being so willing to help."

Doc flashed an impish grin. "Won't hurt that I'm also a generous alum," he said on his way out the door.

He was the reason she'd chosen Ohio State in the first place. She'd worked at the clinic all during high school, first as an unpaid helper and later as the Saturday receptionist. Hearing his stories about the school and the program had made her want to go there, too.

As she gazed at the flowers Joe had sent, she wondered how she'd manage to have the two things she wanted. Her stomach ached when she realized it might come down to a choice. In the past, she'd chosen David over her own dreams. The one thing she knew for certain was she couldn't do that anymore.

Never again would she put someone else's dreams ahead of her own.

"Penny for your thoughts."

Janey looked up to find Mac standing in the doorway. "Oh, hey. What're you doing here?"

He eyed the flowers on her desk. "Just wanted to see my sister. Is that okay with you?"

"That's *all* you want?"

Shutting the door behind him, he dropped into the chair. "Are those from Joe?"

"Maybe."

"Why didn't you tell me?"

"Because I didn't want to."

A flash of hurt crossed his face. "Why?"

"Gee, let's see. Could it be your propensity to overreact or maybe it's your tendency to treat me like I'm twelve?"

"Janey—"

"I'm a grown woman, Mac. I can sleep with anyone I want to, and believe it or not, it's none of your business."

"You're right."

Shocked, she stared at him. She hadn't expected such easy capitulation. "I am?"

"I hate the idea of anyone hurting you. When I first heard about what David had done, I honestly thought I could kill him."

Hearing that, Janey softened. "You're the best big brother any girl could ever have. You know I love you as much as I love anyone. But you've got to let me live my own life, even if it means I get hurt once in a while."

"I'm trying."

Janey scowled playfully at him. "Try harder."

"So you and Joe . . ."

"Me and Joe." Thinking of him brought a smile to her face.

"He's had a big bad thing for you for years."

"So I've heard."

"You really didn't know?"

"Maybe deep down. But when I was with David, I never let myself go there."

"And it was really your idea to, you know . . ."

"Sleep together?"

He swallowed hard. "Yes."

"It was all me. He tried to tell me it was a bad idea, that I'd regret it."

"And did you? Regret it?"

"Not for one second. He's amazing and sweet and he loves me so much, Mac. I've never had anything even close to what I have with him."

"I guess that's saying something in light of how long you were with David."

"What I had with David wasn't anything like this."

"So you're in love with Joe?"

"I don't know. I'd like to be, but I'm not sure yet."

Mac glanced at the flowers. "He's not exactly being subtle, is he?"

Making a face at him, she said, "It would hurt me if this caused a rift between you and him."

"It won't," he said almost reluctantly.

"He loves you so much, and he's thrilled to have you living back here again. I couldn't bear to come between the two of you. That would hurt me more than anything."

"I needed to hear you say he didn't take advantage of you when you were down."

She got up and went around the desk. "He didn't. And you already knew that because you know *him*."

Mac stood and reached for her. He hugged her for a long time and then kissed her forehead. "Love you, brat. I just want you to be happy."

"I'm working on that."

"Let me know what I can do to help."

"Stop being such a buttinsky and forgive Joe."

"I will."

"And Maddie."

"Already did."

"Good. I adore her. She's absolutely perfect for you."

He smiled. "I agree. Do something for me?"

"Sure."

"If I promise to not overreact and overwhelm, will you not keep me in the dark? I like knowing what's going on with you."

She went up on tiptoes to kiss his cheek. "I'm making some plans and decisions. As soon as I know more, I'll tell you all about it."

"I'll look forward to that." He checked his watch. "I'd better go. The boys are coming in on the one o'-clock boat."

"I can't wait to see them," she said of their three other brothers. "This will be a fun week, and at the end of it, you'll be married. Hard to believe, huh?"

"Not anymore. I can't imagine my life without Maddie and Thomas."

"I hope someday I'll be that certain."

"Take your time, brat. Getting it right is well worth the wait."

"So I've discovered."

He hugged her tight against him. "I'm here if you need me."

Janey's eyes burned with tears as she clung to him. "I know." She pulled back and looked up at him. "Have fun tonight."

"Oh, I plan to," he said with a wicked grin. "My last hurrah."

"Hearts are breaking up and down the East Coast."

Mac laughed. "Sure they are." He left her with a wave.

Janey watched him go, knowing that even after he was married, he'd still be there for her. In the midst of chaos and upheaval, there were some things she could count on to stay the same. Her big brother was definitely one of them.

Chapter Twenty

Janey left the vet clinic and decided to take care of something that had been on her mind all day. Steeling herself for a fight, she walked over to Maddie's former apartment, above her sister Tiffany's dance studio. Janey knocked on the door and waited. And then waited some more. After several minutes, the door cracked open, and Francine scowled when she saw Janey.

"What do you want?"

"I'd like to talk to you, if you can spare a minute."

"I have nothing to say to you."

"You've never even met me. How can you dislike me so intensely?"

"You're one of them."

"If you're referring to my parents, I believe you'll recall that my mother gave you ample opportunity to make restitution before she ever reported you. And she wasn't the first to report you."

"She took the most pleasure in it," Francine grumbled.

"You don't know that. You don't know anything

about her. Or me. Or my brother. You haven't given any of us a chance, yet you've decided we're no good."

"I know what I see—and what I hear."

"And what's that?"

"Your mother hasn't exactly been good to my girl over there at that fancy hotel of hers."

"And she has apologized for that. After she learned the truth about Maddie—"

"What truth? What're you talking about?"

"When Maddie told Mac about what my brother Evan and his friends said about Maddie in high school, Mac made them all write letters of apology to the *Gansett Gazette*."

Agog, Francine stared at her.

"Maddie was furious at first because he hadn't yet told her about the letters. But they totally changed her life on the island. No one thinks poorly of her anymore, Mrs. Chester. My brother did that for her."

"Well, your *other* brother caused the whole thing."

"No, he didn't. Darren Tuttle did, but Mac took care of him, too. Evan just went along with it because he was too stupid not to. His apology letter was the most heartfelt of the group. He said he'd always regretted what they'd done to her, and he welcomed the chance to apologize."

"I don't know what you want from me—"

"I want you to come to Maddie's shower tomorrow at my mother's house."

"I most certainly will not!"

"You'd do that to your own daughter?"

"Don't speak to me about my daughter! What do you know about it? What do you know about anything?"

"I know she's the best new friend I've had in a long time. I know my brother loves her with everything he has and my family has fully embraced her and Thomas. Why would you want to force her to choose between you and us? Why does it have to be a choice?"

"She's already made her choices," Francine huffed. "What I think of it apparently has no bearing."

"How can you say that? When the whole island thought she was no better than a tramp, she didn't leave because you insisted on staying here after your husband left. Instead of going somewhere for a fresh start where no one knew her, she stayed here and put up with all the rumors and innuendo about her, because you wanted to be where he could find you."

"*She told you that?*"

"I totally understand why you'd want to stay. I'd want the man I love to be able to find me, too."

Francine sagged against the door frame. "He's been gone twenty-five years. I don't think he's coming back."

"Maybe not, but you have your daughters and your grandchildren, and next week you'll have a new son-in-law who'd do anything for you, if only you'd give him a chance."

"You're asking an awful lot of me."

"Actually, I'm really not. I'm just asking you to give him a chance. He's going to be your grandson's father. If you can't do it for Maddie, maybe you can do it for Thomas."

Francine crossed her arms. "I'm not going to your mother's house."

"You don't have to decide that now. I wanted you to know you're invited. That my mother and I, as well as Maddie and Tiffany, would love to have you there."

"You'd love that, would you?"

"Maddie would, so that's good enough for us."

"You McCarthys like to think you're better than everyone else on this island."

"No, we don't. My mother was big enough to admit she was wrong about Maddie. Maybe you can do the same for us?" Before Francine could answer, Janey turned to start down the stairs. "Two o'clock tomorrow," she said over her shoulder. "I really hope you'll join us."

Based on the warm welcome Joe received from Grant, Adam and Evan McCarthy, he figured they hadn't heard yet about his relationship with their sister. With dark hair and blue eyes, all four McCarthy brothers resembled their father as a young man. Only Janey took after their petite, blond mother.

Evan, a singer-songwriter, had recently landed his first recording contract in Nashville. He was the first to notice Joe's arrival. "Hey!" he said. "It's the fifth McCarthy brother!" Embracing Joe, Evan lifted him right off his feet.

"Dude!" Joe said. "Put me down, for Christ's sake!" Back on terra firma, Joe noticed that Luke had arranged tables and set out the food from Mario's. The cards, poker chips and Cuban cigars Joe had dropped off earlier were sitting in the middle of one table, along with the beer he'd provided, which had been loaded into a huge garbage can and iced. Perfect.

Grant, an Academy Award–winning screenwriter who lived in Los Angeles, greeted Joe with a handshake and one-armed hug. "How's it going?"

"Great," Joe said, going with the truth. What the hell? They'd hear about it soon enough. "Good to see you, man."

"You, too."

Joe admired that Grant hadn't let success turn him into an arrogant jerk. He had a cool, urbane way about him that dated back to high school and probably served him well in Hollywood.

"Can you even believe why we're here?" Adam asked as he hugged Joe. A successful computer programmer who lived in New York City, Adam was six inches shorter than his brothers. They called him "Little Brother," even though Evan was the youngest.

"Never thought I'd see the day, that's for sure," Joe said, his stomach twisting with nerves as he wondered if Mac was still pissed with him. "Where's the man of the hour?"

"My dad is bringing him so he doesn't have to drive," Evan said.

"Oh, good call. Did you guys get to meet Maddie?"

"Briefly," Grant said. "Mac's truly gone over her, huh?"

"Truly," Joe agreed.

"I knew her years ago," Evan said with a hint of chagrin.

Joe winced, recalling Evan's role in sullying Maddie's reputation in high school. "How was it to see her again?"

"She was far more gracious than I deserved."

"That sounds like her," Joe said. "She's amazing."

Luke came in carrying two huge bags of ice. "Oh, hey, man. Everything look okay?"

"It looks great," Joe said. "Thanks for the help."

"No prob."

"Let the games begin!" Big Mac bellowed as he walked in with Mac and Ned trailing behind him. Big Mac spread his arms. "All my boys! How fabulous is this?" When he was excited, his enormous personality got even bigger.

Hit with a sudden burst of nerves, Joe got busy opening catering trays and setting out paper plates.

"Hey," Mac said from behind him.

Steeling himself, Joe turned. "How's it going?"

"This is nice," Mac said, gesturing to the food. "Thanks."

"Luke did most of the heavy lifting."

"I'm sure you did your share."

Joe shrugged off the praise. "I assume you'd do the same for me if my time ever comes."

As Mac studied him with intense blue eyes, Joe couldn't get a reading on what his friend was thinking. "You're damned right I would."

Relieved, Joe couldn't help but ask, "Even if the bride is your sister?"

"Especially then."

"Does this mean I'm forgiven?"

"I'm told you were upstanding throughout the whole . . . um, encounter."

Joe snorted with laughter. "You're extremely ridiculous when it comes to her. You know that, don't you?"

"I've been told that as well."

Cracking open beers for both of them, Joe laughed harder.

Mac glowered at him and snatched the beer Joe offered. "I'm sorry I accused you of taking advantage of her. She said something today I can't get out of my head."

"Which was?"

"That I know *you*, and that should've been good enough. She's absolutely right about that."

Joe clinked his bottle against Mac's. "You certainly know better than anyone how much I love her. I'd never do anything to hurt her."

"I hope you know what you're doing. I don't want to see you hurt, either."

"Don't worry about me. I can take care of myself."

"Joseph," a booming voice intoned.

Uh-oh. Joe looked up at Big Mac and flashed a grin. "Beer?"

Big Mac made no move to accept the beer Joe offered. "May I have a word with you outside?"

Joe glanced at Mac, who snorted behind his hand. "Um, sure. Now?"

"Right now."

Driving an elbow into Mac's ribs on the way by, Joe followed Big Mac outside. As they walked to the end of the long pier, Joe wondered if the older man intended to push him into the murky water and leave him for dead. When they couldn't go any farther, Big Mac turned to him, hands on hips. "What's this I hear about you and my daughter?"

"Well, um . . ."

Thanks to the lights on the pilings, Joe could see that one of Big Mac's eyebrows was raised. That was never a good thing.

"I'm waiting."

"I love her. I've always loved her."

Big Mac stared him down, but Joe didn't blink. "Is that so?"

"Yes, sir."

"So the minute her fiancé was out of the picture, you moved right in, huh?"

"It didn't happen that way. Exactly."

"How *did* it happen?"

"First of all, *she* called *me* when her car broke down."

"And the rest?"

Joe rubbed at the stubble on his chin as a bead of sweat rolled down his back. Being tossed in jail had been far more pleasant than this interrogation. "I'd rather not talk about that. It's personal. Between Janey and me." He cleared his throat. "Sir."

"I can respect that. I suppose. Where do you see this heading?"

"If I had my way, we'd be the ones getting married next weekend. At this point, it all depends on her. She knows what I want."

"She's interested in veterinary school. Are you aware of that?"

"She told you that?" Joe asked, a burst of adrenaline kicking his heart into higher gear. Why hadn't she told him?

"We had a conversation about it. Would you stand in the way of that?"

"Hell, no. Who do you think has been pushing her in that direction?"

"And if she moves to Columbus, Ohio, for the next four years?"

"We'll figure that out when she gets in. No matter what, she's going."

"That's what I want to hear."

"You have to know I'd take good care of her if I'm lucky enough to have that opportunity."

"It might be a while before she figures out what she wants."

"I'm not going anywhere, and I'd wait forever for her if that's what it takes."

Big Mac studied him for a long, *long* moment before

he finally extended his hand. "Be good to her," he said quietly. The tone was in sharp contrast to his usual booming voice.

Overwhelmed by the blessing Big Mac had given him, Joe shook his hand. "Always."

Much later, Joe stood off to the side watching Mac engage in a fight to the death with Grant, who was trying—and failing—to win back some of the money Mac had won at the poker table. The groom-to-be had been unstoppable all night long. Over the course of the evening, most of the old men who hung around on the docks had wandered into the party, and at some point Evan had unearthed his guitar.

Under the influence of his brothers and a considerable amount of alcohol, Mac seemed to be having a fantastic time, which was all that mattered to Joe. However, he couldn't help but wonder what Janey was up to. Since all his guests were happily engaged, he stepped outside to give her a quick call.

"Are you bored at the bachelor party?" she asked. "I told you to get strippers."

Joe smiled, delighted to hear her voice. "You told me no such thing."

"Well, I would have if you'd asked me."

"Where does one get strippers on this island?"

"If anyone would know, I would."

"Do *not* tell me how you know that."

Janey's sexy laugh sent an arrow of desire rocketing straight through him.

"I miss you," he said, looking out at the moon reflecting on the placid Salt Pond.

"You just saw me."

"This morning seems like a *really* long time ago."

"For me, too," she said softly, as if she didn't want someone to hear her.

"Where are you?"

"Over at Maddie's providing the bride with moral support while the groom is out drinking and carousing."

"There's no carousing going on. Just some rather heated hands of poker. Tell Maddie that Mac has relieved Grant of five hundred bucks so far."

He listened while she relayed the message.

"She said that's great, but if he comes home drunk, she's blaming you."

"Fabulous. So, if I bring him home later, maybe you'll still be there, and maybe I can give you a ride back to town?"

"That might be possible."

"I'm not working until twelve thirty tomorrow."

"I'm not working at all. Got the shower."

"Mmm, I'm picturing a lazy morning in bed."

"We're on a diet," she reminded him.

"I'm hoping you'll forget about that about five minutes after we get back to your place."

She released a nervous giggle. "We'll see about that."

"Yes, we will. Don't wait for me if it gets too late."

"I'll wait."

Joe wished he could leave right now and go to her.

"Joe?"

"What, hon?"

"Thanks for the flowers. They're gorgeous."

"I'm glad you like them."

"I haven't gotten flowers in a really long time."

"Is that right?"

"Uh-huh."

"Janey . . ."

"Yes?"

Overwhelmed with love for her, he took a deep breath. "I'll see you soon."

"I'll be here."

Chapter Twenty-One

By midnight, no one else was willing to take on Mac at the poker table, so the cards were abandoned and the bullshitting began in earnest. They covered every old story about Mac's capers as a kid, as well as his considerable dating history. Joe kept them all in beer, whiskey and cigars, even though he'd quit drinking hours ago. No one seemed to notice.

"So you know who was on the ferry this afternoon?" Evan asked. "Remember Sydney Donovan who used to come out in the summer?"

Joe tuned right into the stricken expression on Luke Harris's face. He'd dated Sydney every summer for years before she went off to college and never came back.

"She looked rough, man," Grant added. "Has she been sick or something?"

Since Luke seemed paralyzed, Joe told the others about what had happened to Sydney's family.

"Oh, man," Adam said softly. "God."

"Apparently, she shattered her pelvis in the same accident," Joe said.

"I heard she's here for the rest of the summer," Ned said. "Staying with her folks till she's back on her feet."

"Poor kid." Big Mac shook his head with dismay. "How do you ever get over that?"

"Wasn't she a friend of yours, Luke?" Mac asked.

Luke seemed to snap out of his trance. "Um, yeah. Long time ago."

"She was a friend of Maddie's, too," Mac said. "They worked together at the Scoop." He referred to the ice cream shop in town. "She'll be glad to know Sydney's back on the island."

Mac was slurring his words, and Joe could tell Luke didn't want to talk about Sydney. "What do you say we call it a night? Thomas will have you up early."

A big goofy grin spread across Mac's face. "He's so awesome. Isn't he awesome, Joe?"

Joe helped Mac to his feet. "He sure is."

"I love being a dad. Who knew?"

Mac's brothers snickered as Joe guided him to the door.

Mac tightened his arm around Joe's neck and kissed his cheek. "I'm so glad you're sleeping with Janey."

A collective gasp rippled through the room.

"Oops," Mac said.

If looks could kill, Mac would be deader than dead just then.

"You take him," Big Mac said to Joe. "I'll fill them in."

Joe glanced over his shoulder to find the other three McCarthy brothers and Luke staring at him, mouths agape. Ned, on the other hand, had a satisfied smile on his face.

"Thanks for coming, everyone," Joe said. He moved Mac as quickly as he could to the company truck he'd commandeered for the evening and loaded him into the passenger seat. As Joe secured Mac's seat belt, his friend's eyes fluttered closed.

"Sorry 'bout that," Mac said when Joe started the truck. "Shouldn't have blurted that out."

"Ya think?"

"They love you. They'll be happy 'bout it."

"If you say so."

"I say so," Mac said one second before letting out a huge snore.

Joe laughed to himself and deemed the bachelor party a success.

Arriving at Mac's house a short time later, Joe equated the effort to wake Mac to rousing a hibernating grizzly bear.

"Come on, man." Joe somehow managed to get him out of the car and halfway up the stairs to the deck with no help at all from Mac. Just as Joe's back was about to break from the effort, Mac came to.

"Hey! We're home. Maddie! We're home!"

"Shut *up*, will you?" Joe hissed. "If you wake up Thomas, she'll kill you."

"Shhhhh," Mac said. "Be quiet. Thomas is sleeping."

Joe rolled his eyes and slid open the door to find Janey sacked out on one sofa, Maddie on the other.

Maddie sat up when they came in. "Oh, lovely," she muttered.

"Hey, baby," Mac said. "Come give me some love."

"I don't think so." She pointed Joe to the stairs.

He wrestled Mac up the stairs to his bedroom. After propping him up in the bathroom so he could take care of business, Joe dropped him on the bed.

Mac was out cold the second his head hit the pillow.

"Might be a little ugly in the morning," Joe said to Maddie, who had followed them upstairs.

"That's okay. Did he have a good time?"

"I'd say so."

"That's what matters, then. Thanks for bringing him home."

"No problem."

"Did you two work things out?"

"I thought so, but then he blurted out the whole thing to his brothers, so now I'm going to have to kill him."

"*He did not!*" Janey said from the hallway. "I'll help you kill him!"

Joe reached for her. "We've officially gone public, honey."

She wrapped her arms around him and rested her head on his chest. "How public?"

"*All* the way."

Janey groaned as Maddie giggled.

Mac let out a huge snort and turned over in bed, reaching for something—or someone.

"I guess that's my cue," Maddie said.

"Don't let him breathe on you," Joe said.

They all laughed.

"Thanks for everything tonight, you guys," Maddie said.

"May the Force be with you," Joe said.

"He's going to need the Force with *him* in the morning," Maddie said.

Laughing, Janey took Joe's hand to lead him downstairs. "We'll see you tomorrow." Janey collected her stuff and locked the door before sliding it closed behind them.

On the deck, Joe stopped her from going down the stairs. "Come here."

She dropped her purse and jacket and stepped into his outstretched arms.

"Now that's what I've needed all damned day," Joe said.

"Mmm," she said. "Let's go home."

With his arm around her, Joe led her down the steps and into his truck.

"Smells like a bar in here," she said, pinching her nose.

"Thank your brother for that."

"You didn't have any?"

He reached for her hand. "A couple of beers much earlier. I figured one of us needed to maintain."

"Did you guys talk?"

"Yeah, it's all good, baby. Don't worry."

"That's a relief."

"I had an interesting chat with your dad, too."

"Really?"

"Yep." He decided not to mention what her father had told him about vet school. Joe wanted her to tell him herself—when she was ready. It was enough for him to know she was seriously considering it.

"What did he say?"

"He basically asked my intentions."

"Oh, my God! He did not!"

Joe shot her a look. "You know he did."

"Oh, *God*. What did you tell him?"

Joe brought her hand to his lips. "That I've always loved you, and I always will."

"Joe," she said. "That's so sweet."

"It's true, and guess what? I don't give a shit who knows it. I'm so tired of hiding it from everyone. That gets really exhausting."

Janey released her seat belt and moved closer to rest her head on his shoulder. "How did I get so lucky?"

He let go of her hand and put his arm around her, bringing her tight against him. "I'm the lucky one."

"We're both lucky." Her arm snaked around his waist, and her lips burrowed into his neck.

"Janey . . ."

"Hmm?"

"Driving over here. Don't get too busy."

As if he hadn't said a word, her hand roamed his chest and belly before heading south. When she pressed against his erection, he jolted. With one hand on the wheel and the other arm around her, he couldn't stop her from unbuttoning and unzipping his shorts.

She stroked him, and it was all he could do to keep the truck on the road. "Janey! Jesus. Come on."

She laughed and dipped her head to take him into her mouth.

"*Shit*," he groaned, pulling the truck to the side of the road.

The heat of her mouth and the caressing strokes of her hand brought him quickly to the verge of climax. Then she added her tongue to the mix and took him right over. For many minutes afterward, Joe focused on getting air to his straining lungs. Her lips and tongue on his neck drew him out of the stupor he'd slipped into. Reaching for her, he arranged her on his lap so she straddled him and fused his lips with hers. With one hand firmly buried in her hair, his other hand ventured under her skirt to find her panties damp with desire. The discovery reawakened him, and with just the slightest shift of his hips and her panties, he surged into her.

Her head fell back, and she whispered a startled, "Oh . . ." She clutched his shoulders and rotated her hips. "Thought we were on a diet . . ."

"Not anymore." Cupping her buttocks, he urged her to move and couldn't believe how fast she once again had him fighting for control. Being with her reminded him of his horny teenage years.

"That was a dumb idea anyway," she said.

"The dumbest idea ever." Keeping one hand on her bottom, he dipped the other under her shirt and up to her breast. He pushed her bra aside and rolled her nipple between his fingers. That sent her into overdrive, and her hips began to move more urgently.

Joe pushed her shirt up and replaced his fingers with his mouth. After just one hard tug of his lips, she came with a cry of completion that took him with her. He held her tight against him, absorbing the aftershocks and the scent of jasmine that never failed to arouse him.

"I've always thought diets were so pointless," she whispered in his ear.

Joe chuckled. "Some more pointless than others."

"It wouldn't do for us to be caught like this. I'd hate for you to end up in jail twice in one week because of me."

"Then how about we take this somewhere more comfortable?"

She raised her head to press her lips to his in a sweet, chaste kiss that took his breath away. "Let's go."

Janey hadn't told anyone about her visit with Francine. As the two o'clock hour inched closer, she was riddled with anxiety over whether or not Maddie's mother would show. In hindsight, Janey wasn't sure which would be better for Maddie—if her mother came or if she didn't. Janey took a look around at the festive decorations, the buffet table and the small mountain of gifts she and her mother had contributed.

Linda came up behind Janey and massaged her shoulders. "Why so tense?"

"Just hoping it all goes well today."

"It will. Don't worry." Linda turned Janey so she could see her face. "This has to be hard on you. Throwing a bridal shower for someone else . . ."

Janey shook her head. "I'm okay. You know I couldn't be happier for Mac and Maddie. And I've decided that marrying David would've been a huge mistake." Memories of her erotic night with Joe flashed through her mind. Remembering the bliss of waking up in his arms that morning, Janey smiled to herself. "For a number of reasons." She looked up at her mother. "We need to cancel the wedding plans." Janey thought wistfully of the ballroom at the Samuel Turner Inn, the sunset ceremony and reception they'd planned for next August. The wedding of her dreams—right down to the music, the cake and the dress.

"Let's get past next weekend, and then we'll deal with that."

"Yes, you're right."

Linda raised an eyebrow. "Now, what's all this with Joe?"

"That seems to be the question of the week."

"Do you have feelings for him?"

"Lots of feelings. I'm trying to figure out what they all mean. It's complicated . . ."

"How so?"

"He's had . . . He's been in love with me . . ." She glanced at her mother. "For years."

"I wondered," Linda said with a smug smile.

"You *knew*? And didn't say anything?"

"I only *suspected*."

"Why?"

"His eyes follow you around the room. He lights up when he sees you coming. He listens to you—really listens."

"Yes, he does," Janey said.

"But you can't let his feelings for you pressure you into something you're not ready for. You've just gotten out of a very long relationship."

"Which was over a long time ago, if I'm being truthful."

"Regardless, it just officially ended. If you rush in, you risk hurting yourself and Joe."

"We're kind of past the don't-rush-in warning at this point."

Linda put her hands over her ears. "Lalala. Don't want to know."

Janey laughed. "What would you think, really, of me with Joe?"

Linda framed her daughter's face with her hands. "You'd be one very lucky girl. He's handsome, success-ful, charming, attentive, a hard worker, your parents and brothers already love him, and most important of all, he's *loyal*." With a kiss to Janey's forehead, Linda went to check the oven. "I'm sure you'll agree there's a lot to be said for that."

"It's the most important thing. At least to me."

The screen door swung open, and Maddie came in with Mac, who was carrying Thomas. Maddie wore a pink floral sundress, and her hair fell in soft waves around her face. Janey thought she'd never looked lovelier. Mac, on the other hand, looked like death warmed over.

"Oh, there's my baby!" Linda said, reaching for Thomas.

Mac winced. "Not so loud, Mom."

"Did someone have a few too many last night?"

"A *few*?" Janey asked with a snort. "You were pretty funny."

"I'm never drinking again," Mac grumbled.

"Can I get that in writing?" Maddie asked with a charming smile for her fiancé.

He glowered at her.

"Go home and get some sleep," Linda said. "We'll keep Thomas with us."

"You don't want to do that," Mac said. "He's cruising like a madman. You'll do nothing but chase him all day."

"We don't mind, do we, Janey?"

"Of course we don't. We can put him down for a nap upstairs." She gave her brother a push. "Go. Come back in three or four hours."

"Are you okay with this plan?" he asked Maddie.

"If it'll put you in a better mood, I'm all for it." She kissed him and sent him on his way. After he left,

Maddie hugged Janey. "Everything looks beautiful. Thank you so much. And Linda . . . Thank you."

"Our pleasure, honey," Linda said, helping Thomas with a cookie.

"Five more days!" Maddie clapped her hands with excitement. "The time is flying by!"

"What do you still have left to do?"

"A quick run to the mainland on Wednesday to pick up my dress. That's about it."

"Do you want me to go with you?" Janey asked.

"You'd have to take the day off, and you're already taking half of Thursday and all day Friday," Maddie said. "I can handle it. It's just over and right back."

"If you're sure . . ."

"Don't worry—I'll let you know when I need you this week."

"You'd better!"

Maddie's coworkers from the hotel flooded in a few minutes later, along with her sister and baby niece, Ashleigh.

"Is Mom coming?" Maddie asked Tiffany.

Her sister shook her head. "I tried."

Maddie forced a smile. "That's all right. We'll have fun without her."

Janey put her arm around Maddie to lead her to the guest-of-honor chair, which she had decorated with balloons and streamers. "You bet we will."

Chapter Twenty-Two

Two hours later, the women had eaten and watched Maddie open most of the presents. Thomas had fallen asleep in Linda's arms in the rocking chair, and she'd refused to take him upstairs.

Janey was proud of her mother for embracing the child and making him a part of their family. It hadn't been easy for Linda to get past the rumors that had plagued Maddie for most of her life. But once the letters from Evan and the others ran in the paper, Linda had to admit she'd been wrong about the woman her son loved. She'd apologized to Maddie and had made a real effort to get to know her and Thomas since then. In the midst of the rift with her own mother, at least Maddie would be able to lean on her new mother-in-law.

Janey's cell phone vibrated in her pocket. When she checked the caller ID and saw Doc Potter's name, she took the call because he never bothered her after hours unless there was an emergency at the clinic. She immediately thought of Mrs. Roberts and Molly.

"Hey, Doc." She stepped onto the back deck that

overlooked the hotel, marina, and Salt Pond. The fog that had been worse than usual hung over the edges of the pond.

"Janey! I'm so glad I caught you. You won't believe it!"

"Believe what?"

"I just got off the phone with Dean Richards at OSU."

Her heart slowed to a crawl, and she had to remind herself to breathe. "What did he say?"

"They've had several students in this year's incoming class who were unable to secure financing."

Janey gasped.

"When I mentioned you had financing already arranged, he agreed to facilitate your application—*for this year*! This year, Janey! Like a month from now!"

Her legs went weak beneath her, and she dropped to a lounge chair.

"Still there?" Doc asked.

"Yes, *yes*. I'm just trying to absorb it all."

"I don't think I've ever been more excited about anything! I can tell you now that I always thought it was a travesty how David got in the way of you going to vet school the first time around. I didn't care for that one bit."

"You and everyone else."

"Well, we're righting a terrible wrong, and we're doing it in one month!" He released a deep, pained sigh.

"What, Doc? What's wrong?"

"I just realized this means I'll be losing you at the clinic."

Her eyes filled. He'd been such a constant in her life, one of the most important people in her world. "Maybe you can find a spot for me in the summers?"

"I suppose we can squeeze you in until you're too important to come back."

Janey laughed. "I'll come back the second I'm done, and then you can retire."

"You've got yourself a deal, my friend."

"Thank you, Doc. For whatever favors you called in or the donation you made or whatever you did, thank you."

"No thanks necessary. Just go out there and make me proud."

"I will. I promise."

Janey ended the call and clutched the phone to her chest as she looked out over the pond with unseeing eyes. She was going to veterinary school. It was really and finally happening. She must've been out there for a while because Maddie came to find her.

"I'm sorry," Janey said, snapping out of the stupor. "I totally abandoned you."

"I was well cared for. What's wrong? You're pale as a ghost."

"I got in," Janey whispered.

"To?"

"Vet school at Ohio State."

Maddie gasped. "Oh, that's fabulous! Congratulations! For next year?"

"*This* year."

Maddie's eyes widened. "Oh, my God! Janey! *Oh, my God!*"

Before she knew what hit her, Maddie had wrapped her up in a tight hug.

Janey was in tears by the time Maddie released her.

"What's wrong?" Maddie asked, alarmed. "I thought you'd be thrilled!"

"I am." Janey brushed at the tears, annoyed by them. "It's just . . ."

"Joe," Maddie said, her mouth set in a grim expression.

"I can't do another long-distance relationship, Maddie. I just can't."

"I understand. Anyone would. Joe will."

"What will he understand? He's in love with me. We've spent almost every night together for two weeks. If I walk away from him now, he'll be crushed."

Maddie rested her hands on Janey's shoulders. "You have to go to Ohio, Janey. You have to."

"I know. But I need to break things off with Joe now. Today. I can't let this go on when I'm leaving in a month. He's tied to this island and his business. It's not fair to get any more involved with him." She thought of the date they had planned for later, and her heart ached. She'd gotten awfully used to seeing him every day, to leaning on his quiet strength, to finding unimaginable pleasure in his arms.

"Surely there has to be some way," Maddie said.

New tears spilled down Janey's cheeks. "How? His business is his life, Maddie. He'd be lost without that, and it's not like he can just walk away from it. And he would. He'd do that for me, but I can't ask that of him. I just can't."

"You need to talk to him about this. At least give him a chance to figure something out."

"There's nothing to figure out. He lives here, and for the next four years, I'm going to live a thousand miles from here. Look how it worked out when David was only in Boston. I can't go through that again."

"Comparing him to David would be *very* unfair."

"Do me a favor?"

"Anything."

"Keep this quiet until I figure out what to say to Joe?"

Maddie thought about that for a moment. "I have to tell Mac. I won't keep it from him. I'd like to think I've learned my lesson in that regard."

"You have to swear him to silence. I don't want him to tell Joe until I decide how I'm going to handle it."

"He won't. I promise you that." Maddie hugged her again. "It'll work out, Janey. Joe would wait forever for you."

"I can't ask him to wait four years."

"Maybe you won't have to."

Still holding the sleeping Thomas, Linda came to the door. "Everything all right out here?"

"Yes," Janey said, forcing a smile. "We're fine."

"Maddie, you have a late-arriving guest."

Maddie glanced at Janey. "Who?"

"Why don't you go see?" Maybe Francine had come through after all. Janey could only hope. She followed Maddie inside where Francine waited, gripping a festively wrapped gift and looking exquisitely uncomfortable.

"I'm sorry I'm late," Francine said.

"That's all right." Maddie reached around the box to hug her mother. "I'm so glad you came."

"Could I get you some coffee or punch, Francine?" Linda asked. "A slice of cake?"

"I'm fine, thank you," Francine said stiffly.

"May I?" Maddie asked, gesturing to the package.

Francine handed it to her and followed Maddie to the family room, where the other women had gone quiet.

"This is my mother, Francine." Maddie introduced

her coworkers from the hotel and then sat to open her mother's gift. Maddie removed the paper and opened the box. "Oh. Oh, Mom."

"I gave Tiffany my mother's china. I thought you might like to have her silver."

"I'd very much love to have it," she said, hugging her mother. "It's so shiny and clean!"

"That's why I was late. It took longer to clean it up than I'd expected."

Maddie clutched her mother's hand. "I'm so glad you came."

"Well, your future sister-in-law over there let me know I'd be welcome."

All eyes shifted to Janey, who flashed a sheepish grin and shrugged.

Maddie mouthed the words *thank you* to Janey, who nodded in response.

After she helped to load Mac, Maddie, Thomas and the shower loot into the SUV, Janey turned her attention to the last of the dishes all the while trying not to think about the terrible task that lay ahead.

"Joe," she whispered. "God. What've I done to both of us?"

The irony of the situation wasn't lost on her. In the same instant she'd decided she had to give him up, she'd realized she loved him. *Loved* him loved him. At some point during their exquisite nights together, he had worked his way into her heart, and the idea of losing him hurt more than anything ever had—even finding David in bed with another woman.

Standing at the sink, Janey dropped her head to

her chest, absorbing the blow as all the images from their brief time together flashed through her mind.

Linda came back into the room. "Janey? Honey, what is it? What's wrong?"

Tears clogged her throat, threatening to burst free at any moment. "I, um, I have something I need to do. Would you mind finishing up these last few dishes?"

"Of course not. Go on ahead."

Janey kissed her cheek. "Thanks for everything today. It was a lovely shower."

"Yes, it was, and you did a good thing talking Francine into coming. I'm proud of you for doing that."

The dam broke, and tears flooded her eyes.

"Janey! My goodness! What's going on?"

"It's nothing," she said, even though her heart was breaking. "I just . . . I need to go."

Linda hugged her and wiped the tears from Janey's cheeks. "Call me later?"

Janey nodded, grabbed her purse and headed for the door. In the car, she rested her head on the steering wheel and tried to imagine what Joe would say when she told him they were over. Her heart ached at the thought of hurting him, but better now than in a month, when they'd be even more involved.

"Oh, Joe," she whispered through her tears. "I love you so much." *I hate that I have to do this to him, but I can't turn my back on this opportunity again. Not even for Joe. And I can't expect him to give up his whole life for me. He'd hate me for that someday.*

Blinded by tears, she knew she shouldn't attempt to drive but didn't want to sit in front of her mother's house crying her eyes out, either. She drove slowly on the way home, knowing that once she got there,

Riley and the others would provide the comfort she so desperately needed.

At her house, she indulged in a snuggle with her animals before she let the dogs out and reached for her cell phone. She couldn't delay this any longer. Joe was due to pick her up in just over two hours. As she ran a hand over the black silk dress she'd taken out earlier, she wondered where he'd planned to take her. "What does it matter?" she asked herself as she found his number in her phone.

"Hey, baby," he said when he answered. The sound of his familiar voice sent love and regret surging through her. "How was the shower?"

"Good. It was fine." She wanted to tell him how Maddie's mother had come, how she had made that happen, but she couldn't get the words past the huge lump in her throat.

"What's wrong, honey? You sound funny."

"I don't feel so good." She winced at the lie, knowing she was only postponing the inevitable. "It came on in the middle of the shower, and now I'm miserable." That was certainly the truth.

"Oh, bummer. I had a big night planned for us, but we can do it another time. I'll come over and take care of you."

"No."

He paused. "Why not?"

"I feel gross. I don't want you to see me like this. I'd really rather be alone tonight."

"Is something else wrong, Janey?"

It was all she could do not to break down at the hurt she heard in his voice. "I just . . . I need to be alone. Is that all right?"

"If that's all it is."

"I've got to go," she said.

"Janey—"

"Bye, Joe." She ended the call and stretched out on the sofa as hot tears rolled down her cheeks. She had no doubt it was better this way. But if that was true, why did it hurt so much?

Joe stared at the fog outside the window of his South Harbor office. Something was up. She wasn't sick. How he knew that he couldn't have said. He just knew. "Oh, Janey," he said. "What're you doing?"

He glanced at the suit he'd brought from home to wear on the date that wasn't going to happen now. The way he saw it, he had two choices—sit here and do nothing, hoping she'd come around, or storm over there and demand she tell him what was going on. Neither option was all that appealing, but the idea of doing nothing was unacceptable.

Since it was foggy and chilly, he grabbed a company pullover and headed out of the office. On the short walk to Janey's house, he replayed their brief phone call and tried to figure out why he hadn't believed her when she said she didn't feel good. He knew her. The closer he got to her house, the more annoyed he became. If something was wrong, why couldn't she just tell him the truth rather than giving him the brush-off? That's what he intended to find out.

Approaching her house, he noticed the lights were out and wondered if she was even home. He experienced a moment of trepidation as he opened the front gate. What if she really was barfing her guts up and would be embarrassed for him to see her like that? Well, too bad. He was in for better or worse, and it was high time she realized that.

He knocked on the door, and the dogs went crazy inside.

"Janey?" he said, knocking again. "Come on, honey. I need to see you. I know something's wrong."

The dogs continued to howl, but Janey didn't come.

"I'm going to wait, Janey. I'm not leaving until I see that you're all right. If you don't want me to call Mac—"

The inside door swung open.

One glance at her ravaged face told Joe that something was very wrong. He pulled open the screen door and stepped into the dark room. The dogs danced around his legs. "Baby, what is it?"

"I, um . . ." She looked up at him, her eyes shiny with tears. "I can't do this, Joe."

"Do what?"

"This. Us."

He forced himself to remain calm so he could figure out what the hell was going on. "What happened today? What changed since we woke up together this morning and made love—twice?"

Sobs shook her petite frame, and it took all he had not to go to her, to put his arms around her and assure her he'd fix whatever had her so upset. But he couldn't seem to bring himself to move.

"I never should've let this happen," she said between sobs. "I was messed up. Mixed up. You tried to tell me . . ."

Joe took a deep breath, hoping to slow his rapid heartbeat. "What happened today?" he asked through gritted teeth.

"I woke up from the daze I've been in since everything with David, and now I can't seem to stop crying or thinking about all the years I gave him and how I have absolutely nothing to show for them." She was crying so hard Joe wondered how she was able to breathe. "We were supposed to get married and have four kids. I wanted those kids. That's what I wanted."

This was what he had most feared—that when the shock wore off, she'd discover she wasn't at all ready to move on with him. And where would that leave him? Right here, loving her and losing her.

Needing an outlet for the energy zipping through him, he ran his fingers through his hair and tried to resist the urge to tear it out. "You can still have anything you want, Janey. I'd give you anything and everything. You have to know that."

She shook her head. "I can't. I'm sorry. I just can't."

He felt like she'd ripped the heart from his chest, and right then and there, he realized he'd never get over losing her. Not after all they'd shared.

"Janey, whatever is wrong, we can fix it. If you need more time, take it. But don't try to tell me what's between us isn't love. You'll never convince me of that."

Janey wiped the tears from her face. "Then I won't try."

Hearing that, something inside him broke, and he knew he had to get out of there or risk saying something he'd never be able to take back. "I'm sorry you feel that way. I think we could've had something pretty great, but I'm certainly not going to beg. You know where I am if you change your mind."

Joe forced himself to turn around, to walk out the door and down the stairs. Once he was through the gate, he pulled out his cell phone and dialed Mac's number.

"Sleeping," Mac mumbled.

"Wake up. Something's wrong with Janey."

"What?" Mac asked, instantly awake. "What's wrong?"

"I don't know. She won't tell me."

"What happened?"

"I wish I knew. Will you go over there and check on her?"

"On my way. Are you okay, Joe?"

"I'm confused. Everything was fine this morning and now it's not. Something happened, but she won't tell me what it is."

Mac remained silent.

"You know, don't you?"

"Joe—"

"Forget it. I don't want to know. If she can't tell me herself, screw it. Screw this whole thing. I'm done."

"Wait—"

Joe shut off his phone. Enough already.

Chapter Twenty-Three

Luke dragged his old wooden rowboat onto the sandy beach and stowed the oars inside. The fog was gone, and a full moon lit the big pond. Even without the light from above, he could've found this particular stretch of beach in his sleep. Accompanied by a chorus of crickets, the path to Sydney's summer home was as familiar to him as anything in his life.

How many nights had he arrived just like this, under the cover of darkness, and sneaked into her yard to throw pebbles at her window? How many nights had they spent together on the beach, making love until dawn when she'd tiptoe back into her house and he'd hold his breath waiting to hear they'd finally been caught? Too many to count.

He wasn't sure what had hurt more—hearing that Sydney, *his* Sydney, had married some guy she met in college or that she'd lost her husband and children in a tragic car crash. Luke had devoured every word he could find on the Internet about the accident. They'd been coming home to Boston from a weekend in New Hampshire and were stopped in a traffic jam. From behind them, a drunk driver had come barreling into their minivan, killing the children instantly. Sydney had been asleep at the time of the accident, which safety officials said probably saved her life. Her husband Seth had died later in surgery.

Even though Luke thanked God every day for sparing her life, he ached for her unbearable loss. After hearing last night that she was back on the island, he needed just a glimpse of her, any sign that she was still alive and breathing. So he traveled through the dunes and the dense growth that covered what used to be a well-worn path. A branch full of thorns grazed his face. Judging from the warm sting on his cheek, he figured it had broken the skin, but still he pressed on.

Loving Sydney had made his life. Losing her had turned him into a cranky loner who never again let anyone get close enough to truly touch him. He and Sydney hadn't really broken up, per se, but rather drifted apart. After her second year of college, when she hadn't come to the island for the summer and stopped returning his calls, Luke had gone to her parents' house to find out why.

The wealthy Donovans, summer residents for decades until they retired and became year-rounders five years ago, had never approved of his interest in their fair-haired daughter. However, they'd told him she had an internship, a fantastic opportunity, and wouldn't be coming out that summer. Luke, who'd been unable to leave the island for college because of his ailing mother, had already waited nearly a year to see Syd again. The news that she wasn't coming had crushed him. And that she hadn't seen fit to tell him herself pointed to the unimaginable possibility that she had met someone else.

That summer he became a loner. Of course there had been other women since her but only to provide an occasional physical release. None of them had mattered to him.

He wondered, as he crept through the brush, did she still have that long, strawberry blond hair that reached almost to her waist? How many times over the years had he recalled the way her gorgeous hair would drape them off from the rest of the world as she straddled him and rode him to one incredible climax after another? Did she still get a thousand new freckles for every hour she spent in the sun? Were her eyes still as blue as the ocean and her pale skin soft as silk? Would she ever again let loose with her trademark all-consuming laugh? Had she loved her husband as sweetly and as purely as she had once loved him? Did she ever think about him? About them? About what they'd shared for the four most memorable summers of his life?

As he approached the big yellow house with the wide front porch, he knew he might never get the answers he so desperately wanted. The last person she needed to see in the midst of her terrible grief was an old boyfriend who'd never stopped loving her or thinking about her or remembering her.

But he needed to see her.

In the Donovans' yard, he got as close as he dared to the well-lit porch, thankful for the lingering clouds that dimmed the moon's glow. When he saw her sitting in a rocker, a quilt around her shoulders, he suppressed a gasp. There, after all this time, his Sydney, the love of his life. He hadn't seen her in sixteen years but would've known her anywhere. Her long hair had been cut to shoulder length, but the color was just as beautiful and vibrant as he remembered. It wasn't possible to tell whether she still had freckles or if her eyes were as blue.

She stared out at the distant pond, lost in thought. While he'd like to think she was remembering him and their time together, he knew she was picturing her children playing on the rolling lawn and beach. They'd come every summer, Syd and her banker husband and their two children. Luke had never seen them, had never thought to seek her out, but he'd always known exactly when they came and exactly when they left. Since she was married and lost to him, it hadn't occurred to Luke to try to see her again. That chapter was closed, finished. She had chosen someone else, and Luke had no alternative but to live with it.

As he watched her on the porch, he barely took a breath. His heart beat so hard and so fast he was sure she could hear it. How could she not? And then she began to cry, and it took everything he had to stay where he was, out of sight, out of mind, out of reach. Her anguished sobs reached him in places no one but Syd had ever touched. His own eyes burned and filled, but he didn't move. Time crawled to a stop, and he had no idea if he remained crouched beside the porch for five minutes or an hour. When the cramps in his legs became painful, he eased himself down to the damp grass. He knew he should go but couldn't leave her all alone. Not when she was so sad.

After a while, her mother stepped onto the porch and bent to put her arms around her grieving daughter. Luke watched Mrs. Donovan help Sydney to her feet and slowly guide her inside. Syd moved as if she was still in great physical pain, which was hard for him to watch. For a long time after she went inside and the porch light went out, Luke stayed there, needing to be as close to her as possible.

And then, sometime later when he trusted that his legs would actually carry him, he made his way back down the path to the rowboat at the beach, already knowing he'd come back tomorrow night.

Probably the night after as well.

Janey lay on the sofa staring up at the ceiling. Turning Joe away had been, without a doubt, the most painful moment of her life, and she couldn't seem to stop crying. Her heart ached when she remembered the shattered look on his face. She would never forget that.

A knock on the door startled her. She sat up. Had he come back?

Mac walked in and came right to her. Sitting next to her, he put his arms around her.

As her brother's familiar and comforting scent surrounded her, Janey lost it all over again.

"Shh," he said, brushing a hand over her hair. "It's okay. Everything's going to be okay."

"I hurt him," she said between sobs.

Riley let out a concerned whimper and dragged himself over to her.

Hoping to reassure him, Janey reached out to scratch behind his ears. Among her many concerns since receiving Doc's call earlier was how she would manage eight pets in a Columbus apartment.

"What did he say?" Janey asked Mac.

"He's confused. He can't figure out what happened since this morning."

"Maddie told you?"

Mac brushed the hair off her damp face and smiled at her. "I'm so proud of you. Doctor Janey. How about that?"

Tears spilled from her eyes, and Janey wondered if they would ever stop. "You know why I had to end it with Joe, don't you? I couldn't string him along for the next month and then try to manage another long-distance relationship."

"You're not giving him enough credit."

"He'd walk away from everything that matters to him so I could realize my dreams. I couldn't do that to him."

Mac sat back against the sofa, bringing her with him. She rested her face on his chest, and he kept an arm around her. If he'd asked first, Janey would've told him not to come, but she was glad he had.

"Has he told you about how he came to own the company?"

"Wasn't it his family's business?"

"Uh-huh. Remember his grandparents? They lived out by the North Light?"

"You guys were so much older than me—back then," she said with a small smile. "I never met them. I knew they were important to him, though."

"His dad was killed in a car accident when he was seven. I guess his mother was kind of a mess afterward. Her parents lived out here, so they packed up their place in the city and moved here. His grandfather had started the ferry company just after World War Two. He took Joe under his wing and taught him everything he knew about running boats. Joe discovered he had a natural affinity for anything and everything to do with the water, but it wasn't his first love."

"What was?"

"You must know the answer to that by now."

"Oh . . . the painting!" She sat up so she could see him better. "Have you seen his work?"

Mac nodded. "Quite something, isn't it?"

"I couldn't believe it! Why didn't he go to art school?"

"He was on his way. He'd gotten into one of the best schools in the country, the Savannah College of Art."

"So what happened? Why didn't he go?"

Mac tilted his head, and his mouth twisted into an ironic smile.

"Oh, God. His grandfather died, and he felt obligated to keep the company in the family." Her heart ached when she realized the enormous responsibility he'd inherited at the tender age of eighteen.

"It was never his dream, Janey. He's had a very satisfying life doing something he truly enjoys, but it wasn't his first love."

"I've known him all my life, and yet there's so much about him I don't know."

"He loves you more than anything. You have to know that by now. Is there any chance at all that you might love him, too? Even a little?"

Janey blinked back more tears, bit her lip and nodded. "I love him so much."

"But are you *in love* with him?"

"Yes," she whispered, wiping her face. Any final doubts had disappeared the second he walked out her door earlier. "Very much so."

"It's not fair for you to make these decisions on his

behalf. He's had his choices taken away before. It's really the worst thing you could do to him."

Moaning, she said, "I thought I was doing the *right thing* for him!"

"What would you say to letting your buttinsky big brother fix this fine mess for you?"

She leaned her head on his shoulder. "I'd say please, by all means, do what you do best and butt in."

Mac laughed and kissed the top of her head. "Don't worry, brat. It'll all be fine. I'll make sure of it."

Mac's wedding day dawned clear and sunny. He took a cup of coffee to the deck to look out over the yard and the tent that had been erected the day before. It didn't pay to gamble with New England weather, and Mac was taking no chances that this day would be anything less than perfect. He'd certainly waited long enough to find Maddie. In just a few hours, she'd finally be his wife. And with her came a son who Mac couldn't have loved any more if he'd been his biological child.

Maddie and Thomas had spent the night at Janey's, and Mac couldn't wait to see them later. He'd grown used to his mornings with Thomas and had missed waking up to baby chatter. Mac had arranged for a horse-drawn carriage to pick them up for the wedding. He looked forward to hearing about Thomas's reaction to that.

A hand landed on Mac's shoulder, and he turned to find Joe holding a mug.

"Hey, did you sleep okay?" Mac asked.

"Like a dead man. The boys are still out cold." Joe referred to Mac's brothers.

Mac studied his good friend and saw none of the agitation and despair that had marked his features earlier in the week, before Mac had cued him into Janey's news. Today he saw nothing but serenity and determination on Joe's face.

"Ready for all this?" Joe asked, gesturing to the tent and the arrangement of chairs to the right of the tent where the exchange of vows would take place at two o'clock.

"Absolutely. How about you?"

"Operation Janey is ready to roll."

Mac smiled. "You've thrown her all off-kilter with four days of total silence, you know."

"That's the very least of what she deserves after what she's put me through—for years. Yeah, a few days of suffering is *just* what she needed."

"You two are well matched," Mac said, laughing. "Very well matched indeed."

"You really think so?" Joe asked, showing a hint of vulnerability that tugged at Mac's heart. Hell, everything tugged at his heart these days.

"You know I do." Mac took a long swig of coffee. "So what's the plan?"

"You'll just have to wait and see," Joe said with a smug grin.

"Come on! You can tell *me*. I won't say anything."

"Nope."

"Oh, this is going to be good," Mac said, chuckling.

"You bet it is."

Janey had no doubt that she was far more nervous than the bride. While Maddie had been calm and cool all day, Janey felt like she was coming out of her own skin while she waited to see Joe. She knew for a fact that Mac had told him her news days ago, and yet she hadn't heard a word from Joe since then. If he was trying to punish her, he was doing a damned good job of it.

Night after night she had lain awake wondering where he was, what he was thinking, why he didn't call, why he didn't come over, why he didn't do *something*. The tension had turned her into a basket case as she tried her best to provide steady support to the bride.

The guys had cleared out of Mac and Maddie's house hours ago so the women could finish getting ready, but now Janey heard their voices out on the lawn. She glanced out the window, and her breath caught at the sight of Mac and Joe standing together in black tuxedos. Mac held Thomas, who wore a tiny tux for the occasion. Her other brothers, dressed in dark suits, talked and laughed and joked with them. What a handsome bunch of guys, Janey thought with a smile.

She checked her watch. Ten minutes to showtime. Gathering the skirt of her periwinkle gown, she rushed upstairs and knocked on the bedroom door.

"Come in," Maddie called. She had requested a half an hour alone to finish getting ready.

Janey opened the door and stopped short. "Wow." The dress was simple, elegant and utterly perfect. "Seriously. *Wow.*"

Maddie released a nervous laugh. "Really?"

"Mac won't be able to remember his own name when he sees you."

Maddie flashed a saucy smile. "That was kind of the goal." She reached for Janey's hand. "How are you holding up?"

"I'm a mess." She rested her free hand over her churning belly. "I have no idea if Joe will even speak to me."

"Of course he will."

"I wouldn't blame him if he didn't." Janey shook off that unpleasant thought. "Anyway, it's not about me today. This is your day. My dad should be here any minute to give away the bride. Are you ready?"

"I'm so ready." Maddie's caramel-colored eyes glowed. "I've never been happier in my life. I kept waiting for something to happen to mess it up . . ."

"I told you nothing would happen." Janey hugged her. "Don't start or we'll both be bawling like babies."

"Only happy tears today." Maddie extended her hand. "Deal?"

Janey shook on it, hoping she could hold up her end of the bargain.

Chapter Twenty-Four

Following Maddie's sister, Tiffany, down the stairs to the lawn, Janey looked everywhere but at Joe. She was too afraid of what she might see if she made contact with those hot hazel eyes of his. Instead, she watched her brother's mouth fall open at the first glimpse of Maddie on his father's arm. Janey held Maddie's bouquet during the emotional exchange of vows and took the arm Joe silently offered so they could follow the newly married couple down the aisle.

And still she hadn't dared to look directly at him.

Her stomach twisted and turned, her heart raced and she couldn't seem to get enough air to her lungs. Despite being riddled with tension, she managed to smile for the photographer before they moved into the tent. Luckily, she was seated next to Maddie and Joe was next to Mac during dinner, which Janey only picked at.

Joe gave a beautiful toast about Mac finding the exact perfect partner that brought tears to Janey's eyes. While Mac and Maddie were cutting their cake, Janey finally ventured a glance at Joe's handsome face and found him staring right back at her. Her heart soared with hope at the heated look he sent her, and she couldn't seem to tear her eyes off him. The DJ ended the moment when he announced the bride and groom's first dance as Mr. and Mrs. Mac McCarthy.

Janey startled a few minutes later when Joe's warm hand landed on her bare shoulder, setting off a reaction that rippled through her body like a live wire.

"Our turn," he said.

Looking up at him, she took the hand he offered and let him lead her to the dance floor. As he took her into his arms, Janey breathed him in, flooded with relief at being close to him again. Suddenly, all the tension she'd carried for days faded away, and she relaxed into his embrace.

He didn't say anything, but his fingers lightly skimmed her back as they moved to the music. Later, Janey wouldn't remember the song or the soft summer breeze that drifted through the open sides of the tent. She wouldn't remember her parents dabbing at tears as they watched the four of them from the edge of the dance floor. She wouldn't remember Maddie's mother play-dancing with a giggling Thomas on the sideline or her other brothers watching her and Joe with thinly veiled interest.

Janey would, however, remember the sense of absolute rightness that came over her as Joe held her close to him. She'd remember the distinctive scent of the sea and cloves, the heat of his hand branding her sensitive skin and the brush of his lips over her hair. And she would remember the moment, the *exact moment* when she realized he was holding her the way a man holds the woman he loves. Right then she knew somehow, some way, this was going to be okay. *They* were going to be okay.

"Have you done everything you need to do for Maddie?" he asked as the song came to an end.

Janey looked over at her brother and his new wife, who were totally absorbed in each other. "I doubt she'll be needing me for anything."

"Great," Joe said.

The next thing Janey knew, she had been tossed over his shoulder and was looking at the floor rushing by as he carried her out of the tent.

"*What are you doing?* Put me down!"

"Be quiet or I might be tempted to paddle your ass while I have you right where I want you."

"You wouldn't dare!"

"Wanna try me?"

Janey bit back another retort because she was afraid he would, in fact, spank her with everyone in the tent no doubt watching as they crossed the lawn and headed for the driveway. Over the blood rushing to her head, Janey was certain she heard her brothers hooting and hollering. She'd take care of them later.

"Joe, come on! I'm going to throw up!"

"Throw up what? You didn't eat a bite of your dinner."

She should've known he'd be watching her every move the way he always had.

"*Please* put me down?" she asked, affecting the sweetest tone she owned, since being a shrew had gotten her nowhere.

"And risk you running away from me again? No way."

She'd resigned herself to hanging upside down for a while, so it came as a shock to her when he suddenly stopped walking and put her down. As the blood rushed from her head, his hands on her shoulders steadied her.

Janey twisted out of his grasp. "You're a Neanderthal."

That seemed to please him. "Whatever it takes." He gestured to the horse and carriage Mac had sent for Maddie earlier. "Madame?"

Reaching up, she attempted to bring order to hair that had broken loose from the pins she'd used to hold it up for the wedding. She didn't want to think about how scary she must look with a red face and crazy hair. "What if I don't want to go with you?" she asked, giving him some of his own medicine.

"I can still spank your ass, so you'd better stop talking and get in the carriage." His brows narrowed over those amazing eyes. "*Now*." The last word was uttered with such uncharacteristic menace that Janey did as she was told, even though she'd much rather keep fighting with him.

"This whole caveman act is highly unattractive," she huffed. While that was true, Joe in a tuxedo was among the most attractive sights she'd ever beheld.

He got in behind her and signaled to the driver. "You know what's unattractive? You. Lying to me, blowing me off, making decisions for me. That's *really* unattractive."

"I did what I thought was *best* for you!"

"*Who are you to decide that?*"

Janey stared at him, shocked by the outburst. "So you're mad."

"Seriously pissed is more like it."

"Joe—"

"Don't talk to me right now, Janey. I don't know if

I can trust myself to not give you that spanking you so richly deserve."

While she didn't think for a minute he'd do any such thing, she'd never seen him quite so furious. She was appalled, in fact, to realize she was rather turned on at the moment.

Sitting as far apart as they could get on the wide bench, they rolled along in the carriage with only the horses' hooves clomping on pavement to break the silence. The driver took the long way around the island before pulling up in front of Janey's house.

"Thanks very much," Joe said, slipping the driver a fifty as he jumped down from the carriage.

"My pleasure, Captain Joe. You folks enjoy the rest of your day now."

"Oh, we will." Joe reached for Janey's hips and swung her down as if she weighed twenty pounds rather than a hundred and twenty. Okay, maybe the caveman act was a *little* bit attractive, not that she'd ever tell *him* that.

Janey went in ahead of him and took a moment to greet her pets. Then she turned to let him know what she thought of him pushing her around this way. Before she could say a word, however, his mouth was feasting on hers, and he'd sucked the breath from her lungs. His strong arms came around her, lifting her right off her feet as his tongue engaged in a fierce dual with hers.

He kissed her straight into submission. At that moment she was so grateful to be with him again that she would've given him anything he wanted if it meant he would never stop kissing her. Her fingers sifted into his hair, anchoring him to her.

Many heated minutes later, he tore his lips free, set

her back down and went to work on her neck. "Let's go back to the other night," he said, dropping hot kisses on her collarbone. "When I asked what had happened to upset you."

"I got into vet school for this year," she said without hesitation. "I freaked out about what it would mean for us."

"And you thought it would be easier on both of us if you ended it now rather than later."

"Yes," she said, moaning when his clever fingers molded her breasts through the silk of her dress.

"And was it? Easier?"

"No, it was horrible. I missed you so much, and it was only *four days.* Oh, Joe, how will we ever be apart for *four years?*" The idea alone was enough to reduce her to tears.

He raised his head and found her eyes. "Who said anything about being apart?"

"But you live here. Your business, your whole *life* is here."

Staring down at her, he shook his head, his eyes filled with what looked an awful lot like regret. "I guess I haven't done a good enough job."

"Of what?" she asked, confused.

"I thought you'd know by now that everything I want, everything I *need,* is right here in my arms. The rest is just details, Janey."

She melted into his tight embrace. "I'm so sorry," she whispered. "I never meant to hurt you."

"That's okay. I knew you didn't mean it."

"How did you know?"

"I figured if you really didn't want me, you wouldn't have been bawling your head off."

Janey smiled. He knew her so well, and there was

such comfort in that, even if he had a shocking bit of caveman hidden beneath a usually cool exterior.

With his arms tight around her, he lifted her again and walked them through the house to the bedroom. By now, her obedient pets had the routine down and headed for their own beds, knowing they'd be locked out of her bedroom for a while. Joe put her down next to the bed and started with her hair, tugging each pin free while never taking his eyes off her face.

As she reached up to release his bow tie, Janey's heart hammered at the intense expression on his face. "I need to tell you something else," she said.

"What's that?" He unzipped the gown, pushed it off her shoulders and let it fall into a puddle at her feet. His eyes went wide when he got a look at the sexy teddy she'd worn under the dress.

With both hands on his face, she directed his eyes up to meet hers. "I *love you* love you."

He sucked in a sharp deep breath. "Really?"

She nodded.

"Since when?"

"Since the second I thought I had to give you up."

"You don't have to give me up, Janey."

"But what about—"

His mouth came down on hers, a frantic meeting of lips and tongues and teeth. His hands were everywhere, pulling at buttons and hooks and vests and pants. "Goddamned tuxedos," he moaned against her lips. "Too many pieces."

Janey laughed and helped him get rid of the last of his clothes. The second they were both naked, he lifted her and slid into her.

"Oh!" she cried, her arms wrapped tight around his neck. "*Joe.*"

"You really thought you could live without me?"

She shook her head. "I knew I couldn't, but I wasn't about to ask you to give up everything for me."

Without losing their connection, he brought her down to the bed and hovered over her, moving his hips slowly, just enough to make her crazy. "Yesterday, I hired someone to run the business in my absence, and I made two of my part-time captains full-time."

Janey stared at him, trying to comprehend what he was telling her. And then he pushed hard into her, and she ceased to think at all.

"Nothing," he whispered against her neck, "means anything to me without you. I would go anywhere in the world if it meant I got to be with you."

"It's four *years*, Joe. You can't be gone that long."

"Yes, I can." He withdrew from her, leaving her bereft and wanting. His lips laid a trail from her neck to her breasts. "I can do any damned thing I want to. I own the freaking company, Janey." His tongue circled her nipple, and she tried to direct him, but he wouldn't be rushed. "That freaking company makes a lot of freaking money, which gives me the freedom to do any freaking thing I want to." He tugged hard on her nipple, making her cry out from the sensations that darted through her. "And what I want, what I *really* want, is to go to Ohio with you."

His lips shifted to her belly, his tongue flirting with her belly button as his broad shoulders pushed her legs apart. He had her so ready, so primed, that just a few strokes of his tongue over her most sensitive area sent her flying higher than she'd ever gone before. A cry that sounded more like a sob erupted from her throat, and then he was back inside her, riding her hard and fast.

Janey had no choice but to hold on tight and go with him to the place that only he could take her.

"Tell me again," he said, breathing hard as he looked down at her. "Tell me."

"I love you love you, Joe, and I always will."

"I love you love you, too, Janey McCarthy. More than anything in this whole damned world, and I always will." He pushed into her one last time and threw his head back as he came. His powerful release triggered another for her.

For a long time afterward, he rested on top of her, still joined with her.

"You're really going to come with me?" she asked, her hands caressing his back.

"I really am. Someone has to take care of you and the menagerie while you're studying."

"And you're sure that'll be enough for you?"

"I figure we can come back here in the summer so I can get my fix on the boats, and I'll have the rest of the year to paint and help you study."

"You can't help me. You'll be too much of a distraction."

"We can fight about that later. In fact, I'll look forward to it."

Janey let out a little squeal.

"*Jeez*, you gotta do that right in my ear?"

"I'm just so happy! I get to have vet school and you, too. I never imagined I'd get both."

He raised his head to press a soft kiss to her lips. "I never imagined I'd get you." One kiss became a second and then a third. "Can I ask you something?"

"Anything."

"That dream wedding you planned for next

summer—how much of that was you and how much was him?"

"One hundred percent me."

Joe rested his forehead on hers. "Don't cancel it."

Her eyes widened. "What are you saying?"

He withdrew from her and shifted onto his belly to reach for his suit jacket on the floor. When he came back up, he held out his hand. A diamond ring sat on his palm. It was easily twice the size of the one David had given her. This one came with everything that mattered most to her—things that had been woefully lacking last time.

Janey covered her mouth as tears sprang to her eyes.

"I think Dr. Janey Cantrell has an awesome ring to it." He reached for her hand, slid the ring onto her finger and kissed the back of her hand. "Don't you?"

"Yes, I think so, too."

"I've loved you for so long I don't remember a time when I didn't love you."

"It took me a little longer to catch up, but now that I have, I can't imagine my life without you."

His face lifted into that sexy grin she so adored. "You'll never have to."

Janey reached for him and held him close. "Thanks for waiting for me, Joe."

"You were well worth the wait, my love. Very well worth it."

"Are you ever going to say anything?"

Her familiar voice electrified Luke, startling him as he squatted in the dark beside her parents' porch.

The peal of laughter that followed her question reminded him of the happiest time in his life, when she'd laughed at all his corny jokes, before she'd gone away to college and met someone she liked better.

"Luke?"

He stood slowly, not sure if he was more relieved or mortified to have been caught watching her. "How long have you known?"

"Since the first time you came last summer."

Okay, mortified. Definitely mortified. Luke released an unsteady laugh. "And here I thought I was being so sly."

"As if I could ever forget the sound of your boat scraping against the beach. I used to listen for it every night."

The reminder of those unforgettable summer nights made his heart race. When he'd heard through the island grapevine that she'd arrived on a ferry earlier in the day, he'd told himself to stay home, to leave her alone. But knowing she was here, knowing she was just across the pond . . . Like the summer before, he'd been unable to stay away.

"I'm sorry," he said. "You must think I'm some sort of creep. I swear I'm not. It's just when I heard about what happened . . . to your family . . . I had to come. To make sure you were okay. Well, of course you weren't okay . . ." He ran his fingers through his hair. "Jesus, I'm screwing this all up."

She smiled, and he was relieved to see it reach her expressive eyes the way it used to, back when she smiled at him every day. He took it as a sign that she'd recovered, somewhat—as much as anyone ever could—since he last "visited" her a year ago.

"Do you want to come up?" she asked.

"Oh, I don't want to bother you or your parents—"

"They're off-island for a few weeks. Family reunion in Wisconsin."

"You didn't want to go?"

She wrinkled her nose. "I'd rather be here in the summer than anywhere else."

Somehow he worked up the fortitude to climb the five steps to the porch, his heart pounding so hard he wondered if it would burst through his chest. Keeping his hands in his pockets so she wouldn't see them tremble, he was unable to remember the last time he'd been so nervous. Speaking with the love of his life for the first time in seventeen years would make any man nervous, he supposed. "You always did love it here."

"It's my favorite place in the world."

"I wondered if you were going to come this year." Her smile faded a bit. "I had some stuff I had to

take care of before I could come out to the island."
She gestured to the rocker next to hers. "Want to sit?"

"Um, sure. I guess. For a minute." Under the glow
of the porch light, he took a furtive glance at her. He
was relieved to see that she did, in fact, look a thousand times better than she had a year ago, just a few
months after the accident. "Who's your friend?" he
asked, referring to the gorgeous golden retriever who
lay between their two rockers. The dog had taken a
long measuring look at Luke as he approached the
porch but had remained silent.

"This is Buddy." She reached down to scratch his
ears, and even as he clearly enjoyed the attention,
the dog never took his solemn eyes off Luke. "We
gave him to the kids the Christmas before . . . the
accident . . . He loved them both, but he and my
son Max had a very special bond. I thought poor
Buddy would die himself of a broken heart after what
happened. He whimpered and cried for months."

Luke's heart ached at the pain in her voice and at
the image she painted of the devastated dog. "He
wasn't with you last summer."

"I was still recovering from my own injuries, and we
worried I'd trip over him or he'd knock me over without meaning to. He stayed with our neighbors at
home for a few months. I'm so glad to have him back
with me now. The poor guy has been through a lot."

So have you, Luke thought but chose not to say. As
if she needed the reminder.

"I owe you the world's biggest apology," she said,
startling him.

"I was the one stalking you. How do you owe me an
apology?"

"You were *checking* on me. Big difference." She

curled her legs up under her and turned to him. "The apology I owe you is for seventeen years ago."

"Oh. That."

"Yeah. That."

"Sydney—"

"Luke—"

He cleared his throat and folded his hands tight in his lap. This was far more excruciating than he'd ever imagined it would be—and he'd imagined it plenty of times. Thousands of times, to be honest. What he might say. What she might say. If either of them would have anything at all to say. "Sorry," he said. "Go ahead."

"What I did to you was unconscionable. I know it's no consolation, but I thought of you so many times. I wanted to write to you or call you or something, but what does one say in that situation? 'I'm really sorry I left for the school year and never came back'? Would that have made anything better?"

"It helps to know you thought of me."

"Oh, God, Luke, how could I *not* think of you? Those summers . . . The time we spent together . . . Other than when my kids were born, it was the most magical time of my entire life."

No, he decided, this was far more excruciating than anything he'd ever imagined. "If that's how you felt, then why—"

"I was an idiot."

Shocked by her bluntness, he gave up any pretense of trying not to stare at her. The thick, strawberry blond hair he'd loved running his fingers through was shorter than it used to be, but the summer freckles that had popped up on her nose after long days in the sun were still there. The bright blue eyes that had been so tragically sad last summer seemed to have recovered some of their sparkle.

"I had this idea, you know, of how my life should be. Who my husband should be. What he would do for a living. Where we would live. I was a snobbish fool."

"I suppose the boy you'd left behind on the island, who worked at a marina and never made it to college, didn't quite fit the bill." Luke tried like hell to keep the bitterness out of his tone, but after so many years of suspecting what had driven her away, hearing confirmation of what he'd most feared was hardly a balm on the still-open wound.

"I know there's nothing I can say to change what happened all those years ago, but I want you to know I regretted the way I treated you. I *always* regretted it."

Hearing that didn't help as much as he'd thought it would.

She looked down at her hands. "Sometimes I wonder if what happened . . . to me . . . was payback . . ."

"Don't say that. No one deserves what happened to you."

"Karma can be such an awful bitch," she said ruefully. "Maybe I asked for too much, you know?"

"I can't believe in a God or any higher power who'd take the lives of innocent children to pay their mother back for being cavalier with the feelings of an old boyfriend."

Sydney winced. "Cavalier. Ouch."

"What would you call it?"

"Horrible. I was horrible to you." She leaned her head back on the rocker and studied him. "You haven't changed at all. I'd know you anywhere."

"Your hair is shorter, but otherwise, you look exactly the same, too."

"Tell me you found someone else, got married, had a boatload of kids. Tell me it all worked out well for you."

"No wife, no kids, but a good life. A satisfying life."

"I ruined the wife and kids thing for you, didn't I?"

He fought to maintain a neutral expression, to not let her see the pain. "Don't give yourself too much credit, Donovan. You weren't all *that* important."

Her laughter danced through the night, making his heart flutter. "Whatever you say, tough guy."

He never had been able to fool her. "Could I ask you something?"

"Sure."

"Your husband . . . ?"

"Seth."

"You were happy with him?"

"That's a very complicated question."

Luke expelled a tortured moan. "Come *on*. Tell me it was worth it—at least for one of us."

They sat in uncomfortable silence for a long time. "Seth was a good man, a wonderful father, a devoted husband and I loved him."

"But?"

She looked over at him, their eyes connecting with a powerful sense of awareness that left him breathless. "What I felt for him . . . It was different than what I felt for you."

He wanted to ask her what she meant by that. *How* was it different? Different better? Different more? Different less? But he couldn't seem to form any of those questions, so he had to settle for what she'd given him.

"I shouldn't be admitting these things, especially to you. See what I mean about karma?"

Luke shook his head. "The universe doesn't work that way. It just doesn't."

"Some days, it's hard to believe I didn't have it coming. I wasn't always a good person."

"You can't honestly believe that. A drunk driver killed your family, not you."

"That's what my counselor has been trying to get me to believe for fifteen months now."

"Getting any closer?"

"Good days, bad days."

"I hope seeing me won't make this a bad day."

"Seeing you is wonderful. I've wished for years to have the opportunity to tell you how sorry I was to have left without a word. Sometimes when we'd come for a summer visit with my parents, I'd think about going down to McCarthy's to see you."

"Why didn't you?"

"That would've been so unfair to you, for me to show up out of the blue like that after all that time just so I could make myself feel better about being a shit to you."

"I would've liked to have seen you, to have met your kids. More than anything, I've missed my friend Sydney. The best friend I ever had."

Her eyes sparkled with tears. "I'm so sorry, Luke," she whispered. "I'm so very, very sorry. Can you ever forgive me?"

"I forgave you years ago. You were nineteen. You didn't owe me anything."

She reached over and rested her hand on top of his. "I owed you so much more than what you got from me after four magical summers together."

The brush of her skin against his brought back a flood of sweet memories, the sweetest of all memories. He turned his hand so hers was caught between both of his, and the emotion hit him so hard it took his breath away. Suddenly, it became urgent that he leave before he said or did something he'd regret. "It was good to see you, Syd."

"Thanks for checking on me."

Luke grimaced. "*Checking* is a much nicer word than *stalking*."

She squeezed his hand. "It touched me last summer to know you were here, that you cared, despite the way we left things. I hope you understand I wasn't ready yet . . ."

"Please. Of course I understand."

"Will you come back again?"

Startled by the question, Luke said, "Do you want me to?"

"I missed my friend Luke. I never stopped missing him."

Overwhelmed by her, he couldn't find the words.

"I can see I've caught you off guard. I've been doing that to people a lot lately. Ever since the accident, I don't see much reason to hold back. Life is short. What's the point of hedging?"

"No point, I guess."

"I don't mean to shock you."

"You haven't shocked me so much as given me a lot to think about."

"Do you accept my apology?"

He nodded. "Clean slate."

"That's far more than I deserve."

"The slate is clean, remember?"

She smiled at him the way she used to when she

still loved him, and Luke swore his heart stopped for an instant.

He forced himself to release her hand, to get up, to walk down the stairs, to make his escape while he still could. He'd made it to the lawn on the way to the beach when she called out to him.

"Come back, Luke. Please come back again."

Luke waved to show he'd heard her and continued toward the shore on what used to be his well-worn path between her yard and the beach. His old rowboat, the same boat he'd had way back when, waited for him to make the trek across the Salt Pond to the same small house he'd once shared with his mother. Her illness had kept him tied to the island when Sydney and his other friends were leaving for college.

He'd never regretted giving those important years to the woman who had raised him on her own, but he couldn't help but wonder what might've been different for him—and for Sydney—if he'd been able to accept the scholarship he'd been offered that would've made him a marine biologist. Would that profession have been good enough for Sydney? The Sydney she'd been back then?

Probably not. She'd married a banker. A guy who studied algae and pond scum probably wouldn't have made the cut. Either way, it didn't do any good to speculate now. What difference did it make? She'd made her decision a long time ago, and he'd had no choice but to accept it.

Except, as he rowed slowly across the vast pond, guided by the light of the moon and stars, he was filled with an emotion he hadn't experienced in so long he'd almost forgotten what it felt like: hope. She'd never forgotten him. She'd thought of him, missed him, regretted their parting. *God, what did that mean?*

She was no longer married. Her husband and children had been gone for more than a year. He could see just by looking at her that she was doing much better accepting the awful hand life had dealt her than last summer when the pain of her loss was still so fresh and new.

"Ugh," he said out loud as he rowed. "Don't go there, man. It was over and done with years ago. Leave the past where it belongs."

But even as he told himself there was no point, that pesky burst of hope refused to be ignored.

Books by Bestselling Author
Fern Michaels

___**The Jury**	0-8217-7878-1	$6.99US/$9.99CAN
___**Sweet Revenge**	0-8217-7879-X	$6.99US/$9.99CAN
___**Lethal Justice**	0-8217-7880-3	$6.99US/$9.99CAN
___**Free Fall**	0-8217-7881-1	$6.99US/$9.99CAN
___**Fool Me Once**	0-8217-8071-9	$7.99US/$10.99CAN
___**Vegas Rich**	0-8217-8112-X	$7.99US/$10.99CAN
___**Hide and Seek**	1-4201-0184-6	$6.99US/$9.99CAN
___**Hokus Pokus**	1-4201-0185-4	$6.99US/$9.99CAN
___**Fast Track**	1-4201-0186-2	$6.99US/$9.99CAN
___**Collateral Damage**	1-4201-0187-0	$6.99US/$9.99CAN
___**Final Justice**	1-4201-0188-9	$6.99US/$9.99CAN
___**Up Close and Personal**	0-8217-7956-7	$7.99US/$9.99CAN
___**Under the Radar**	1-4201-0683-X	$6.99US/$9.99CAN
___**Razor Sharp**	1-4201-0684-8	$7.99US/$10.99CAN
___**Yesterday**	1-4201-1494-8	$5.99US/$6.99CAN
___**Vanishing Act**	1-4201-0685-6	$7.99US/$10.99CAN
___**Sara's Song**	1-4201-1493-X	$5.99US/$6.99CAN
___**Deadly Deals**	1-4201-0686-4	$7.99US/$10.99CAN
___**Game Over**	1-4201-0687-2	$7.99US/$10.99CAN
___**Sins of Omission**	1-4201-1153-1	$7.99US/$10.99CAN
___**Sins of the Flesh**	1-4201-1154-X	$7.99US/$10.99CAN
___**Cross Roads**	1-4201-1192-2	$7.99US/$10.99CAN

Available Wherever Books Are Sold!
Check out our website at www.kensingtonbooks.com